Long Island Butcher

Dark Mafia BWWM Romance

Long Island Mafia Romance
Book 2

Jamila Jasper

Thank you, Tasha & Nini J for helping me name Geno Vicari, Valeria & Natasha for helping me name Giovanna, and to all my other patrons for your support with this story.

www.patreon.com/jamilajasper

Thank you to my most supportive readers:
Andi-Mariee, Keisha, Jennett, Fredericka, Candece, Lydia, Sabrina, JM, Jackie, Mo, Ashaunte, Tolu, Lori, Dionne, ZLB, Nicol, Elbert, Jesi, Brenda, Desiree, LaShan, Only1ToniD, Debbie, Tiffanie, Shawnte, Lisema, Christine, Trinity, Monica, Juliette, Letetia, Margaret, Dash, Maxine, Sheron, Javonda, Pearl, Kiana, Shyan, Jacklyn, Amy, Julia, Colleen, Natasha, Yvonne, Brittany, June, Ashleigh, Nene, Nene, Deborah, Nikki, DeShaunda, Latoya, Shelite, Arlene, Judith, Mary, Shanida, Rachel,Damzel, Ahnjala, Kenya, Momo, BJ, Akeshia, Melissa, Tiffany, Sherbear, Nini, Curtresa, Regina, Ashley, Mia, Sydney, Sharon, Charlotte, Assiatu, Regina, Romanda, Catherine, Gaynor, BF, Tasha, Henri, Sara, skkent, Rosalyn, Danielle, Deborah, Kirsten, Ana, Taylor, Charlene Louanna, Michelle, Tamika, Lauren, RoHyde, Natasha, Shekynah, Cassie, Dreama, Nick, Gennifer, Rayna, Jaleda, Anton, Kimvodkna, Jatonn, Anoushka, Audrey, Valeria, Courtney, Donna, Jenetha, Ayana, Kristy, FreyaJo, Grace, Kisha, Stephanie E., Amber, Denice, Marty, LaKisha, Latoya, Natasha, Monifa, Alisa, Daveena, Desiree, Gerry, Kimberly, Stephanie M., Tarah, Yolanda, Kristy, Gary, Janet, Kathy, Phyllis, Susan

Contents

Mafia Playmate

Forced To Surrogate

ISBN: 979-8-3303-3510-7

* * *

This is book two in an interracial mafia romance series with dark themes and potential triggers. If you enjoy steamy and spicy BWWM romance with a black woman/white man romance, you will enjoy this story. For readers of the Pagonis family or Doukas family series, strap in... You'll enjoy this deliciously wild ride.

Created with Vellum

Description

Alexis stumbles home after a frat party and witnesses a murder.

Before she can run for help, John Vicari, a bearded, muscular killer, intervenes.

The curvy, nerdy college student falls into the lap of the most dangerous crime family in Long Island.

To earn her freedom, Alexis has no choice but to give John complete ownership of her body and mind.

He craves a lifelong unbreakable bond to keep her safe and loyal.

Get on your knees, cupcake — and submit to my desires.

* * *

If you enjoy WMBW mafia family romance stories with action and dark themes, you'll love this enemies-to-lovers

Description

dark romance story. Get Book #2 in this series of interconnected standalone stories.

Series Titles

https://bit.ly/longislandseries

Content Awareness

dark bwwm mafia romance

This is a mafia romance story with dark themes including potentially triggering content, violence, frank discussions and language surrounding bedroom scenes and race. All characters in this story are 18+. Sensitive readers, be cautioned about some of the material in this dark but extremely hot romance novel. There's a morally grey alpha hero in this story, along with a black female heroine.

* * *

Enjoy the spicy interracial romance story…

Note From Jamila

Hello Reader.

Are you ready for the second book in the series?

John is even more unapologetic than Lucky and I need you to brace yourself for the twisted way he will keep Alexis in his clutches.

If you enjoy the bad boys who are truly fucked up... welcome.

A life of murder and crime leaves John screwed up in the head, but *very* skilled with people. If you find the good in the bad boys and enjoy stories with these possessive alphas who completely melt for the **black women they love...** *welcome.*

Be warned, the content in this story may be sensitive to some readers but if you want to walk with me on the wild side and dare to have dark fantasies about twisted alpha heroes and black female leads — turn the page and begin the second installment in the series...

The completed series:
https://bit.ly/longislandseries

Chapter 1
The House Party & The Murder
Alexis Carter

I hate walking to parties alone at night. It sucks, but at least it's better than hanging around all night while my best friend sucks the face off some annoying frat boy at a pregame. Chloe loves parties, and she loves the attention she gets for being a petite, outgoing Asian girl even more. I'm always the awkward third wheel. I have a boyfriend, but he's normally too busy proving himself as the school's reigning beer pong champion.

Chloe thinks I just need to have a few "sneaky make outs" with other guys when Cameron ignores me, but I just… I don't want to hook up with anyone. I just want a boyfriend who gives a crap. Maybe if I had a boyfriend who gave a crap, I wouldn't have to walk down these city streets in uncomfortable high heels alone.

I'll never get our generation's obsession with hooking up. I'll never understand how everyone is so fucking satisfied with these shallow relationships where you barely know each other's last names, much less each other's interests, likes or dislikes before you shove your tongues into each other's mouths. Is it too much to want a guy to ask me my middle name before he puts his hands in my pants? I just find the obsession with getting numbers up and treating people like consumable products so shallow and stupid.

Chloe sends me a nervous text message. She's probably already drunk, but at least she's checking in to make sure someone hasn't mugged me. Columbia students are notoriously naïve. We get mugged all the time around here.

My phone buzzes as I close in on the door to the party. I glance down at several texts from Chloe, most of which are blurry images, followed by a brief text.

Chloe: Alexis… Where r u??????????

Chloe always writes an excess of punctuation. One question mark is more than enough.

Me: I'm outside.

I'm nervous, but since there are parties all over the five-block radius around this brownstone, it's unlikely I'll stumble upon anything more criminal than fraternity brothers peeing against the wall to someone's house

Chloe: Thank GOD!!!!!!!!!! Thought you were DEAD!!!!!!

She is the most dramatic texter ever. How the hell could I text her back (and keep her updated with the occasional photo) if I were dead? When she drinks, her anxiety climbs by one thousand percent. She bursts out of the brownstone with a drink in her hand and a bright red flush that tells me she's already wasted.

"Oh my God, ALEXIS!" she shrieks. "Get in here. Gabe is about to beat Cameron in pong and the house is going fucking nuts. Their shirts are off, you have to see this."

Ugh. I hate when my boyfriend drinks enough to take his shirt off. Random girls always come up to me and congratulate me on sleeping with him as if Cameron were some kind of achievement and not a flawed person, just like anyone else. Chloe thinks I'm way too cynical about him, but I don't know. I just hate house parties and when you date a student athlete at Columbia like Cameron, parties come with the territory.

Cameron never portrayed himself as the type of guy who got drunk every weekend when he first slid into my DMs, but every weekend, his idea of a date is inviting me to watch him get shit-faced with his buddies and then we have sex in his room.

The sex is bad. He finishes after three to four minutes and then watches porn with his headphones on. At least he doesn't mind if I finish myself off afterwards in the bed next to him. There are good parts to our relationship, or I would have dumped him by now, but it's easy to forget those good parts when I desperately want to feel... loved.

Cameron loves reminding me I'm a strong college feminist—I don't need a man to orgasm. If I try to argue with that, things normally spiral out of control, so I stopped bringing it up. Arguing with Cameron is about as effective as arguing with a lacrosse ball.

Before I can ask Chloe any follow-up questions about Cameron's drunken state so I can assess how much trouble I have to deal with, she drags me into the house. Her hands are conspicuously sticky, which means she's drunk enough to have spilled liquor on her hands and not even noticed. The Fanta smell wafts to my nose and my shoes stick to the floor because of all the beer.

How much time have they even had to get this drunk?

Once I enter, Cameron comes up to me with his arms outstretched, holding two red solo cups sloshing with the foamy, cheap beer college guys use to get girls absolutely shit-faced. Cameron knows there's no way in hell I'm drinking two solo cups of beer. I take one from him and offer a polite sip.

"Mmm... yellow." I can't think of any other positive words to describe the flavor.

"I know, right," Cameron nods with an oblivious and self-satisfied smile. Boyfriend. He's your boyfriend, Alexis, and he's adequate.

I stare with confusion at Cameron's splatter of bad tattoos and wonder if perhaps he is significantly less than adequate.

"You can chill in my room if it gets too rowdy for you, babe," Cameron says, leaning forward and giving me a kiss that's far too wet. I grimace and he mistakes it for an approving smile. He's so dumb. Chloe whoops loudly and starts shaking her ass to *I Kissed A Girl*, the overplayed Katy Perry song booming in the background. Three of the black guys on Cameron's team dance behind her, sandwiching Chloe as she does some drunken approximation of twerking. What she lacks in skill, she makes up for in enthusiasm.

"I'm fine," I tell Cameron, wanting to be cool for once. "I'll kick it for a bit. Don't you need to kick Gabe's ass at beer pong or whatever?"

"Yeah."

Cameron smiles and returns to the pong table, giving me a goofy smile like he really wants to impress me. He's good-looking, but aside from that, Cameron's not impressive. He's a decent boyfriend compared to my ex but he's lazy, constantly farts because of his gross strawberry flavored protein shakes, doesn't understand anything with the slightest hint of complexity and he drinks too much. He's sweet though and we've dated since freshman year, which is basically marriage by Columbia standards.

Cameron tosses the tiny ping-pong ball across the table and lands it smoothly in Gabe's remaining cup. It's up to his roommate to tie the game. Gabe squints and aims for Cameron's cup with his ball. Chloe shakes her hips in the corner of the room as everyone ignores her in favor of the pong game she's drunkenly oblivious to.

Gabe tosses the ball and misses. Badly. The crowd groans, and Gabe looks visibly pissed.

"Fuck this, man. Fuck this…"

Gabe's drunk too and he's the only guy in this house who can out-drink Cameron, which is saying a lot. Cameron pumps his fist and then beats his chest like an ape. He makes me cringe, but… having a boyfriend is better than not having one — at least according to Chloe and every other female friend I have.

"Suck it," Cameron taunts him.

"Fuck you, man," Gabe shoots back half-heartedly. He stumbles off into another room. Cameron wraps his arm around me and plants a wet kiss on my cheek. He stinks like liquor and I hate when he gets all slobbery and gross like this. He bites my lower lip and a few people in the room cheer after our kiss. So embarrassing. Cameron grins at me.

"Wait in my room, babe. I'll come see you soon."

Cameron knows I hate parties like this, so I'm grateful he's giving me a way out. Chloe's having too much fun dancing with a few other girls in our year and two of Cameron's other roommates. I tell Chloe I'm heading upstairs and she begs me to have more shots with her.

I know Cameron would probably appreciate it if I at least tried to have fun, so I grab him by the hand and drag him over to Chloe. We do shots together and then I dance with Cameron and Chloe for a few more minutes before Cameron has to return to his beer pong tournament.

By the time I slink upstairs, I'm drunk. It doesn't take much to get me wasted, which is why I try to avoid nights like this one. I hope I can nap and sober up before Cameron gets upstairs so we can hang out and talk. We need to talk about our relationship. Drinking always makes me want to talk about our relationship, which goes about as well as you might think.

But seriously… Cameron can't keep relying on cheap tricks at the pong table to impress me. He can't just call me "babe" and assume I'll be his forever. He knows what I want out of life. I'll be in New York city until medical school and I need to work my ass off to get to my dream school, Harvard medical. Cameron just failed *Introduction To Sexuality Studies* because he claims it wasn't what he expected. He'll have to stay an extra semester and he doesn't have any plans.

Columbia relationships are weird and I'm not the type of girl who likes relationships without labels, which makes me totally incompatible with most guys. Cameron at least likes labels like "babe" and "girlfriend". That's the best you can hope for, right? An average guy, living his average life... with an average dick... with average grades. Average is good.

I slip my shoes off and crawl into Cameron's bed. It's comforting that it smells like him, but I don't love the fact that his pillow is damp. He sweats a lot and doesn't stick to the wash schedule I made for him at all.

I pull the covers over my head, and the room seems to swirl around me. Woah. Maybe I had more to drink than I realized. My stomach lurches. I can't hate Cameron. His smell is everywhere and his inability to stick to a wash schedule is not the biggest deal in the world.

I text Cameron out of habit.

Me: Babe. I'm drunk. Upstairs. Miss you.

I don't know if I've ever missed Cameron, but it's what you say when you have a boyfriend and I don't just have a boyfriend — Cameron is hot. Other women on our campus want to date him and most wonder openly what a white bread prep like Cameron wants with a black woman like me...

Asking him something so blunt is out of the question. He cares about me, and that counts for something. Cameron doesn't respond to my text message before I fall asleep, but I don't mind. He's probably the undefeated beer pong champion somewhere.

The bed moves, and there's a thud. Boots hit the floor. I'm up and there's warmth in my bed. The invasive smell isn't Cameron's, and then I feel a large weight pressing into me. Holy fuck.

My head spins and I feel even more drunk than before, if that's even possible. I try to mutter the word "no" but nothing comes out. An elbow presses into my stomach with no regard for presence and the oxygen evacuates my lungs. I assume the body on top of mine is Cameron's, but as the elbow jabs into my stomach, a strong, unfamiliar male smell invades my nostrils. I don't know who the fuck it is, but I know it's not Cameron.

Not Cameron.

I panic. My heart races and I hate that I freeze as I feel a hand slide under my shirt. I cry out loudly as roving fingers touch my breasts. No. I try to push him off, but I'm too drunk and the man on top of me is way too strong. Uncomfortably wet lips press against my earlobes. My stomach tightens with nausea. He's going to rape me.

"I always wanted to fuck you," Gabe whispers. "Now I'll get the chance. If you scream, I'll cut your fucking throat."

He runs his tongue over my neck, and I don't scream. He pinches my breasts again and I try to knee him in the balls. He slaps me across the face with his free hand and I cry out. Who the hell could hear me anyway over the music? Panic surges through me. I have to get the fuck out of here.

I feel something soft and warm poking against my thigh and my frozen response transforms as the threat looms. I collect myself enough to knee him hard in the gut, forcing him off me with all the strength my adrenaline can provide. Gabe groans and I attempt to push him off. I don't do enough to get him off me, but I hit him hard enough to really piss him off.

"You little bitch," he grunts, pushing my face to the side and holding me down as he attempts to take my pants off. I know if he gets my pants off, I'm finished and he'll have me right where he wants me. I have to fight harder. I knee him in the balls this time and remember something I watched online once. I squeeze my fingers together and when Gabe looks at me, I jab him in the eyes.

The surprise forces him to jump off of me and I leap out of

bed. He got most of my pants off and my shirt up. Gabe lunges at me as I run for the door. He grabs my forearm and pushes me hard.

"Stupid fucking slut," He snarls, his beer-breath threatening to knock me unconscious.

He grabs my throat and slams me against the door. I knee him in the balls again and this time, I throw the door open and hit Gabe in the head as he doubles over. That's it — I have time to escape. I run down the stairs and run past the rest of the party. I don't see Chloe or Cameron and I don't look for them.

He tried to rape me. Cameron's roommate tried to rape me. I'm in shock and my clothes are hanging off my body, and I don't have any shoes. Oh my God. I'm outside in Manhattan with no shoes on. Tears stream down my face as I heave and gasp for breath.

This wasn't supposed to happen to me. I'm not the type of girl who goes to house parties and ends up beneath some strange guy. Tears stream from my eyes as I heave for breath, the realization hitting me that there was never any "type" of girl that this happens to. Some of us just tell ourselves that so we can go through life feeling safe, never worrying that some guy will viciously steal our dignity.

I pick a direction and run as fast as I can. Then I take a turn, thinking I'm heading back to campus, but I'm facing down an alley and I'm not alone. The best course of action would be keeping my head down and sprinting in the opposite direction. That's not what happens. The two men are speaking to each other, arguing about something, and they're both holding guns. There's a lump on the ground that I try to discern the identity of.

I've never seen a gun in real life before. I'm too fucked up and traumatized to think things through before reacting. I shriek— loudly. The men snap their attention to me and I freeze as the taller one raises his gun to me. The other one glances to the ground and my eyes follow the direction of his.

My screaming gets louder. *Fuck*. They have a dead body and

I've never seen a dead body either, but that's definitely what's lying on the ground beneath them. The pool of red blood looks black in the darkness, but there's a tangy metallic smell that finally reaches my nostrils.

The taller man turns the gun away from me and shoots the guy on the ground right in front of me. If he wasn't dead before (perhaps just dying) he's dead now. I scream again and turn around, readying myself to run but knowing that I'll die right here, two blocks away from Cameron's house with my clothes ripped by bullets in my back. I have to do something and there's no fighting two killers with guns.

I run as fast as I can, filled with the knowledge that it's entirely hopeless.

This is how my story ends.

* * *

Chapter 2
The Alley Girl
John Vicari

Lucky has to hold him down after the first shot so I can make the second shot humane. There's no way to make this job cleaner, really. It's a dirty fucking job and we're dirty fucking people for doing it. He squeals like a pig and I shoot him again. He goes limp, and he's instantly still. There should be no other sound but my breath and my brother's. Instead — there's a scream.

Lucky whips around after my third and final shot, pointing his weapon at the girl standing at the edge of the alleyway. Her knees knock together and she seems like she's going to faint. *Pretty African American girl.* Nice figure. Ripped clothes. Gorgeous lips.

"Don't shoot," I command him gruffly. The girl makes a strange sound between a moan and a cry. Her eyes bug out of her head like she plans on passing out right in front of us. Fuck, this is bad. I never felt great about this job and now that Sammy's son is dead, it's hitting me like the fucking F train. The girl makes another anguished cry and nearly drops to her knees.

"We have to do something," Lucky growls at me, talking in as hushed a tone as possible, which isn't enough to stop the girl from hearing.

She just witnessed a crime and every inkling in this obvious good girl's body is probably telling her to run her ass to the cops. She glances over her shoulder like she's going to run and despite my instructions, Lucky raises his pistol to her. Fuck.

I have to stop her before she takes off and provokes my idiot brother's killer instincts. We've already pushed the boundaries of human depravity tonight. He's dead. The kid I helped raise is dead on the ground because my father commanded it. Don't I feel an inkling of regret? Can't I fucking feel anything?

My heart pounds, reminding me that even with all the crimes I have committed against other living beings, my heart still physically beats. Lucky gives me an impatient look, his hand hovering too close to the trigger finger for my liking. If we don't kill her we have to do something. This isn't how the fuck we go down, it's just not how the Vicari family falls. This kid on the ground between us… This is family business, not police business and we can't have this pretty as fuck, reckless as fuck college kid screw this up for us.

"She's going to bolt," Lucky snarls. "I'm not going after her." Motherfucker. The girl runs and I sprint after her. She's barefoot in a disgusting Manhattan alley for whatever fucking reason. She won't get far.

She glances over her shoulder and screams when she realizes I'm getting close. That won't help her. I get closer and yell at her to stop running. She stops and turns like she's going to fight. The brave little thing reassesses the situation when I get closer to her. I tower over her by at least a foot. Someone tore her clothes, and she looks like she's been through hell.

"Don't fight," I growl at her which I mean to calm her down, a goal I fail at completely. She freezes until the last second when it's far too late for her to escape my clutches. My first impressions were that I thought she was pretty, but I haven't exactly had a good look at her appearance outside of the shadowy silhouette in the alley. The first thing I notice about the witness to our late night butchery is the softness of her body as she smacks into mine. Holy fuck, she's soft. I wrap my arms around her to stop her from any attempts at escape.

Guilt rushes through me but I can't help it. I squeeze her body against mine and allow myself to enjoy how delightful it is to feel her scream and struggle. Trust me, cupcake, it's better me than my brother and certainly better me than my cousin Sammy. I hold her close and smell her perfume. She's spent the night drinking and by the smell of beer coming off her, she's had too much. Her soft breasts press into my forearm and my cock throbs as I struggle to subdue her.

I don't chase women of her complexion, but I don't consider this a chase in the traditional sense. I tighten my grasp on her as she enters the headspace prey animals do when they feel they have nothing to lose.

Our witness makes a loud noise between a howl and a squeal as I wrap my hand over her mouth and attempt to subdue her. She has ripped clothing. No shoes. She's black, and it's one of those nice copper brown shades, a dark ochre color that gets me really fucking hard, especially when I see my pale hand contrasted against her exceedingly beautiful skin tone. I can't touch her. I can't. I've done it before and been punished before and it's never worth the trouble just for a woman, even one who gets me instantly aroused like this one.

My stomach tightens. I feel like a bastard just for noticing her skin tone and how my hand feels against it. We can't do that anymore, can we? Notice shit like skin color. We have to pretend it's fucking invisible, even when we can't get it off our minds...

This world we live in is all fucked up and I'm a part of the fucking problem. She thrashes around, but ultimately, she's no match for me and by the time Lucky gets his ass over to me, she has to fight both of us off, which would be fucking impossible for any regular sized human male, much less a college student. No wallet, no phone, we won't have much trouble hiding this one on the other side of the city.

"Get her in the car," I grunt. The girl breaks out into a full-blown panic. Lucky bites his lip to stop himself from saying something disrespectful. What? He doesn't expect me to kill the chick, does he? It's not my style any more than it's his.

We get her in the back seat and she fights like hell until Lucky points his gun at her.

"Shut the fuck up, kid or I'll blow a hole through your skull."

Christ, Lucky. That'll calm her the fuck down. I swear my brother has the brains of a fucking sea sponge.

"Settle down," I tell her. "We need to get you out of here."

I glance at Lucky and he knows what I'm asking. I have other problems tonight, apparently. That alley should have been quiet, but we had to take our chances. That's one of the many problems with the morgue. You're forced to gamble and those gambles don't always pay off.

"I'll take care of the body," Lucky mutters. The girl whimpers in the backseat. If I let her out of my sight, she'll run to the cops. I sense it. Lucky reacts visibly when he hears her whimper. I don't know what to tell him. I'll work on her.

"Thank you," I mutter, shifting uncomfortably as I come to terms with the fact that I don't have a single clue what the fuck I'm going to do with this chick. She goes to one of the most expensive private schools in the country. It's not like she can disappear and no one will notice. It's not like she's ever seen anything like she's seen tonight. She'll want to tell someone and the second she runs her fucking mouth, we've got a problem.

A bigger problem lies dead wrapped in a tarp in the back of my SUV. I killed my nephew and I am definitely going to fucking hell for that.

"Should we talk to Sammy?" Lucky asks. His mind is the same place mine is, not like that's any fucking good. I shake my head. There's no point talking to Sammy. When he finds out Enrico's missing, he'll know because he's in 'the life' and he knows how my father treats traitors. Alfonso Vicari comes from an era of shooting first and asking questions later.

Better yet, dad doesn't ask any fucking questions. He's led

the Vicari family for the past twenty years and he's more stuck in his ways than anyone I know. You don't get to be that old in 'the life' without an iron fist, at least that's what dad always said...

Crazy fucking Sammy will also know that this order could have only come from one person — the big Vicari boss who runs my fucking life. But how will he ever forgive me for going through with this? My mind races with thoughts, but I'm also plagued by a strange numb feeling, like I've gone too far. Dad's halfway across the world and he made me kill my best friend's son.

Dad... Without him, I wouldn't be the man I am today but he drives me fucking nuts leaving me here to absorb the backlash from carrying out his commands. I don't have time to have a fucking life and it's beating me into the ground all the plotting and killing and chasing down the fucking Murray bastards and giving up everything that made me human for what... .

Power? Is power fucking worth it?

I drive Lucky to his car, and he takes the body. I don't know who he'll get to help, but my brother is very resourceful. I enter the driver's seat again once he's gone and take a proper look at the girl who witnessed our crime for the first time in the rear-view mirror. I plan on getting a quick look at her and glancing away quickly. The less we see of each other the better if she plans to survive tonight. Once my eyes land on her, that's not what fucking happens. My eyes don't break away from her and I can't stop drinking her in. Her chest heaves slowly with each nervous breath and my gaze lingers inappropriately on her voluptuous bosoms.

She's pretty as fuck. I can't help how I respond to that. She has smooth, golden ochre color — and deep brown eyes. Thick hair, all loose. She looks like a fucking mess and while she might be a beautiful mess, it's clear that this chick has seen some shit. I pull my car away from the spot where Lucky parked.

I glance at her in the rear-view mirror again and she cries once her eyes catch mine. I terrify her and I barely think she perceives me as human. Fuck, I didn't mean to make her cry. She's right to think I'm a monster after what she saw. What kind of man kills another in an alley without even flinching? There's no way to change who I am. As long as my father remains the boss of the Vicari family, which he will for the rest of his life, it's my duty to obey him, not question him.

I ain't that fuckin' scary, am I?

"You don't have a fucking thing to worry about, kid."

"I'm not a kid," she says with a trembling voice. "I go to Columbia University and someone will report me missing. They'll find you and take you to prison. Forever."

"Okay, Columbia University."

I have to get her out of Manhattan. If I let Miss Columbia out of my fucking sight, I can almost guarantee that she will take her ass straight to the cops and fuck me all the way up.

"Where are you taking me?" She says.

"Enough questions, Columbia."

"That's not my name."

"Probably better if you don't tell me your name."

She gets a scared rabbit look in her eye again and leans back, silent. It takes over an hour to get out of the fucking city and she doesn't say a word or try to escape.

"Where's your cell phone?" I ask her once we're out of Manhattan and I know I can deal with any bullshit without losing her. Lucky enjoys life in Westhampton, but I prefer staying closer to the casino. My first girlfriend and I bought an apartment in Bayside, Queens together. After our relationship fell apart, I bought out her half and could never bear to get rid of it. I like the simplicity of everything and the quiet little neighborhood where everyone knows my name and the Italian restaurants still serve a manly amount of pasta. I would have to fall head over heels in love to leave this place.

Lucky thinks I'm a little too fucking sentimental. He collects real estate like baseball cards. I bond to places for life and I feel bonded to this place—my witness's new prison.

I bought this place during the good times before I had this much fucking responsibility. I know what my father would say about her. She's not worth keeping alive. She ain't one of ours. A chick like her goes missing, nobody gives a flying fuck. I could have killed her and easily gotten away with it.

Maybe it ain't right, but it's the way the world fucking works and there ain't a damn thing you can do about it. I don't want to do what our father would want tonight. Killing Enrico was bad enough. I need to show mercy for once. This is my chance to show mercy. She looked at me like she was looking at a monster and the tiniest most human part of me is absolutely fucking desperate to prove her wrong.

"I asked you a question. Where's your damn cell phone?"

I don't mean to sound tense and upset. It's not her, really, it's just the blood on my hands and my racing heart as I try to keep calm and remember all the shit I need to do to stop this from blowing up in my fucking face.

"I left it at my boyfriend's house," she responds. She doesn't have a city accent, so I don't have to worry about fucking gang bangers tracking me down to Queens. She has a flat, Midwestern accent that tells me her parents are far away and she's from a classy sort of place that will polish out the grammatical inadequacies and unnecessary use of slang from a woman's speech. I guess the smart cookie didn't end up at Columbia by accident.

"Your boyfriend?"

"Yes. My boyfriend," she repeats, glaring at me as she repeats the word.

Boyfriend. I don't know why that word fills me with instant rage. I wonder what pretentious rich kid who probably doesn't even deserve to get laid gets to have this chick in his bed. She's a fucking knock out.

"What's his name?"

She hesitates, but she eventually spits out his first name. "Cameron."

A prick named Cameron. I can use that information later, I bet.

She doesn't tell me his last name, which is probably pretty fucking smart since the thought immediately crosses my mind that I might have to kill that motherfucker if I get my hands on him.

"Where are your shoes? Why the fuck were you wandering around alone this hour of the night?"

I don't like that she's afraid of me, but for now, it's to my advantage to use her fear to get answers. She'll figure out that I won't hurt her soon enough and I need my answers before she realizes she's completely safe with me.

The girl glances at me in the rear-view mirror and when my eyes meet hers, she starts crying. And I mean she starts fucking bawling. I've never encountered any shit like this in over three decades of life so I sit in the front seat fucking stunned by her emotional display. Crying makes me very uncomfortable. *Fuck.* What the hell am I supposed to do now? How the fuck am I supposed to react to this shit, huh?

"Hey, listen… you don't have to cry…" I mumble, hoping that pointing out the obvious will stop her tears. Her crying only intensifies. Fuck.

"If I knew I was going to die tonight, I would have called my mom," She sniffles, her soft sobbing getting louder with each shivering sniffle.

Jesus fucking Christ. Does she really think I plucked her out of an isolated Upper West Side alley to kill her? If I were going to kill her, it would have been much smarter to do it several miles away from my home. I think better of pointing that out to her as my better instincts tell me that would only make the crying worse.

Thankfully, we don't have far until we get to my apartment. I own the entire building, but I live on the top floor. Getting her ass up the top floor will be a big fucking problem if she doesn't cooperate. She stops wailing and sniffling when I stop the car at least. That's a fucking relief.

"I need your cooperation, Columbia," I tell her plainly. "Once I have that, you'll make it."

"Stop calling me that."

"I gotta call you something."

I get out of the car and she tries her door again. Child locks. Gotta love those. I open the door and she doesn't sprint out, apparently remembering my brother's threats. I'm armed, but my gun is unloaded. Still, she looks pretty fucking green and she goes to college for rich kids so an unloaded gun is probably more than enough to scare the ever-loving crap out of her.

"Come on, Columbia. Out of the car," I tell her, gesturing towards me so she knows it's okay for her to leave the back seat as long as she stays close. If she makes one wrong move, I'll have to take this a step further when I would really prefer not to. The girl steps out of the car and doesn't run. So far, so fucking good.

"My name is Alexis," she says snootily. "And I don't care what your name is, I need you to take me back to my dorm. If you aren't going to kill me… let me go."

Is she serious? How the fuck do I benefit from leaving the one witness to a murder I committed to run back to her college campus and blab to everyone she knows. I have to bond with her —and quickly. There's always the obvious, but she's twenty years old, which is too young for me and it's too much wrong for one night. I'll just have to keep her close and fight the temptation I felt the second I wrapped my arms around her.

"No chance you're leaving my place tonight."

I know the truth about why I took her, and I have to suppress it at all costs. We close in on the stairs to my place and the smell from downstairs gets stronger as we approach the stairs in the back. Basil. Marinara sauce. Mozzarella cheese. Alexis sniffs loudly as she follows me up the stairs to my front door. My chest tightens as I get close to the door and question what the hell I'm doing here with this girl.

"You live above a pizza place?" Alexis asks after conducting her investigation.

Watching her examine my apartment fills me with discomfort. I want to impress her, which is pretty much impossible since she just saw me kill someone and clearly views me as a monster. "Yup."

I also own the pizza place, but she doesn't need to know that. Aside from the casino, I like having a few solid small businesses in my portfolio. I used to love that pizza place when I was young. Fuck, I miss being young... If I were younger,I wouldn't think twice about dragging her to my bed and forcing her to enjoy me. *I'm different now. Older. Wiser. Less cruel.*

I'm no angel and with a woman like that, it's worth the effort of convincing her that she really does want my tongue between every crease of her skin.

I want redemption from her. I want to wipe the horrified look off her face and prove to her that I'm human. It's foolish, but maybe it's a sign I'm really getting old. It's just another reason I should stay away from her.

Alexis walks close to me as I guide her up the stairs and unlock the door to my place. I don't need all four bedrooms, but I enjoy imagining that one day I could have a family to fill the place up with. I don't keep many friends around.

Once we're in my apartment, I have to turn up the heat on this chick. I know I'll scare the crap out of her, but I have to make sure she doesn't fucking talk.

"Get a chair and sit the fuck down," I growl at her, trying to sound especially stern.

My gruffness even surprises her. "What?"

"You heard me."

"I thought you said you weren't going to hurt me," she replies pleadingly. She thinks pain is coming next. No, little thing. I can't hurt you. I give myself plenty of time to consider her face. She has very round cheeks, a lot of hair and curves. Curves everywhere. Since when are twenty-year-olds this full-figured. Her breasts move a lot with each breath and she has a round ass that I'm not thinking about smacking. Or tasting. Or fucking.

It's normally easier to control myself. If I didn't have to force myself to survive killing my nephew, perhaps I wouldn't have taken her at all. Her lips quiver as I get close enough to see her properly. Smudged makeup. Ripped dress. Something else happened to her.

She gives me a look of utter despair that sends a gut-wrenching surge of guilt through me. I killed my nephew tonight. There's more blood on my hands now than ever before and there's a woman in my house who sounds so weak and vulnerable. I can't hurt her.

Every instinct in my body that would normally tell me to eliminate anyone who could send my ass to prison becomes instantly suppressed by the strong feelings Alexis draws from me. Is her skin really as soft as it looks?

I want that gentle ochre color, curled up by my side. Murder makes you crave comfort, no matter how hardened you are to the life. Alexis looks like she would be very comfortable and just as soft as I need.

Her voice is enough to make my cock stiffen completely and her very presence at such a tumultuous adrenaline-ridden moment tempts me beyond belief. I fight the urge to shift my cock in my pants and battle the even stronger urge to remove my clothes completely and have the comfort I desire with none of the stumbling into things. I want to dive into this bad fucking decision.

"I won't hurt you if you talk. You witnessed some shit tonight that you shouldn't have seen and I'm taking you out of harm's way so we can talk about what the fuck you saw and what you're going to do about it."

Now I fucking terrify her. She glances around as if some avenue of escape will suddenly materialize, which it doesn't.

Alexis takes a chair and sits. Her eyes well with tears again, forcing me to notice how young she is. When the fuck did college kids get this small? She's about 5'5" and curvy. Very curvy. She has a few extra pounds on her in all the right places and a nice, tawny skin color that gets me stiff when I shouldn't be.

I need to ditch the guns. I have to call Lucky. There are a million fucking things for a mob boss to do when he just whacked his fucking relative but here I am — home with a strange girl I found.

"Tell me everything that happened to you tonight," I tell the terrified and so undeniably beautiful woman. "I need details. If you expect to get out of this alive, I need to know everything about you including your full name. Do you have a wallet on you? Forms of ID? I need everything."

With a skin tight dress like that which leaves nothing to the imagination and has rips all over it regardless, I doubt she can hide anything, but I can't be too careful. I trust Lucky to get rid of the body and my cousin to suppress the missing person's report, but there are too many factors when you kill someone to worry about. You can't afford to get careless. I keep my eyes glued to Alexis, searching for signs of deception. If I keep her alive, I need to keep her loyal.

There's one thing that works with women and fuck, I want it so badly it hurts. I want her bent over. I want her mouth. I want to take this college girl to bed and fuck this horrible night into my past.

Alexis shakes her head.

I speak gently with her to provoke the truth. "If you lie to me, I'll know. I'll find out."

She nods, like she believes me and then she blurts out her name quickly. "Alexis Carter."

"Alexis Carter," I repeat, committing both her first and last name to memory. This will come in handy when I check on her school records and need to search her associates to find that Cameron asshole.

I continue questioning her. "Freshman? Sophomore?"

"I just started junior year. I'm studying for the MCAT."

"Where are your shoes?"

She gasps for breath and then buries her head in her hands again. What the fuck is with the tears every time I ask about where she was tonight? Christ. Lucky would be so much better at this than I am. He does the feelings shit perfectly which is why women are always falling head over heels for his irresponsible fucked up ass. I've never had his luck with women just using my personality. My looks get them into the bedroom, but I spent the past decade waking up alone. My last ex said it best – no one can stand being in a relationship with a cold, unrepentant fuck up.

Could things be different with this one? I push the idiotic thought out of my head. I'm too old and messed up to think anything romantic. Guys don't give a shit about romance anyway, not even Italian men. We're dogs and we just want to fuck, right? I don't know if that's true, but tonight I question the gender philosophy my father taught me. I can't bear the thought of touching her without knowing who hurt her. I want to punish anyone who could bring tears to this woman's eyes without remorse. I feel something on the same night I did the most horrendous thing a man could ever do. I killed a member of my family.

Alexis still can't bear to look at me. I don't have a fucking ounce of Lucky's charm and most women can't bear to look me in the fucking eye — including this one. I know I have to say something that isn't completely foolish to get her to talk.

"Alexis. Talk to me. What happened? Be honest with me and I'll help you."

I don't know how the fuck she's getting me to talk so much and to sound so... sensitive.

"I promise I'll help you," I continue. It doesn't feel like I'm the one speaking because these don't sound like John Vicari's words, but a promise made by a man much better than I am.

"I can't tell you," Alexis whimpers, sobbing softly. "No one will believe me."

Her desperate tone tugs at my heartstrings.

"Try me. What's the worst that could happen, huh?"

She stops sobbing briefly to hold her head up and look me straight in the eye as she answers, "The worst already happened to me tonight."

I knew she would say something like that. She might be frazzled and all over the place, but Miss Columbia ain't an idiot.

"Tell me," I compel her, fighting the urge to go over there and force her to open up. I can't fight my instincts and damn it, I want answers. Alexis is too stubborn to succumb simply to my stern tone.

She grits her teeth and shakes her head. I walk over to her chair and grab her cheeks, forcing her to look me in the eye. She shivers as my hands touch her face. Yes, her skin really is as soft as I thought and fuck, that brown ochre color looks just as good as I thought against my pale hand. Alexis gawks at me like a terrified doe.

"Fucking tell me," I snarl at her, toughening up to get the answers I want despite my desperate desire to protect her. This isn't the time for disobedience. Alexis might live in a world where she has independence and freedom but that world no longer exists. The moment she stumbled upon Enrico Zagarella's body in that alley, the moment she saw what we did to her, she became mine. I have the responsibility to protect her now and I want to protect her. That instinctive urge is the strongest I've felt in years.

Her life sits in my hands, and a part of her must be profoundly aware of it. She's close to cracking. I know kissing her could pull the words out of her, and I'm very tempted to kiss those soft, gently parted lips. Instead, I plead with her again.

"What happened to you tonight? Who ripped your dress? Where are your shoes? Why were you in the streets so late at night?"

Her lips tremble. I fight the desire to run my tongue over them. She's so fragile…

"My boyfriend's roommate tried to rape me," she says, tears falling from her eyes and running down my fingers. Holy fuck, she has gorgeous eyes. Her tears only draw more attention to the beauty of her face as they run down the soft curve of Alexis' cheeks.

I run my tongue over my lips and fight the urge to have the most inappropriate reaction to her confession.

"What's his name?" I growl. There's no chance in hell I let this shit go.

Chapter 3
The Mobster's Firm Biceps
Alexis

I refuse to answer him. I suddenly realize how much danger I'm in and it hits me that the less I say, the better off I'll be. He hasn't told me his name yet, and this seems to come to his realization as I try to hold strong.

"My name is John," he says. His voice sounds as smooth as honey and his Long Island accent makes me forget he's a murderer. "You heard of me?"

I shake my head. Where the hell would I have heard of someone named "John". It's not like he even gives me his last name. There have to be over a billion Johns in the world. I glare at him, which is the worst I can do to hurt him and completely ineffective to boot.

"Good," he says. "Good. I need you to talk, cupcake. That's what the two of us need. Conversation."

Cupcake? I'm going to throw up. I hate this man and the way he looks at me makes me feel all gross and wriggly inside. John makes me feel weird just for looking directly at him. His jawline is way too sharp and well-defined for him to be a murderer. And since when do murderers have time to build so much muscle? This man is a psychopath and corny nicknames won't make me forget that. I watched him kill someone, and he didn't even flinch. He's fucking insane.

"I have a class at nine in the morning," I try to reason with him. "If you let me go to that, no one will know this happened."

"You don't understand what the fuck just happened, do you?"

Is he fucking joking? I'm a Columbia student. I have the mental capacity to understand what the fuck just happened when a man shoots someone in front of me. I'm not a complete idiot despite John's low opinion of me. What an old-fashioned, proper sounding name for a guy who looks like a fucking thug and acts with no compassion. Except for saving me. He could have killed me so easily that it scares the crap out of me.

John's killer eyes are a deep shade of arctic blue, and one of his pupils is wider than the other. He wears his rough life all over his face. Two scars on his lip. Giant muscles that look stuffed. He looks like he's broken his nose twice. Those fucking eyes… they're haunted. This man has seen more horrible things than what I witnessed in the alley. My palms are sweaty as I try to think of a way out of here. A smarter person wouldn't have frozen up but after what I went through with Gabe…

Despite my best efforts, I tear up again and John surprises me by approaching me and wiping away the tear with his thumb.

"Listen, cupcake. I need you to stop crying. I've been harsh. I get that. But I need you to calm the fuck down and tell me everything. Boyfriend. The friend. I need the names."

I know if I tell John more about Cameron, especially his last name, John will end my boyfriend's life. If I tell him Gabe's name… he'll probably kill Gabe too. They hurt me, but killing is wrong. John is far too comfortable with the idea of murder. I steel myself to talk him down from his murderous ledge.

"I don't want you to hurt him."

"What about the sick fuck who hurt you?" he asks, wiping away another of my tears and rubbing the tear off on his black jeans. My chest catches every time he touches my face. Part of me wants him to stop but another part of me yearns desperately for contact between myself and someone who can take the pain of what happened away. I can't even text Cameron. He'll have no idea where I am and I don't know what the hell Gabe will say about everything that happened.

"I…"

"Tell me what happened," John commands firmly. I don't know what makes me tell him the truth. I blame his gorgeous blue eyes. It's not my fault this monster has alluring eyes like that. He reminds me of a vampire.

"I crawled into my boyfriend's bed and I tried to go to sleep," I whisper, unsure why I'm telling the horrifying hulk of a man standing in front of me what I went through before he only dumped more trauma onto me.

"Mind if I smoke here?" he interrupts me. Of course I don't want the gross smell of a nasty ass cigarette. Only old people smoke anymore and this guy obviously hasn't learned the dangers of nicotine. When I'm a doctor, I guess I'll have to deal with stubborn people like John.

"Whatever," I mutter, glaring at him. He doesn't give a fuck about my silent protest and pulls out one of his gross cancer sticks. Ew. He should at least have the decency to crack a window or something. He moves towards his kitchen window which only unnerves me more. This place is nice, but it's not exactly the sort of place I expected a big time mobster to live.

It's not lavish at all—just a modest, well-furnished apartment in Bayside above a pizza place. Maybe he's not that important in the mob.

"Tell me about the fucking guy," he says, puffing out the window. He has a sexy, Long Island accent I wish didn't get me instantly wet. That's been the best part about moving from boring old Ohio to New York City. The men here have delicious accents and the white guys here aren't afraid to look twice at you. Not like John's looking at me at all, or that I want him to. I just like his accent. It makes him seem safer.

Alexis

What is wrong with me?

John gazes out the window, waiting for me to continue. I'm too scared to move much from my chair. I don't want him to snap and decide I have the next face that needs a bullet. I can't let my momentary pangs of attraction to him make me forget the truth.

"He crawled into bed with me. I tried to fight him off. I could feel him… He was trying…" I gasp for breath as the memories rush back to me. This night has been one horrific moment after another and if I let one negative memory in, all the others rush into my head in an unceasing thrum. I feel numb and my hands won't stop shaking.

"Stop," John interrupts my story with a gentle plea for me to stop. I'm grateful because I can't get the words out and I can feel these stupid fucking tears coming again. He doesn't ask me to stop crying. He sets his cigarette in an ashtray and comes over to me, putting his hand on my shoulders.

He puts his hand on my shoulder, and I shudder. His touch has no right to be this gentle. "Unless you tell me his name, you aren't going back there."

"You won't let me go anyway," I tell him. "I went with you to a second location. You're going to kill me."

His face doesn't relax even a little. Fuck. He really does plan to kill me. Involuntary tears start again and his hand moves from my shoulder to my face.

"I won't kill you," he says. "But if you want to survive, I'll need your obedience."

"I won't do anything sick or twisted," I mutter weakly. I hate how pathetic I sound. I'm crying. My feet are cold as fuck. I look like a hot mess and this strangely attractive murderer could break me in half with his ham-sized biceps even if he didn't have any firearms. There's no use pretending I have any chance against a man who kills for a living or worse, for a hobby. I don't know which and that scares the crap out of me too. It's not like I can ask.

"What you witnessed puts you at risk. My brother and I are not the only people who will want to know the truth. NYPD. Our enemies. There are many people who will want a witness."

"I'll shut up if you shut up," I tell him. I hope he can tell I'm pleading for my life. I just don't want him to kill me. I've survived this far… I want to keep surviving and I want to get out of here. This man is too strange for words and he has a weirdly calm expression on his face when he looks at me. And he's handsome. I especially hate that he's handsome, and that fact is impossible to get off my mind.

John smiles. A strange flutter throbs between my legs. His smile makes him look like the type of suave Italian guy you catch the eye of across a bar. No. He looks better than that. He looks like if your brunette celebrity crush got into three too many bar fights.

"Yeah," he says. "That won't work, cupcake. I don't know you, I don't trust you and I have too much to lose. You're staying here. I don't have much space so you're sleeping in my bed."

"What?" My bladder feels like it's about to give. John glares at me.

"Christ," he snarls. "I don't mean like that. Fuck the guy who did that to you. Give me his fucking name and I'll take care of him."

"I don't want you to do that."

"Fine," he says. "I have bigger problems. For now. You're staying here. Get off the chair and get a shower."

"I don't have any clothes."

"It's your lucky day, cupcake. I happen to wear clothes once in a while."

Does he have to be so sarcastic? Despite his instructions, I'm too terrified to move. How can he expect me to loosen up around him when I just watched him put a bullet in a guy's brain and walk away like it was nothing? He's nearly done with his cigarette. Maybe that's when he plans to drag my ass away and kill me in the shower. I have to keep my guard up.

"What the fuck are you thinking?" he asks.

"I don't need a shower."

"Yeah, you do," he says. "You've been through hell tonight. A shower will do you good. We'll talk in the morning after you get rest."

I don't want to get naked. I don't want to look at my body at the spots where Gabe touched me and acknowledge how absolutely violating this entire night has been. My heart pulses nervously. I can't get what happened out of my head and it hurts so fucking much to acknowledge the pain of knowing that running felt like my only choice. Cameron wouldn't have handled this well.

I can't stay in this man's bed overnight. How the hell could I explain that to Cameron? He would never understand the position I was in and even if I explained, he would insist on going to the police or something stupid that could blow up in both our faces. I'll have to face him, but I'll do it after I get free from John's grasp.

"I'm serious," I attempt pleading with him. "I can't stay here overnight. People will ask questions."

My boyfriend being the main person I'm concerned about. Chloe will probably wonder what happened to me, but she won't notice I'm missing until tomorrow morning when she realizes that I didn't sleep over at Cameron's.

"They won't get any fuckin' answers," he says confidently. "You're mine tonight, cupcake. Get in the damn shower and I'll get you clothes."

"Where is your shower?" I ask nervously. He's too stubborn to argue with and maybe he's right that running hot water over my skin will do me good. I can wash the places where Gabe touched me, scrub myself clean of his gross and violating hands. I'll scrub my cheeks where John touched me too. My cheeks haven't stopped burning since he put his hands on me and I can't help my mind wandering cruelly to imagining where his hands would feel somewhere else.

I tell myself the inappropriate thoughts are a result of the trauma. I feel numb and disconnected from my humanity, so my gut instincts send me careening into the nearest warm body which happens to be John's. I have to fight this instinct. I'm no cheater and I love Cameron. Trauma doesn't give me an excuse to betray him.

"Inside the bedroom, first door on the left," John says gesturing toward the bedroom door. As I look towards the door, I notice his eyes on me. His gaze is deeply discomforting. John puts out the last of his cigarette and I get off the chair and walk towards the door to his bedroom, steadying my breath.

He keeps his place meticulously neat, and it's extremely sparse. It's like a ghost lives here. When I walk into John's bathroom, it smells like bleach and there are three stacks of freshly folded white towels on the counter. Okay, he must have a housekeeper because there's no way this thug folds his washcloths in the shape of a swan.

I take note of this housekeeper as a potential means of escape before I step into the shower. When I take my clothes off, I feel numb and like I'm floating outside of my body. No matter how hard I press my fingers into my skin, I feel nothing. Despite sobbing freely in front of John, alone in that apartment bathroom, I can't bring myself to cry.

Survive this, Alexis.

I step beneath the stream of warm water and allow it to wash over me. There's nothing in the world more important than my survival right now. I can't allow myself to worry about Cameron or Chloe or even what the fuck will happen to Gabe. A mobster picked me up off the streets of Manhattan and now I'm stuck with no shoes and no cell phone miles away from my university with no clue about how to get back and not a dollar to my name.

Don't forget the streets of New York are fucking dangerous and if you let your guard down in the jungle, you give predators an opportunity to pounce. That's what happened with Gabe. That's how I ended up here… I need to find a way out.

Once I turn the shower off and dab my body dry, John knocks politely at the door. He voice sounds gentler on the other side. Maybe nicotine calmed the gruff beast.

"I have socks, sweatpants and an *Islanders* sweatshirt," he says. "Hope you like hockey."

I've never watched a hockey game a day in my life.

"Thanks," I tell him before opening the door. John doesn't bother attempting to avert his eyes when he sees me. He clears his throat and then his gaze drops from my eyes to my feet as he surveys my entire body.

A flush of warmth spreads through me as he gives me the most intense stare down I've ever received. I want to disappear into the ground.

"Take the clothes, cupcake. I'll be out here."

* * *

Chapter 4
My Precious Captive College Girl
John

She exits the bathroom swamped in my clothes. This chick is fucking beautiful. Eventually, I'll find out who touched her and end the motherfucker's life. Tonight, I need to get her ass to sleep so I can close my fucking eyes and deal with all the bullshit that happened tonight in the morning. She's a flight risk, so once I get her into bed, I'll have to double lock the doors and set the alarms.

I'll have to come up with a good reason to keep her here tomorrow, but I'll need sleep to come up with that.

Alexis looks me right back in the eye. She does a terrible job of hiding how much I scare her. Women didn't always fear me. I would prefer her awe or her attraction.

When I was my brother Lucky's age, women leapt at a chance with me. I could ask anybody on a date — anyone in the entire fucking city. Not like that's worth anything if you want to have a family.

I'm pushing forty now and twenty-year-old women like Alexis are far out of my fucking league. I need another cigarette when I think about the fact that I gave up my chance at happiness by not settling down. I'm not like Lucky, so I can control myself around the harder shit. Cigarettes are prescriptive. Without them, there's no fucking rest for my sick head.

Looking at Alexis only makes my guilt worse. A girl like her deserves a good guy, not an asshole like me and not an asshole like the one who left her alone in an alley to stumble into my unfortunate clutches.

"I need you in bed," I say to her gently. "For your own protection. I'll sleep over the covers, you get under."

She bites her lower lip and looks away from me. "What are you going to do to me in that bed? Please, just say what you want…"

"I want to get the fuck to sleep."

If she keeps talking about what she thinks I'll do to her, I don't know how much longer I can push the fucked up thoughts out of my head.

Alexis shoots another nervous look in my direction. She doesn't protest, and she walks out of the bathroom towards my bed. There's plenty of room in there for both of us to fit without stepping on each other's toes. We don't have to succumb to the human instinct that happens when a man and a woman get close to each other and those thoughts cross their mind.

She wouldn't be the one to think of me that way. No, she probably wants to be back at her university with her sweet and terribly gentle college boy. My stomach wraps itself in a knot of guilt and envy just thinking about him. I can command her, protect her and control her, and her stupid boyfriend can't do any of that now. *She's mine.* Alexis looks fucking nervous.

I wait for her to get into bed and then she pulls the covers all the way up over her head. Good. I don't care if she doesn't want to see me as long as she listens to what the fuck I have to say.

"Wait here," I tell her, leaving the room to double check the locks on my doors and call my brother. Fuck. It'll be hell to keep this girl in the house, I can tell. But there's no one else I trust to deal with this.

Once I leave the room, I call Lucky.

"It's done," he says. "Geno has the gun, he's taking it to Boston and we have our team suppressing any possible missing persons if any of the Zagarella people are stubborn enough to go to the police."

My father commanded this not caring that it could rip our families apart. If enough of our cousins disagree with his choice to end Enrico's life, we could have a war on our hands. I don't want to lead an unholy fucking war like that. There aren't enough cigarettes to keep me calm, so I don't bother lighting another.

"Good," I sigh with nicotine tinged breath. "Did you find anything on the body?"

I have to be cold now. I'll have plenty of time to let the bullshit get to me when Sammy finds out. He'll hate that I didn't make him do the hit, but how the fuck could I do that to my own cousin? It wasn't his fuck up.

"Yes," Lucky says. "We have everything we need about the Murray renegades. They're camped out in the Bronx somewhere, but when word gets out, they'll scatter. Their man is done for and they know it."

"Yeah. Did you hear from Padraig?"

"Geno has word from his son. They're sending someone in a few weeks to help us rat out the renegade Murrays, make sure they're flushed out of their fucking rat hole."

"We could use the help," I admit, even if it rankles my pride to admit we could need the Boston mob of all people for help with anything.

I don't want to waste more man power hunting down the renegade Irish. We need time to let this blow over before we go commanding people to start a war with violent Irish motherfuckers who could build alliances with the Hispanics or some of the other city gangs.

It's better to let their own get the fuck over here and stay in charge of cleanup. The news about the Boston fellas chills me out a bit.

"We can't go back there for a while," I remind Lucky. "Did you call Freddie?"

"Freddie's got us covered. No cops," Lucky says. "What about that girl? Do you still have her?"

Do I still have her? She's in my bed and it's getting very fucking hard to quell the dark thoughts in my head about how I can keep her both close and quiet. I can't afford more problems right now, especially not with the Irish boys interested in the city.

"I have the girl," I respond gruffly. I hope my brother doesn't suggest I kill her. Lucky is far too smart or maybe even far too human to suggest such a thing, but he doesn't shy away from his point.

"It's been a long time for you, hasn't it," Lucky says. He sounds too serious. The last thing I need a serious fucking lecture about my sex life from my younger brother. He doesn't know a fucking thing about the responsibility on my shoulders.

"Shut up."

"She's pretty. And way too young for you," Lucky says in an almost teasing tone. Does he feel as badly about tonight as I do? How can he joke about anything at all when we did... nevermind. We each have our own way of coping with 'the life'. This is mine — rescuing a beautiful woman who I should have never laid hands on and... protecting her.

"I didn't take her home to screw her," I growl at Lucky.

Lucky chuckles. "John. You're my brother. We come from the same fucked up fruitcake batter."

I need to send Lucky on a trip to New Jersey...

"Shut the fuck up."

"Where is she?" Lucky asks.

My mouth feels dry. I know how he'll react to this. I pull out and light a cigarette before answering him. "My bed."

Lucky chuckles. "Making her earn her keep?"

"I'll call you in the morning, fuckface."

I hang up on him and smoke for a few minutes. Lucky's right about me. I can't stand going back in there. The second my skin touched hers, I got an immediate erection and it can barely subside for more than a few minutes when I'm around her before I'm hard again. She's too fucking young for me, she's black which is out of the fucking question, and some other fucking asshole just tried to force himself on her.

SHE'S TOO VULNERABLE.

YOU KNOW you like women in this position, John. You love a vulnerable fucking woman so you can ride into her life on a white fucking horse and rescue her. Didn't you learn the hard way that trying to save people never fucking works?

I CAN'T BE a coward forever so I put out the cigarette, saving some for breakfast, before walking back into the bedroom. She's still under the covers. The lump beneath the covers tempts me to take my clothes off and break every soft promise I made to her, but greater sense prevails over my animalistic desires. Sex can wait.

Maybe not for long... but it can wait.

As my weight shifts onto the bed above the covers, I hear her attempt to stifle a nervous gasp. She doesn't know if this is the moment I'll break my vow to her and press her into my bed.

"Don't try anything foolish," I whisper. "I could break your neck before you get to my front door."

She whimpers, which is enough of a response for me. If I have to scare her to keep her safe and keep her in this bed to me,

John

I'll steel myself to that reality. Tomorrow's gonna be a fucking shit show.

I WAKE up early to the sound of soft snores from the lump beneath the covers next to me. Her butt presses up against me and fuck, I'm hard as a rock. I don't want to move and wake her up, fearing that she'll feel my erection but my little college captive has her perfect round ass inadvertently pressed against my dick.

If it weren't for my fucking back, I would have slept on the couch. Maybe I should have slept on the fucking couch anyway considering the slightest movement will probably force me to ejaculate. She murmurs in her sleep and wriggles her ass. Blood rushes to my cock.

You need to put your dick in that ass.

I cough, hoping to wake her up and move away from her before she becomes completely sentient, but that doesn't work. She wriggles her ass under the covers more, rubbing the soft flesh against my stiffening cock.

Fuck this. I leap off the bed, trying to get myself away from the horrible temptation and wake her up instantly. It's not like I could expect her to fall into a deep sleep in a stranger's bed. I terrify the fuck out of her and it's clear by the hurried way she darts out of what appeared to be a deep sleep.

Alexis throws the cover off and stares at me in a panic. Jesus... What happened to her hair? There's a clump of it sticking to her face and several clumps in several directions. Alexis wipes her eyes, still red and puffy from last night. She's a few shades lighter than walnut with thick, untamed hair and I can't get the thought of her lips around my cock out of my head.

It has been way too fucking long since I got laid.

"What's going on?" She says. "Why are you awake? Can I go home yet? I have class at nine in the morning. Please... I promise I won't go to the cops."

Too many questions spill out of her mouth and I am fucking desperate for nicotine, even if I never have late night cigarettes anymore.

"Quiet, cupcake," I snarl. I'm hard, unable to do anything about it and not in the mood for any of her fucking whining about the cops or leaving my apartment. I have bigger problems —like a raging erection unlike any I've had in years.

"What is wrong with you?" she hisses at me with frustration. I can't control myself. I need to make her obedient and there's only one way I know how to achieve that. I have to show her I mean business, that I intend to take control here and push her to obedience by any means necessary.

I'm not her fucking college boyfriend. I'm a nightmare.

"What happened to you last night was wrong," I growl, pacing at the foot of the bed. I'm losing my mind. I'm losing it because this is so wrong and…

Alexis keeps staring at me and I feel possessed.

I murmur half to myself before glancing over at her. "I can fix everything that went wrong."

She gives me a bewildered look like she didn't see this coming and maybe she didn't, but fuck she should have felt it coming. I didn't exactly hide my hardness from her and she must have felt my body against hers. I run my tongue over my lips, preparing for her resistance. She's been through hell and this could break her… But I don't know.

She won't regret a fucking second with me, but I know at first, this will hurt her. Confuse her. I have to do this if I want to keep her safe. I have to have a way to control her and this is the best way how.

"What do you mean?"

She pushes her hair out of her face, raking her fingers through her thick curls in a desperate attempt to untangle them. Her chest juts out crudely forward and I can't help imagining those gorgeous walnut-colored breasts spilling from her shirt. I want to lick her nipples until she screams.

I want to take her so she knows she's mine and send her back to the Upper West Side to turn her fucking life upside down. It's too late for Alexis to go back now. She witnessed John Vicari pulling the fucking trigger in an alleyway.

The only way I can protect this chick is to keep her. But she's too fucking wild like this. I have to break her.

"I mean... I saved your life. I housed you for the night. I'll even consider sending you back to your fancy university during the daytime for your classes if you prove to me I can trust you."

I tried my hardest to resist her, but I found it impossible. I tried to be a better person, but I wasn't even a good person.

"How the hell would I prove that?" Alexis asks, genuinely bewildered. Guilt forms a painful lump in my throat. I told myself I wouldn't go this far, but my erection is too much for me to bear and if I climb into that bed again to face her soft ass pressing into my body, I'll lose myself.

I need her agreement before I recklessly indulge in our chemistry for each other.

I can't tell if Alexis suspects my intentions yet or if she's always been suspicious and she's just damn good at hiding her feelings. I don't care. I sense from the doe-eyed look on the innocent college student's face that I will get exactly what I want from here and that will make my job a hell of a lot easier.

I just can't let Lucky find out I'm screwing the college student. I'm the responsible one, not the fuck up. But it's been so fucking long and I'm so fucking hard—and there's a girl in my bed who I need to break.

"Women are loyal creatures," I tell her. "Angels, every single one of you. If I fuck you, cupcake, I'll have your loyalty and that's what I want."

She doesn't miss a beat. "Are you out of your fucking mind?"

Yes. You have to be out of your fucking mind to survive the mob and you have to be the craziest motherfucker out of millions to make it as the boss. Even if dad comes home soon, this will fuck me up forever. I've had to do shit I never thought I would and order hits I never thought I could pull off. I pulled the trigger on my own fucking family and I'll keep that shit with me the rest of my life.

"You have a choice, princess. You stay here and I protect you, but I don't fucking trust you, or you give me your body. Once we get this out of our system, you go back to your college, dump your lame ass boyfriend and we work out a deal about classes and that other bullshit."

"What kind of deal?"

That wasn't exactly the answer I expected. Honestly, I thought she might push back more about the boyfriend thing. I try not to read into it. I'm not here to fuck this girl's heart. I only need her to agree to give me her body—her supple, twenty-year-old, way too fucking curvy for her own good body.

Deal, John. Think of the fucking deal.

"You go to classes. You live your life. You come here every night and do exactly what I ask."

"You expect me to trek out to Long Island every night?"

"I'll come get you. I will always maintain responsibility for your whereabouts."

"Why the fuck would I do that?" she responds. There's still some bite in her but the more forceful Alexis is, the more I crave taming her.

"Because you don't want me to fuck you anyway and then kill you."

I'm taking a risk, pushing her like this. I could never hurt her like that but... she doesn't know that. It's not to her advantage for her to know how far I would *really* go to keep her safe. *She's mine. I can't fight that possessive urge towards her.*

Her face wrinkles in disgust and she shrieks at me like she's my fucking mom or something.

"You are disgusting," she hisses. "I won't respond to your cruel threats."

I grit my teeth, running my tongue along the inside of my lip desperately forcing myself to be patient while my erection throbs and I force dirty thoughts out of me head. I know I'm past the point of control, but I want this woman to agree to having me and I need her agreement before the sun crests over the horizon and floods my Bayside apartment with daylight. I want her before the night we shared disappeared.

The only way out of this is by bonding us together. There is nothing in this world more physically bonding than sex. The sweat, the smell, the taste of a woman and the delicious flood of hormones make tangling in the sheets the fastest way to secure our futures.

Unlike Lucky, I can't wait a fucking decade for the woman I want. Bringing her to my place was a mistake I stumbled into on purpose. I can't help myself. Even when I'm trying to be the fucking good guy, I turn into a goddamned predator.

"This is the only way I can guarantee your loyalty," I snarl at Alexis gruffly. "You come to my bed, or I cannot let you out of my sight. I'll have no reason to trust you. I might as well kill you if I can't trust you."

She glares at me like she's lost the spirit of her fear.

"I'm not going to just sit here and let you kill me. I'll bite your dick off," she threatens again. I still see very little sense in relenting to her.

"When you have your lips around my cock, you won't bite," I tell her. "Now get off the bed."

First, I have to touch her.

"What? Are you out of your mind?" she hisses, scrambling to the other side of the bed and dragging a pillow between us as if it's some sort of defense.

"I won't fight you, Alexis. If you need help, I'll make you cum first."

"Ew!!!"

She clutches the pillow tighter as her voice reaches nearly a fever pitch. I have her trapped on the bed and have no intention of letting her out of my sight until she makes a sensible decision.

"Quit the fucking drama, cupcake. Get over here."

She lobs the pillow at my head and scowls at me, crossing her legs defensively as I catch the pillow and toss it aside.

"It's not drama," she responds indignantly, glowering at me from my bed and looking even more fuckable than she did when her soft ass pressed into my cock and awakened this beast of desire in me.

She blurts out quickly, "I don't want to be hurt again. That's not a crime."

"I'm not a fucking rapist. I need loyalty, not pain. I promise I won't hurt you. No anal, nothing like that."

Not tonight, at least. There's definitely going to be anal in Alexis' future.

"I have a boyfriend," she gasps, her chest heaving as it finally hits her that I'm dead fucking serious and she's not leaving my apartment unless I get my cock wet.

"Do I look like I give a fuck? Once we're done, dump him. Fuck, if it'll make you feel better, dump him first."

"I can't dump Cameron!" she shrieks. "And I am NOT under any circumstances a cheater."

Jesus fucking Christ. My dick is too hard to handle hysterics right now. I need compliance. Obedience. Are there still people in New York who don't take orders from John Vicari? I stop myself from being harsh with her.

"Why the fuck not? Give me his number, I'll dump him for you."

I reach for my cellphone and Alexis gives it a wistful look like she's considering lunging for it and then considers making a better decision that doesn't endanger her life.

"No!" Alexis says quickly, giving me a forlorn expression that she better not think will change my mind. "I'll do it."

I'm not falling for her sad girl act. She's a college student. I hand her that cell phone, she'll have the cops over here in two shakes of a witch's tit.

"I'm not giving you the phone. You give me the number, I'll put it on speaker. Then you dump him."

John

She gives me a desperate, pleading look that makes my dick want to burst out of my pants even more. Does this woman know the fucking effect she has on me? She drives me fucking wild and I haven't even touched her yet. Maybe I should call Lucky. Maybe he could talk me off the precipice of being a fucking idiot.

I won't be as stupid as my brother. I won't knock this one up.

"I can't do that," she pleads with me. "Cameron… I haven't even told him about Gabe and then I have to drop this on him and dump him… He'll never believe I didn't cheat on him. Please don't do this. Please, just let me go. I promise I won't tell."

Gabe. That must be the motherfucker who touched her. Duly noted.

Fuck, she's crying. I don't want her to cry. Pain isn't the point of this. I guess maybe I can't avoid hurting her somehow. It's either this or I find some other fucking way to ruin her life. I already ruined her life. The moment Alexis Carter's eyes landed on John Vicari's, her life was over.

This won't ruin her life—this will be the tiniest pleasure in the sea of fucking hell this chick will go through.

"Cameron doesn't fucking deserve you."

I don't have to know the guy to know I'm fucking right. First, Alexis is drop dead gorgeous. She's one of those women who clearly doesn't know that she doesn't have to beg and plead for loser fucking guys to give her attention. She's a rare fucking gem and the right guy would have never put her in the fucking position to have some loser get into bed with her. No fucking way.

"You don't know my boyfriend," she says defensively. "We've been together forever. You don't know what we have. What we have is real love. You're a murderer. You don't know what real love is. You're probably doing this because your mother didn't love you. I'm sure there's some psychological reason that-

Christ. She's like a parrot.

"Alexis, quiet," I snap at her, mostly because I need us to

focus here and leave unpacking my psychological issues for my future grandkids' shrink. She silences right up, which suits me fine.

"Cameron doesn't deserve you. Gabe doesn't deserve you. None of those fucking losers deserve you. Get your clothes off. You'll dump the fucker after."

"I'm not a cheater," she whimpers, shaking her head furiously. "I'm not a cheater."

"You're not. You're in a desperate, vulnerable position and I need this to ensure your loyalty. You're obeying me. You're saving your life, Alexis. It's noble."

She ditched her one line of defense, my pillow, and now she gives me a weak, defeated look. I have her. I'm so fucking close to having her and this feels worth it.

"It's not noble," she whimpers, her hands falling to her side and tears streaming down her face. This won't work if she's cowering in a corner. I need her to come to me. I stand near the bed and point to the ground at my feet.

"Get over here and get on your knees. This can be quick."

"My knees?"

She gives me that sad, pleading look again. I'll always remember her face frozen at this moment in time—our first night in my apartment. I know it the moment she looks at me with the purest fucking defeat. Her face tugs on my heart strings for a split second and there's this warmth inside me that I swear I killed years ago and that warmth spreads only in her direction.

There's this fucking energy between us that I can't explain and her eyes don't leave mine as she slithers across the bed reluctantly and sobs as she drops to her knees. We both know she's about to suck my cock and we both know that given the choice, she would run back to the Upper West Side and never hear from me again but instead... we're making this memorable.

She won't forget any fucking word out of John Vicari's mouth. It's the quickest way to ensure her loyalty. For her own good. Yeah, that's what I have to tell myself to believe that I'm not completely broken and fucked up in the head beyond repair.

Once she's on her knees, her eyes drop away from me and she drags herself to the exact spot I guided her to. She's twenty. I have to be fucking careful. She doesn't seem like the type of chick who does this often. She also doesn't stop crying.

I put my finger under her chin and tilt her face up so I can look her in the eye.

"Stop crying, cupcake."

"I can't," she whimpers, tears streaming down her face.

"What's the matter? You don't want to suck my cock?"

She runs her tongue over her lips and whimpers, "I have a boyfriend, John. I… I love him."

"Hush, woman," I whisper. "You don't love that mother-fucker. He doesn't deserve your love. If you were mine, I would kill any motherfucker who dared climb into a bed with you. I'd bring you his fucking testicles as a necklace."

Her crying intensifies. Fuck.

"That's cruel."

"I'm not your college boyfriend, sweetheart. I know what to do with my dick and I know what to do with your body. So hush up, open your sweet mouth and let's stop wasting time."

I need to be smarter than this, but I'm not. I convince myself that this way I don't have to kill her. I convince myself that I can keep her in my Bayside apartment at least most of the time if she just does this. I let go of her chin and she rushes to avert her gaze from me.

"Fine," she whispers. "I'll do it and then… I'll dump him."

"Good."

"But you have to promise not to kill him," she says, those tears falling hard again.

"I'll promise you anything if you stop crying."

"Then promise that," she whispers. "Please, promise that you won't kill him."

I need my cock sucked.

"Yeah, whatever. I promise."

"Okay."

She sniffles and then wipes away her own tears before reaching for my pants. I have her. Holy fuck, I am so close. It's been far too fucking long since I had a woman and I definitely don't deserve the one on her knees in front of me.

* * *

Chapter 5
On My Knees For The Butcher
Alexis

His bedroom smells nice. At least his bedroom smells nice. It's neat with a bottle of black cologne on the bedside table next to his pistol. I can hardly take my eyes off the pistol but John seems to view this dangerous weapon as just another feature of his bedroom. He gazes down at me with those terrifyingly intense blue eyes and my chest catches as I come to terms with what I'm about to do.

Cheat on Cameron.

I don't want to cheat on Cameron, but John makes it pretty fucking clear that he won't let me leave unless I suck his dick. He won't let me have my way about anything unless I dump Cameron, but I'll worry about that after I handle the dick thing. I've struggled to ignore John's raging erection, but ignoring his dick becomes out of the question on my knees in front of it.

He's well-endowed, which makes this worse. I didn't want to think about how big his dick was. An average dick might have allowed me the privilege of ignoring his dick size, but as I run my hand over the outside of his pants, I can't help but visibly react to his cock.

He smirks. I hate that he's smirking like he's about to win a prize at the state fair, so I quickly remove my hand and act like

Alexis

I'm not losing my fucking mind about the size of John's dick. He was stiff and swollen with arousal. I could tell without removing his cock from his pants that I wouldn't have the ability to get my mouth around it.

He wants to put that thing between my legs. No way.

I touch his belt and give John another pleading look. So far the pleading looks have done nothing to activate his latent empathy. It's dawning on me that John doesn't have any latent empathy. He's a monster who I watched kill another man in cold blood and he's making me sleep with him because he's a misogynistic asshole who derives sick pleasure from the power he holds over me.

"Are you waiting for an invitation?" he asks in a thick, oddly sexy Long Island accent. "Because I already gave you the fucking invite, cupcake. Get my dick out."

He has the social graces of an ostrich in high heels, but John has absolute power over me and if I say a single word to offend him, he'll end my life. If I do this... I live. If the cost of my survival is breaking up with Cameron, it's a sacrifice I'll have to make.

I unzip his pants and John grunts prematurely as I peel them away from his hips. Holy shit, he has a muscular ass. I'm not the type to keep my eyes glued to a man's butt cheeks but John has an especially voluptuous ass with muscular glutes, well-shaped thighs and a deliciously chiseled stomach, which he lifts his shirt to bare to me.

I don't have time to catalog his tattoos, but there are enough to require a catalog, all in black ink. My mom always taught me that tattoos were expensive and time-consuming and men who had too many were broke with too much time on their hands. John doesn't seem broke but maybe she's right about him having too much time on his hands considering every inch of his body underneath his shirt is covered in ink. I can't make sense of all the tattoos, but they all piece together a collage of who he is... *A beast's secrets.*

52

As I run my fingers beneath the waistband of John's underwear, his fingers unceremoniously slide through my matted curls. I just woke up. The last thing I want to do is have a white man playing with my messy hair while shoving his dick in his mouth. John appears to revel in tangling my hair further with his fingers.

He grunts before I even get my hands on his dick and long before I get his underwear off properly. John's hefty, throbbing mass of man-meat juts forward greedily as he grunts, "I love your fucking hair."

A strange and unwelcome gush of juices spreads between my thighs and my cheeks warm with guilt. Nothing John says or does can turn me on. I refuse. Ignoring the warmth in my cheeks, I run my fingers outside his underwear again, feeling the shape of his cock to tease out what kind of mess I got my ass into.

He's too big to get into my mouth. I know it. Slowly, I remove his underwear and John's dick springs forward crudely, thick drops of pre-cum pooling at the monstrous, bulging head. His dick is a mysterious, dusky pink color that sends that weird gush between my legs again.

My fingers brush John's dick and he makes a frustrated grunt like I'm teasing him. I attempt to wrap my hand around his dick but I can't fit the entire thing in my grasp. He's way too thick if I can't wrap my hand around it, but as I hold on to him and marvel, John's cock only grows in my hand. My stomach tightens.

How the hell can I fit a dick that big inside me?

John grunts again as if taking my time represents some unique violence against him. His cock strengthens in my grasp, veins bulging from the side of the thick dusky pink shaft. He's making me do this but my body responds as if I want this more than anything. The back of my mouth waters at the size of the impressive dick I hold tenderly in my grasp.

"I need your mouth," John gasps. I close my eyes. There's no need for me to watch the inevitable train wreck of John desperately struggling to fit his enormous dick into my mouth.

I run my tongue slowly on my lips to get them nice and wet for his dick. It's the only chance I have to fit his big dick in my mouth without cracking my jaw. John's dick juts forward impatiently. With closed eyes, I stick my tongue out and touch the tip of his thick, oozing dick. The clear liquid oozing out of his tongue drops onto my tongue as it touches the head of his cock. He tastes like diluted maple syrup and my tongue instinctively swirls around the head of his dick to catch every drop of his arousal.

John makes an ungodly groan like he's never had a blowjob before. I assume a guy who looks like him has sex all the time. Hell, he wants to have sex with me and he just met me. I'm no different from any other woman. If anything, I'm less special. More broken. I close my eyes to push the thoughts out of my head and focus on producing that ungodly sound from John again.

It's much better than him silently glowering at me. I run my tongue in a slow circle against the head of John's dick and he groans again. It's a different sound, but still pleasure. I stretch my mouth as wide as possible and barely get the head of his dick between my lips. As I slide my mouth down an inch, John makes that sound again and his fingers slide into my curls.

My body tenses nervously as John's pale fingers twist between my curls. I have a rule — I don't let white people touch my hair. This isn't exactly the position to make demands in, but I don't think John would care. His fingers sink lewdly between my curls with no regard for my curl pattern, the almond oil and various butters that keep my coils neat, or my hair style. He grabs a handful of my hair and holds my head in place.

"You have a hot fucking mouth," he whispers. "It's been so fucking long for me, cupcake. I need more…"

John's statement is more of a request than a warning. Holding onto my hair like a handle, he slowly eases more of his dick into my mouth. His dick stretches my mouth to capacity and I can't feel any oxygen coming into my lungs because of John's dick filling every inch of my mouth.

"Fuck, that feels good," he grunts, and he pushes deep into my mouth. I stretch my lips as wide as they can possibly go, and I struggle to take the full length of John's thick, veiny shaft in my mouth. Holy fuck. I grab his thighs and run my tongue along the underside of John's staff. He groans and pulls his dick away from my mouth.

I gasp for breath and tears stream out of my eyes from the lack of oxygen. John still holds my hair, too dominant and possessive of me to let go. I run my tongue over my lips to get spit off and then glance up at John. When I look up at him, John grins. His blue eyes send a shiver straight through me.

He smirks. He's enjoying this way too much.

"Didn't mean to choke you with my dick, princess," He murmurs gently. My pussy throbs again. I want to hate him, but he provokes the filthiest reaction from me and I'm stuck here. I'd better enjoy him since he's hellbent on having me in his bed no matter what.

He takes his thumb and rubs away my tears, taking them away from my face as he smiles.

"I'm not done until I cum."

"I can't fit that thing in my mouth."

"Yes, you can. I have to be patient. But it's fucking hard. It's so fucking hard," he grunts. The pain is visible on his face. Why the fuck does it hurt John so bad not to have his dick in my mouth? He must be some kind of player. This can't be an uncommon occurrence for him.

John guides my head, holding onto my hair and forcing me to put my tongue on his dick. I open my mouth wider and John pushes his dick between my lips again.

"You have the perfect full lips for sucking cock," John grunts in his sultry Long Island accent. He doesn't sound proper, like Cameron. He doesn't sound foreign, like Gabe. His voice makes me want to obey him more than anything and it's not just fear. There's a gush between my thighs and John pushes his dick deeper than the first time. I try to breathe out of my nose and it works. John moves my head further down his shaft and I take him deeper, moving forward of my accord.

John grunts again, and I run my tongue along the underside of his shaft. John's grasp on my hair tightens, and he groans again, "Fuck, I'm gonna cum."

So soon? I grab onto his thighs again and attempt to get John's dick to touch the back of my throat. That happens with less than half his dick in my mouth. I gag as John's enormous dick touches the back of my throat and the slight contact with the deepest part of my mouth pushes John over the edge.

His grasp on my hair tightens, and he twists my hair around his hand as his dick explodes in my mouth. Hot cum gushes from John's cock and he groans as the thick liquid forms a syrupy plug in the back of my throat. I gag and then John removes his cock quickly, allowing the hot gush of his seed space to slide down my throat. My swallow reflex stops my gagging as every drop of John's cum slips down my throat.

I stop gagging, but I'm still nauseous. His cum tastes like diluted maple syrup again with a hint of coffee – no hint of the tobacco he seems to smoke constantly. The nausea hits me hard because I just did the unthinkable. Cameron. Genuine tears spill from my eyes as John's cum slides down my throat.

I'm a slut. This is proof. I'm worthless. Gabe thought he could take me and John… I voluntarily got on my knees for John. That makes it worse. John's cock softens before my eyes, still maintaining an impressive size. His dick can't be natural. I don't know what else it would be but… he has to have one of the largest human penises in existence.

My jaw hurts and my throat aches and the taste of John's sweet cum makes me feel lower than dirt. He finally relinquishes control of my hair. I crumple forward in a tangled limp mess of guilt and flailing limbs. I can't stop myself from crying. Sobbing would probably be a better description for it.

My tears provoke no sympathy from John. He stuffs his cock into his underwear and pulls his pants up.

"Listen, cupcake. You did a great job."

My crying intensifies. Cameron complains about my "lazy bitch" blowjobs and regularly reminds me that I'm a prudish pillow princess. Having the tattooed man who shoved his gigantic cock down my throat tell me I did a great job feels like strange mockery.

There's also pride, but I suppress that feeling. It's disturbingly unfeminist to pride myself in my ability to suck a mobster's cock to climax. I refuse to get up unless John makes me. If he wants me to have sex with him and if he wants me to feel this loyalty towards him, he'll have to work. He already degraded me with a full helping of his sloppy, creamy white cum down my throat. Maybe I'll get lucky and he won't make me go all the way.

"Don't think you're getting out of this," he says gruffly, dashing all my hope that he would give up his lust for sex with me. "I want your cunt and I'll be ready for you soon."

I whimper on the ground and John roughly grabs my forearm, dragging me to my feet. I hate myself for cowering in front of him, but there's something humiliating about this entire experience that finally gets to me. Congratulations, John Vicari–you broke my spirit with your enormous dick and the thick warm helping of cum still sliding down my esophagus spreading guilty warmth through every inch of me.

"Don't worry," he snaps. "I don't want kids, so I'll use a condom."

I won't lie about the relief that floods me when he says this. The thought of John putting his cock in me scares me enough. I don't want him to cum inside me. That would only make this terrible situation worse.

"Okay," I whimper from my position in front of him.

Alexis

"Stop acting all fucking scared," he commands. "I haven't hurt you yet."

Yet. That's a key word there and it's a word that sends a chill straight down my spine. He's dangerous. I have to remember to keep this man happy because he's fucking dangerous and if I piss him off, he could put a bullet in my head next.

"Christ," he snarls. "You're shaking like a fucking rabbit."

"What do you expect?" I snap. "You shoved your dick in my mouth and…"

I hate myself for breaking down, but I can't stop my natural reaction. I cry as I finish my sentence. "You made me cheat on my boyfriend."

I'm trapped here. I'm just trying to survive. I can't let him get into my head. He's a monster and he's making me obey his filthy commands. I don't have to let myself fall for his icy blue eyes or his immoral desires. I'm stronger than him and I'm stronger than this. Resist him, Alexis.

Resist him.

* * *

Chapter 6
Getting Rid Of The So-Called Boyfriend
John

Each time she mentions her boyfriend, I get so fucking pissed off. I want to find the bastard in whatever preppy enclave on the Upper West Side he insulates himself from the rest of fucking society in and kick his ass back to Connecticut or wherever the fuck the prick is from originally.

"You don't have a boyfriend," I growl at her. "You broke up the second I grabbed you in that alley and he won't be a part of your life after tonight, so forget about him."

"But… cheating is wrong."

"Yes," I snarl at her. "So make sure you stay loyal to me and only me after tonight. Once I put my tongue or my cock in any part of your body, your boyfriend no longer owns that part of you."

"You're sick…" she whispers.

"No," I respond flatly. "I simply understand human beings. Your boyfriend abandoned you tonight, and he lost the right to claim you. I won't make that mistake."

Alexis bites on her lower lip hard and fights back tears.

"You are mine," I tell Alexis firmly. "You were mine the moment I touched you and by the time you break up with that asshole, you will be thoroughly and utterly done with him because I will have claimed you. Understood?"

"I'm not that person…"

"You're my person," I growl. "And you will always be mine."

Goosebumps break out over her skin as I say the word "mine". I need her to surrender to the inevitability of belonging to me.

There will be no boyfriend after tonight. Every inch of this college student will belong to me. The thought of another man touching Alexis after feeling her warm lips wrap around my dick drives me wild. That will never fucking happen. This woman is mine. Sex will earn her loyalty and that works the other way around.

I release her forearm and Alexis keeps her arms up as if she could successfully shield herself from me if I really wanted to hurt her. I want her to settle down and enjoy this. We both need this to ensure our safety.

"I can make this easier on you if you get on the bed and take your pants off."

"There's no way putting your alien dick inside me will be easy."

Alien dick. There's a first. She's a college girl, so she must be into sci-fi shit. I run my tongue over my lips. This time, my dick won't be the part of me I put inside her. If I want Alexis to turn to putty in my hands, I need to eat her pussy like the last supper and suck her lower lips until she turns into a gooey, sweaty mess in my hands.

"Not my dick, cupcake. Ever had a man put his tongue down there or have guys stopped doing that?"

She can't still feel any shyness around me after having my dick in her mouth. But she sure acts that way.

"I don't want to tell you that."

"Why not?"

"I don't know you. The only thing I know about you is that you're a killer."

"That still has you fucked up?"

"What are you? Who are you? Because you are way too comfortable with all of this."

She's wrong about me. Every fucking thing about this is way too uncomfortable for me. I didn't expect to find her. I didn't expect to like how she looked. My desire for her came out of fucking nowhere and I'm still thinking of a way I can follow my protective instincts and keep the shrieking college girl from spilling her guts to the fucking cops and forcing me to do something massively fucked up.

I don't want to kill a woman. I don't. It's what really fucking changes you and turns you into someone you don't want to become – not even in the mob. It's the type of shit that makes you drink too much and do drugs and all that other bullshit. You gotta keep your head clear.

"I'm the man who will keep you safe if you do exactly what he says."

"How is oral sex going to keep me safe," she says with a clinical tone and a sneer. I don't think she can help it. College girls all sound like they're smarter than you and it's probably because they are. I gotta give her a good answer that she can wrap her mind around.

"It won't keep you safe. I'll make you cum and make you feel good without all the bullshit knocking around you head."

"An orgasm won't make me forget what I saw."

"What about three?"

She rolls her eyes. "Bragging like that is really unattractive."

I chuckle. Her fire gets me hard again faster than I expected. Damn, I'd better get my tongue between those pretty caramel thighs if I know what's good for me. Alexis has the softest brown skin and I want to put my tongue all over it. Every inch of her needs a fucking kiss and as for her pussy...

Unattractive? I don't give a fuck if she thinks I'm unattractive. All I need is Alexis on the bed so I can split her lower lips with my tongue and suck her pretty pussy to a climax.

"Whatever, cupcake. As long as you do what I say."

"Does being a demanding asshole really work with women? You know… women you aren't forcing?"

We both know I'm not forcing her into this position. She lay in my bed and knew I wouldn't hurt her. Now morning light filters in through my window and we can both smell the pizza crust dough from downstairs.

For the first time in ages, I crave her more than a cigarette. I don't want to leave this bed before touching her, holding her, and giving us the only bond that can keep us safe. *There won't be another woman like this. I'm old enough to know that.*

"I haven't been with a woman in years. Now get on the bed or I'll tie you there," I murmur, sounding far more threatening than I intend to.

She pipes down really quick like she's afraid I'll fucking do it. I haven't restrained her at all and I've given her absolutely nothing to fear.

"Don't joke about that," she snaps. "And you're still… you're still making me cheat on Cameron."

"It's only cheating if you climax," I tease her, taking her by the waist and pulling her against me. I'm tired of Alexis shying away from me when I want her this fucking badly.

"That's not funny, John," she lectures. "I–

"Pants off. We're done discussing this."

She glares at me but the pants come off. There's relief and then my dick gets hard as fuck. She has the plumpest hips, thick curves with stretch marks and then her ass…

"Turn around," I grunt. I don't want her to see how fucking red I'm turning looking at her. She has a perfect body and I haven't seen a perfect body in a long time. She's not too thin. There's weight on her stomach and her hips and her ass. They don't make asses like this in Long Island. No. This is the perfect, ripest pair of ass cheeks I've ever seen. She has two giant pumpkins bulging out of her behind and they look so fucking soft. My cock jerks in my pants and I don't know if I'm strong enough not to enter her.

"What are you staring at?" she says, even if she can't see me staring. Her instincts are on fire.

"Your perfect black ass," I growl. My dick can't stand this. I need her so fucking badly it physically aches.

"John," Alexis replies with sharp indignation. "That's really inappropriate."

"Why? It's perfect. You're black. You've got the perfect black ass like a girl in a music video."

"Shut. Up," Alexis breathes. I want to take a big bite out of that perfect ass.

"Why?"

She sounds all choked up when she answers me. "My boyfriend never talks to me the way you talk to me."

"Christ, Alexis. I'm tired of this fucking boyfriend. Bend over. Get on the bed."

"John, wait–

"Do as I fucking say."

She stumbles forward and bends over my bed. I drop to my knees behind her and kiss her thighs too quickly. She squeals nervously as my warm lips contact her shy, untouched thighs. They're exactly as soft as I expected, but her nervous response pisses me off. She's thinking of her boyfriend, isn't she?

"Stop feeling guilty," I snarl. "He doesn't deserve you. He never deserved you if he allowed another man to get near you. With me, that will never fucking happen. I will destroy any man who comes near you."

"John…"

"Quiet," I snarl. "I'm tasting you."

I don't want her to respond or complain or protest. Once I choose a woman, an obsession roots in me. It's mutual insurance for Alexis' safety. We both need this. She whimpers to silence her desire to moan as I kiss her thighs. Alexis has perfect voluptuous thighs that spill into my palms as I roam up her ass and spread her cheeks apart.

I need those panties off immediately, so I rip them off, causing Alexis to moan and her face to collapse forward into my apartment bed. I bet her boyfriend never eat her pussy like this. I drive my tongue between her legs, sliding my tongue from her ass to her clit. I like to start with my tongue on a woman's asshole because it's the softest, tenderest most forbidden part of her and it's the part I like to own the most.

Teasing her with my tongue only gets me hotter for what I plan to do with that soft, tiny and super fucking tight asshole. Alexis moans as my tongue slips over her furry outer lips and then between them until my lips wrap around her clit and I suck on the little nub until she screams. She has no time to react to the intrusion of my tongue between her legs. I control every movement and surprise her with how swiftly I move from her clit back to that tight puckered asshole.

I don't want her to cum – I just want to taste her sweet black ass and push my tongue in every fucking hole she has before I make her cum in my mouth.

"I love your ass," I whisper. "You have a nice tight asshole."

She whimpers and tries to say something which comes out in muffled moans as my tongue probes her back door curiously. Yeah, she's never had anything back there, I can tell. My tongue slides over her tender, puckered folds and Alexis squeals like nothing I've ever heard before. Every noise that comes out of her mouth is so fucking hot. I don't think she gets how fucking crazy she makes me.

I want to cum inside each one of her perfect, tight brown holes. I'm nobody to give Lucky shit because of his sexual prefer- ence when I'm the fucking same. It's a curse how much I love these fucking women and it's a greater curse to have to keep this a secret. To keep her a secret. I spread her lower lips again with my tongue, moving from her tongue-fucked back door to her neglected vulva.

Her pussy lips taste fucking delicious. Alexis moans again as I slide a finger over her entrance and tease her outer lips with my tongue. Her moans drive me fucking crazy and I don't want to stop fucking her sweet pussy with my tongue. She gushes clear juices all over my finger once I slide inside her. Alexis' hips buck back against my lips and I suck on her lower lips as I slide my index finger inside her tightness and enjoy the sound of her screams and the way she pumps her hips back against my finger, desperate for pleasure despite her initial reluctance to have me inside her.

Her head might feel guilty but her heart and her body both know exactly what they fucking want. Her pussy tightens around my finger as another gush of fluid drips out of Alexis' tightness. She smells really fucking good. I forced myself to forget how much I missed the smell of a tasty, wet pussy. Pushing my tongue and fingers between her legs is almost enough to make me cum with no extra effort.

Not until she finishes. I can't allow my cock inside this tight, perfect brown pussy until she cums hard enough to forget her loser ass boyfriend. I have to break them up. I rub my tongue in slow circles around Alexis' perfect clit. Her body responds by tightening around my fingers and I know I almost have her. Pushing her over the finish line should be easy.

I add another finger to her tightness. At first Alexis wriggles and moans in mock resistance to the intrusion of a second finger. Feeling how fucking tight she is with my fingers nearly makes me explode in my pants. She is insanely tight and heat pulses straight to my cock as I push my fingers deeper into the tight pussy I plan to fuck tonight.

"Fuck, you're perfect," I whisper between kissing her soft little clit. Alexis' moans grow soft as she gets closer. I rub her g-spot with slow circles and keep kissing her clit until she succumbs to the pleasure she so desperately wanted to deny herself. My little cupcake cums hard, her juices gushing out of her pussy and flooding my hands and fingers with her essence.

John

Her soft whimpers drive me fucking nuts. I lick her juices off those pretty brown thighs and slowly remove my fingers from her dripping pussy.

After licking my fingers clean of her pussy juice, I give Alexis a soft smack on the rump.

"Okay, cupcake. Time to dump your shitty boyfriend."

Alexis collapses forward, like she can bury her face in my bed and disappear. Nothing she does will change the fact that I just tongue-fucked her pussy to an orgasm and I bet it was better than anything she got from her shitty college boyfriend.

"Can you stop," she groans. "Just… stop."

I don't want to get angry with her. She probably loves the fucking guy, I get it. But if she loved the guy, she might have fought harder. She might have stopped herself from cumming in my mouth. She might have begged. Alexis didn't do any of that. She wants me.

"Get the fuck up," I snarl at her. "I made you cum. I took you off the streets and I'll keep you safe. But that only works if you do what you know is right. Dump him. Now."

* * *

Chapter 7
F**king To Feel Better
Alexis

Tapping Cameron's number into John's phone could kill my soon-to-be ex-boyfriend. I don't know how far John's crazy extends, but I sense he has the power to use that phone number to track down my boyfriend and take him out. He already knows Cameron's first name, and he has enough information to find him and Gabe...

My throat tightens. My cum drips down my thighs, a guilty reminder that I don't have a choice anymore. I have to dump Cameron.

I'm a cheater and he doesn't deserve a cheater. A part of me feels dirty, but there are nervous jitters that I could mistake for excitement if I didn't know better.

"Give me the number," John says gruffly, all too excited to get his way with me. Asshole.

I recite Cameron's number from memory. His is the only phone number I have memorized aside from Chloe's, my best friend from home's number, and my parents' number.

Cameron doesn't pick up the first time. My stomach sinks. He must have noticed that I wasn't in his room last night. I guess he has no reason to pick up a call from an unknown number. John's eyes flick to mine and a self-satisfied smirk crosses his face. I hate the cocky expression on his face.

"Cameron's probably asleep," I mutter. "It's almost 6 a.m."

He probably passed out somewhere and doesn't even know I'm gone.

"Call him again," John demands.

There's something seriously fucking wrong with John. But the way he moved his fingers inside me... Oh my God. Why did he do that? Why did he put his tongue in my ass and then suck my clit until I came all over his face? Why did he call me perfect?

It's all too confusing to think about and what's simple is what's cruel—following John's orders.

"Put him on speakerphone," John insists. He won't back down an inch. If I do this, there's no turning back from John Vicari. If I dump Cameron, I submit to his will, his protection and soon... his dick. He promises to keep me safe, but as far as I know, he's the biggest danger in my life. I can't anger him.

I call Cameron again and quickly put him on speakerphone before the first ring. Cameron picks up after three rings this time and a knot the size of a cane toad forms in my throat.

I'm not strong enough to do this.

"Alexis? Where the fuck are you? Where did you go? I came up to my room, and you left all your shit and your fucking phone. Where are you calling me from?"

Cameron doesn't give me time to answer, which shouldn't shock me. That's just Cameron. He's the alpha, the top dog on campus and he always gets everything he wants—including me. He doesn't have to ask about my feelings. He doesn't have to be gentle. My chest tightens. Maybe I won't regret dumping Cameron. I have to get used to the idea that we're no longer going to be together, anyway.

I still don't know why John needs me to do this, or if Cameron's feelings for me extend past the flood of pride he gets from having a girl on his arm.

He still doesn't deserve this. I glance at John who presses a finger to his lips. At least he won't make this worse, which is a pathetic and tiny comfort.

"I'm… I'm fine," I whisper, because I can't tell him I'm in Queens. Cameron would do something stupid like try to come get me. Or worse, he wouldn't come get me and I'll be stuck here with a pissed off murderous mobster. "I'm using a friend's cellphone."

God. Hot shame courses through me. John is the furthest thing in my life from a friend, but he smirks when I say the word. What a bastard…

"What the fuck happened? Why did you leave?" Cameron presses, his voice growing more and more aggressive.

"I didn't mean to… I…"

What do I have to lose now by telling him? John won't let me out of his sight unless I dump Cameron and considering where John just had his tongue, dumping Cameron is the right thing to do.

"What the hell happened?" Cameron says forcefully. Why the hell does he sound angry? His tone sends the first shiver of pure rage through me for the night. None of this would have happened if Cameron's roommate hadn't climbed on top of me, if he hadn't tried to shove his dick inside me when I was drunk and passed out in Cameron's bed.

The tightness in my throat disappears.

"Your stupid fucking roommate tried to rape me," I snap at him. "That's what happened. So I ran out of the house and–

Cameron doesn't let me finish my sentence. I don't know how I would have ended it. Telling him about John or anything I witnessed tonight could get us both killed. I might have already done enough to get Cameron killed.

"Are you talking about Gabe?"

"Do you have another roommate?" I snap at him. This isn't the time to start an argument, but Cameron's voice sends adrenaline through me and this time, I have the power to fight.

My body burns with so much anger that I feel itchy. I want to throw the phone across the room already because the disbelief in Cameron's voice cuts like a fucking razor blade.

"No. I mean… Listen, Gabe is totally passed out in here. No way he could have done something like that. He was way too drunk."

I want to throw up.

"He tried to rape me, Cam. He climbed into your bed and I woke up and–

"Christ, don't fucking describe it," Cameron snaps. "Why would I want to hear some gross shit like that?"

"Excuse me?" I yell at him.

"I don't want to hear you talk about how you almost fucked another guy," Cameron says coldly.

I hate that John's hearing this. The stabbing sensation in my chest twists into a layered knot. I've never felt so much humiliation in my life. John's expression darkens. I can tell he wants to wring Cameron's neck and he might want to wring mine too.

Cameron's indifferent tone leaves me momentarily tongue-tied, but I find the words, eventually.

"I did not almost fuck him," I say forcefully. "He climbed into bed and–

"I told you I didn't want to fucking hear it," Cameron interrupts again. "Listen, babe. Gabe had a lot to drink. He probably thought you were someone else. I'll talk to him in the morning and get his side of the story."

"How the hell will talking to him help anything? He ripped my clothes off, Cam. You don't need his side of the story. He's a rapist."

John clenches his hands into fists. I doubly regret giving him a way to track Cameron down.

"Jesus, did it get you fucking horny, Alexis? This is the third time I asked you not to describe the nasty shit you did in my fucking bed, but you won't stop. What the fuck is wrong with you?"

John glances at his gun on the nightstand and then back at

me. I scowl and stare at his cell phone. John's pending emotional hurricane is the least of my concerns right now.

His brazenly displayed emotions give me a jolt of excitement. He's so comfortable feeling things I'm not allowed to feel. I hate that he makes me feel excited but the less I fear him, the more the butterflies in my stomach feel like the good kind.

I can't ever admit this out loud, but it's true... It's the trauma. It has to be the trauma. I can't let myself feel butterflies with a killer.

"Don't you care that your fucking roommate tried to rape me?" I scream at him.

"Allegedly," Cameron shoots back. "Allegedly tried to rape you."

"Cameron..."

"Get the fuck over here and we'll talk about this."

"I'm not coming over. I'm..."

I have to do this now. John looks like wants to skewer something alive and since I'm the only living thing in the room with him, I need to end this damn phone call and work out a plan not to become his next victim.

"I'm breaking up with you," I blurt out so fast that it all sounds like one word. My five-word-one-word-break-up apparently hits Cameron like a smack to the face because he sits on the other end of the line in stunned silence. Even John glances at the phone impatiently to make sure we didn't accidentally disconnect.

He wants Cameron out of my life and I don't know how far he'll go to make sure that happens.

"What the fuck are you talking about?" Cameron responds. "Did you actually fuck him?"

He doesn't believe me. My stomach twists in a painful knot as I force myself to acknowledge that while I didn't want to break up with Cameron, while I told myself this was something John forced me to do—now I really have to do it.

I know what happened with me and Gabe. I'd never felt so frozen or viscerally terrified in my life. Gabe knew what he was doing and Cameron should have my back. I run my tongue over my lips and close my eyes for the inevitable breakdown. There's nothing you can do to stop a breakup from hurting, even if you're beyond done with the asshole you're dumping and you know you're doing the right thing.

When you care about someone, when you love hard, breaking up always fucking hurts, but sometimes, it's the best thing you can do to free your heart and theirs to find someone else.

"I didn't fuck him," I hiss angrily. I want to say something cruel that I can never take back. But I don't. "But this is still over."

"You did," Cameron says. "Holy shit, you did... I'm gonna kick his ass."

"It's over, Cameron," I repeat loudly. "It's over."

I mean it. This time, I mean it from the heart.

"Whatever, slut," Cameron hisses and then he hangs up, and that's it. We're over and the last two words my boyfriend said to me were "Whatever, slut". It's a gut-punch of an end to a relationship that I thought would last forever. I toss the phone onto John's bed and give him the most furious look I can muster.

He gazes at me expressionless at first. I'm just happy he isn't smiling and gloating like the maniac he is.

"You're better off without that asshole," John says with far too much self-assuredness for my tastes.

Tears stream down my cheeks, but I lose my fear of John in one immediate flood of adrenaline. Anger, hatred, betrayal, sadness, disgust and loathing pour into me and then overflow in an immediate burst.

"I fucking HATE you," I scream at him. I take the phone off the bed and hurl it at John's head with as much force as I can muster. Even if it's completely senseless and impossible, I genuinely want the phone to strike his temple in exactly the right spot and knock him dead. I'm angry enough to lose the sense of danger keeping me safe. I lunge off the bed for John and punch him right in the stomach with an uncomfortably feral screech.

I sound and feel like a caged animal burning with every desire for escape. John's muscular stomach offers stiff resistance to the first hit from my fists. Two more hits land against his chiseled stomach before he stops me by wrapping his arms around me and physically stopping my flailing.

I know how fucking crazy I look but I don't care. I try hitting him again and when I realize how easily he has me subdued, I lean forward and bite his shoulder with genuine intent to hurt him. If I cause John any pain, he doesn't show it.

"Stop fucking fighting!" he yells.

"I hate you!"

He clamps down around me tighter. I couldn't escape him if I wanted to. Dumping Cameron sealed my fate and failing to fight back adds the final nail to the coffin.

I attempt to bite his shoulder again and John flings me backward onto his bed. All the air in my lungs flies out with a huff and then I start scream-crying again. John paces at the foot of the bed as I roll over and press my face into his pillow, sobbing and weeping because of everything. It's all hitting me and there's nothing I can do about how painful tonight was aside from those brief moments of pleasure when John made me climax.

JOHN STOPS PACING, but I don't stop crying and his voice sounds surprisingly sweet when he next speaks.

HE PRESSES his hand to my cheek and uses his thumb to wipe away one of my tears. He forces me to look at him, forces me to sit up in bed and he turns my face towards his as he holds me.

John runs his tongue over his lips and says in a calm, deep voice. "That asshole doesn't deserve you and he doesn't deserve your tears. If you were my girl... which you will be... I would hunt down any fucker who laid a hand on you and feed his balls to my cousin's dogs."

I can't muster more than a whimper in response. John might have had a moment of sweetness, but he hasn't lost track of why I'm here and what he wants from me.

"LET'S FINISH THIS, cupcake. You're single now. So take those clothes off and we'll fuck until you feel better."

"I have class."

"Not today," John murmurs. "I'll handle your deans. I think you deserve a week off…"

He means a week in his bed. He wants us to stay here and have sex for an entire week. The lump in my throat quickly turns to throbbing between my legs.

"Go on," John says sternly. "Clothes off."

✳ ✳ ✳

Chapter 8
Belongs To Me
John

I know I'm a dick. I'm not proud of being a fucking dick, but it's who I am and I gotta own that. With her, I have to own it because she's already seen the worst of me. This beautiful woman has already seen firsthand how sick I am. There's nothing to hide from her and right now… I need that.

Sex after killing was easier when I was younger. I used sex to forget the flood of emotions and the horror of what I'd done. The older I got, the less I could get by with using sex to forget. My emotions heightened during sex and I had to stop casual sex because it was all too intense and I needed sex to be the place I could feel.

Alexis rolls over with a face stained by makeup and tears. After all that bullshit, she's still the prettiest fucking woman I've ever seen and I can't stop staring at her.

"I'm not done with you."

"Haven't you had enough?" she asks sadly, sitting up and dangling her legs off the side of my bed. I haven't had a woman in this bed in so fucking long that it's almost ethereal watching her sit there, watching her perfect ass leave an imprint in my sheets and knowing that her smell will be in my bed long after she leaves it.

That is, if I let her leave at all.

"That guy is a dick," I remind her. "You pulled the trigger, cupcake. You deserve one good fucking thing to happen after the hell you've been through."

"Your monster dick splitting me in three pieces doesn't sound like a good time."

She doesn't know how hard it gets me when she's all smart-mouthed like that. Women from her background are spicy as fuck with an attitude that you don't get in the suburbs. None of that passive aggressive bullshit–black women say exactly what they mean.

Alexis has a point. Her tiny lips could hardly wrap around a few inches of my cock. Burying my entire length inside her tight little pussy could definitely hurt her more than she can handle. I don't want her to fear me. Tonight should bond her to me – not push her away. I run my tongue over my lips and try to be more than just a wise guy for a second.

"I'll go slow and it'll feel just like making love," I tell her. She wrinkles her nose in disbelief. I made her cum, so she knows I can deliver on my promises. Her little game of resistance is… enjoyable. Putting in the effort to chase a good woman only brings me absolute pleasure.

"Calling it making love doesn't change what you're doing," she says, sniffling and giving me a fierce look. Her little fierce looks intended to scare me only make her look more adorable. I want to kiss those pouting angry lips and suck on her neck until her tightened brows relax, and she melts in my arms.

I shrug. "I can fuck you, make love to you, it doesn't matter to me. I won't be the one hurting."

She scowls at me and searches for a pillow to throw at me. They're both on the floor already and nowhere near her furious little hands. I don't want her trying to fight me again. My shoulder hurts like fuck and once I get inside her, I'll have to punish her. I don't want to punish her, but if I want her to stay with me, grow to love me, if I want her to need me – I'll have to punish her.

"You're a bastard."

"I'm not. I'm the good guy, cupcake. I'm saving your fucking life. Now open your legs. Let me see that pretty pussy."

Alexis squeezes her eyes shut and bites down on her lower lips. She doesn't want to acknowledge what she's doing for me any more than she wants to acknowledge how fucking wet it makes her to spread her legs for me. I felt her squealing and mewling against my tongue. I tasted the depths of her juicy pussy and I know how wet I make her. Her body screams for me. After the hellish night she's had, that perfect body needs release.

She spreads her legs as I kneel on the bed, slowly dragging myself between her legs. I want her more than I've ever wanted anybody.

"Take your shirt and bra off, princess," I whisper. "I want to see your tits."

She keeps her legs spread and obeys my commands to remove her shirt. She's incredibly sexy in this position and I don't want to bother with self-control right now. Self-control was what I needed to shoot a family member in the head. Self-control has no place here.

With her tits bare and her body ready for me, I grab her by the hips and pull her towards me, leaning my weight into hers and pressing her into the bed. Alexis heaves as my bare chest touches her. The contact sends a thrill of desire straight through me and gets my dick instantly hard. Alexis whimpers as I kiss her neck and then run my tongue over her soft skin until I get to her breasts. Her nipples harden from the touch of my tongue and Alexis moans as I swirl my tongue in teasing circles around her nipples.

Her nipples response to my teasing fills me with an even greater desire to enter her. She has the most perfect pair of breasts ever. The large brown globes swell in my mouth as I lick her succulent flesh to arousal and prompt Alexis to several guilty moans. Still, she's holding back. I don't need her to hold back tonight.

I press my crotch against hers, careful not to spear her tight entrance just yet and kiss her neck before whispering into her ear, "Touch me. I want your hands on me."

She reluctantly slides her hands behind my neck, stroking the nape of my neck and then running her fingers down my bulky shoulder muscles. My cock yearns for her more than ever as her soft fingers tease one of the few parts of my body untouched by ink. When her fingers spread the strands of my chocolate brown hair apart and she grabs onto it, I have to give her what she wants.

I hoist her legs apart and grab the head of my cock to line it up with her entrance. Alexis whimpers once she feels the ooze of pre-cum dripping against her pussy. Despite her wriggling and her fear, I want her to enjoy this. Alexis had too much pain tonight that she didn't deserve. Now it's time for pleasure.

I press the head of my cock against her entrance, pushing slightly this time and Alexis gasps despite my inability to enter her. She's so tight that the first movement between her legs proves not forceful enough for me to get a dick my size inside her. She needs more than a gentle thrust for her body to accept a big cock.

She wriggles away from me, succumbing to her fear when the first thrust between her legs doesn't work. No. I can't let her get away from me after the slow burn between us the entire night. Alexis grasps onto my shoulders but her face speaks of pure terror. I plant a soft kiss on her lips to calm her down.

"The first thrust might hurt," I warn her in anticipation of the force my hips will need to apply for me to fit my dick between her extremely tight pussy. I don't know if it's because she's twenty or if Alexis is just unusually tight. The fucked up part of my brain wonders if it's a race thing.

Alexis shakes her head. "No..."

"I promise," I whisper, cupping her ass and pulling her

against me so she can't escape at the last minute. "I will make up for the pain."

She bites her lower lip and shudders with sudden acceptance of just how futile her resistance against me might prove to be. Alexis keeps her eyes shut as I kiss her neck and force the head of my cock to pierce her reluctant entrance.

I can almost feel the pain myself as my cock bursts through the tight ring and my hips force their way between her legs. Alexis lets out an ungodly sound between a yelp and a moan. My hips move forward again of their own accord causing her more pain but ensuring my cock burrows deeply between the most perfect set of milky brown thighs I've ever laid eyes on.

She's far too fucking young for me and I know it, but there's another force guiding me tonight that has nothing to do with logic and everything to do with the bizarre combination of guilt, grief and emotion that comes with murder—and getting caught. Don't forget the getting caught. I sink my teeth into her neck instinctively, adding to her pain as I claim her with a gigantic cock that pins her naked body to my apartment bed.

I grunt as my cock throbs and fills the young woman moaning desperately beneath me. My kisses don't take away the pain the way I think they will and tears stream down her cheeks as she moans, "It's so big… It's so big…"

At first I think she's moaning in pain and then I move my hips slightly and Alexis' response can only be described as the most intense female orgasm ever experienced. I feel her pussy tighten around my dick and she loses control of herself, moaning and bucking her hips up to take my cock deeper. I thought I hurt her, but she grabs my ass and digs oddly sharp fingernails into my ass cheeks before pulling me inside her.

Holy fuck, taking her this deep feels euphoric. The deeper I get, the more I can feel her tight inner walls and experience the absolute fucking euphoria of joining our bodies together. She smells even better than before now that I'm inside her and I want more than anything to be completely fucking irresponsible and empty my seed inside her.

Condoms. We should have used condoms. She doesn't know that it doesn't really matter. I can't have kids. I've tested my fate too many times for that not to be the case. It's not exactly something a dude brags about, but it has its perks.

When Alexis cums that hard, she gives me the freedom to succumb to my animal instincts without hesitation. I pump my hips into her harder and grab her hands, pinning her to my bed as I fuck her deliciously tight pussy with reckless abandon. Alexis skin flushes nearly purple and I suck on her neck as I take her pussy. She gets wetter and wetter, climaxing again as I pin her to my bed.

I want to cum, but it's far too risky to cum inside her. I pull out of her, my face red with desire and growl, "Turn around. Wait for me to get a condom."

Alexis nods. My chest swells proudly at the hickeys on her neck. Three red circular scars from where I sucked her pretty brown skin so hard I left welts. My cock juts forward still desperate for more of her. Alexis folds herself slowly into a position on all fours that presents her ass like a giant fuckable heart for me to enter.

Her deliciously tight asshole soaked with her juices and my spit beckons to me. I won't get that precious hole tonight but I won't leave Alexis' tight asshole untouched forever.

I hastily get an XL condom which still struggles to fit on my cock. I had custom for a while but when the women dried up in my life, so did the desire to keep getting custom rubbers. This will have to get us through tonight. Once my cock has a sheath over it, I'm eager to plunge between the buttery smooth folds dripping with juices of arousal that Alexis presents to me.

My mouth waters with desire to press my tongue into her sexy back door again but this time, my cock rules. I ease between her legs and hold her hips to prepare her body for the intrusion of my powerful cock. Alexis trembles with initial anticipation, which I ought to expect but fuck, she's terrified. Despite her pleasure, her relatively small body and extremely tight pussy can't help experiencing utter terror at the presence of my mammoth dick.

I rub her ass cheeks slowly to soothe her.

"Easy," I whisper. "I'll go easy on your sweet ass pussy."

I give her ass a much needed kiss and wish I could stop to leave hickeys all over these voluptuous brown ass cheeks. My cock slowly probes her entrance. I rub the engorged head over her slippery pussy lips and then find her slit slightly reddened from a mixture of pain and arousal. Touching her soft skin, I rest the head of my cock against that entrance and attempt to enter her more slowly this time so I don't bruise the sensitive pussy I just fucked hard without a care in the world.

She wriggles her hips back to meet me more aggressively but I hold her back, pushing against her ass and entering her at my own pace. Taking her slowly brings more pleasure than I can imagine. The burst of euphoria spreads through me instantly and once I get the head of my dick past her tight slit, I can't help myself. I push the rest of my dick inside Alexis.

Like the last time, just the friction from slow entry by a gigantic cock makes her cum instantly. Once I feel my thatch of pubic hair resting against Alexis' wetness, she trembles and moans with the force of an intense orgasm. Her pussy clamps around my cock and her orgasm makes it impossible for me to hold back... nearly.

I need to make her cum one more time before I finish. I hold her hips tenderly and ease my cock into her with slow, rhythmic strokes, watching her perfect black ass bouncing on my dick as I make love to her from behind. Watching her soft, pillowy cheeks jiggle as my cock disappears between her legs drives me wild.

This is too much to bear. I lean forward and cup her breasts to pull her body against mine. After a few more thrusts, I allow myself the sweet pleasure of release. I kiss her neck again and ease my hips forward to cum. My seed bursts from my cock into the thin rubber between us. I want her. I want her. I grip her body against mine as I cum.

THIS IS OUR BOND NOW.

I KISS her shoulders and withdraw from Alexis. She shudders and collapses forward on my bed. I'm keeping her here for a week and teasing every hole in her body until Alexis breathes loyalty to John Vicari.

She wriggles beneath me and I draw her to me even more tightly.

"You are mine from now on," I murmur. "And I'm yours. Anything you need from me, anything you want... I will provide."

She moans as I kiss her neck one last time. My cock stiffens against instantly.

WHAT WILL HAPPEN with her tomorrow? *Foolishness. Because I like her and I like our chemistry and I'm always a fool with women and feelings. That's why I've never allowed myself to have them. How did this young woman pierce my armor? I'll never have the answers.*

* * *

Chapter 9
A Taste Of Freedom
Alexis

John allows me to leave his apartment in time for classes the next Monday, but he keeps me captive as long as he promises, sending "his men" to get my clothes from my dorm and my stuff for school.

All week we have sex and John trains me on how to behave and conduct myself so that if the cops show up, he can get me out of trouble. I'm sore all over and my body burns with guilt for how I spent the past week.

John doesn't understand what I'll have to face going back to school after a week absent and that disappearing like that at a private university filled with incredibly gossipy nerds will raise questions. John doesn't seem to care about university or my grades or the fact that dumping Cameron will be important campus gossip and I need to find out what people are saying.

I at least want my cell phone. I need to contact Chloe. I'm shocked she hasn't gone to the police by now. Then again, maybe she has. John forbids me from having a cell phone of my own, but he's allowing me to attend classes on Monday as long as I don't "screw up". He threatens to have people watching me, but I've only ever seen him interact with one person aside from me —the other creep in the alley.

"One word to the cops or anybody about what you saw and you're dead, cupcake," he whispers before giving me a deep tongue kiss and dropping me off outside Buell Hall.

It's weird and old-fashioned that he calls me "cupcake" but after what happened this weekend, hearing it makes me feel all funny between my legs. How the hell can he threaten to kiss me and then kiss me more deeply and more possessively than Cameron ever did?

I have to remember that despite dropping me off at classes and promising to look after me and buying me a burner phone and kissing me on the lips—John is not my boyfriend. He's not Cameron, he's a dangerous killer who feels completely entitled to having my body whenever he pleases. I'm simply lucky he doesn't want my body now.

I open the door to the car and burst out. No one sane would ever describe the air on the Upper West Side as fresh, but coming from captivity, it feels like I'm in the Alps. I shut the door and John watches me walk to the building door. Chloe has this class with me too so I can apologize to her and try to explain my fucked up weekend without saying anything that will get us both killed.

Cameron doesn't have classes until noon, so if I'm lucky, I can get away with avoiding him all day. John demanded before we left his place that I meet him exactly ninety minutes after my classes are done with my bags packed to stay at his place when I'm not at school or studying.

He'll take me to college classes every day but outside of that, he expects me to stay right under his nose and he claims it's for my safety. I've run through all my options and sadly, listening to John seems like my best option.

I don't know if I believe this is for my safety. Something strange happened in that bed with the terrifying Long Island man and there isn't a person alive I can talk to about it.

"OH MY GOD. OH MY GOD!"

I hear Chloe screeching from the other end of the hall and

she literally shoves a lacrosse player out of the way to get to me. He gives her a bewildered look, but doesn't react otherwise. Chloe doesn't apologize. She jumps on me, nearly knocking me over. I only fall against a wall at which point Chloe gets ahold of herself. Slightly.

"I called the cops! I called the cops, I swear, but they told me you were safe and they had proof. They're liars. Fucking liars! What happened? Oh my God, what happened?!"

Chloe is the loudest person I know. You can hear her voice across a loud room and she has a distinct shrill that you could never mistake for someone else. I love my overly enthusiastic best friend but she's asking me so many questions, I don't know which one to answer first.

"I'm fine," I say to her, trying to sound strong but unfortunately appearing exhausted and frail. It's not that John didn't want me to sleep. During our tangled weekend together, I was the one begging with him for more.

Even now, I feel sore between my legs and the anxiety of wearing a scarlet letter on my chest. Chloe grabs my face and gazes into my eyes with ferocious intensity.

"Were you traumatized?" she asks seriously, not knowing how close she is to the truth. Traumatized twice.

I bite my lower lip and despite myself, my eyes fill with tears. I promised myself I wouldn't break down in front of Chloe because she couldn't handle hearing about what happened to me all weekend. I can't avoid telling her at least a part of the truth. I'm just surprised she hasn't heard about my breakup with Cameron yet.

"Why do you ask?" I choke out, avoiding Chloe's intense gaze.

I quickly get my face out of her grasp and wipe the tears away from my eyes before they make Chloe freak out even more than she's already freaking the hell out.

"I heard Cameron dumped you for cheating on him but it's

obviously a stupid lie," she says. "There are dumb rumors about everyone from the party."

"Cameron said that?"

I expected word to get around, but I didn't expect Cameron to lie. Unfortunately, we have to cut our reunion short because of the bell for class.

"Shit!" Chloe says as the bell blares throughout the hall and interrupts her response to my question about Cameron. My ears burn with heat. Do I really have the right to get pissed off at Cameron? I spent all weekend tangled in the sheets with a terrifying, muscular monster covered in tattoos. Every time I close my eyes, I see his icy blue eyes. Guilt rages through me, but Chloe's oblivious and just thrilled that I'm okay.

"Fuck Cameron and fuck all the boys on campus. Promise me you were safe this weekend. That's all I want to know," she says, her face still exhibiting deep concern.

I give her an ambiguous response that won't get me out of trouble for long.

She might let this go temporarily, but Chloe won't let me disappear for an entire weekend without pressing me for details about all the hours she missed.

I wish I could focus throughout our entire lecture. Sitting next to Chloe and occasionally sharing the chai latte she brought to class helps keep me locked in the moment, but the weekend events keep flashing before my eyes. Not just John and the crazy things he did to me in his apartment. Like his tongue against my asshole. I think about the murder I witnessed and how the guy who gave me the best orgasms of my life killed him.

Class seems boring, but at the end, we have a pop quiz, so I seriously regret half-assing the reading to hop into bed with John again and I definitely regret everything about the entire weekend. Orgasms are no reason to throw my morals out the window. I slept with a killer and I liked it. I'm definitely going to hell.

Thoughts about my fate burning in the eternal flames distract me throughout the entire pop quiz. When I turn it in, my confidence is in the gutter. I'm sure I bomb the quiz. Failing any quiz threatens my chances at medical school, so I feel like I'm walking on a tightrope when I hand it in. Chloe doesn't seem to care if she failed or not. School doesn't make her anxious at all. She finishes before me and waits for me outside of class. I don't have another class until noon.

"Want to go to JJ?" Chloe suggests. Dining hall food doesn't exactly excite me, but I want to have a normal day — just one normal day before I dive back into John's world.

John Jay dining hall has been the site of many of our post-weekend gossip sessions and normally I wouldn't hesitate to get food there—Chloe has the unlimited meal plan and doesn't mind sharing—but I know Cameron will be there with his team and possibly Gabe. The thought of facing Gabe again makes my head swim.

Still, I can't pull off being "fine" if I turn down Chloe's offer for food. Women who have their shit together aren't too scared to go to the dining hall.

"Sure. I'm starved," I lie through my teeth because I don't want my best friend to worry. I don't know how I'll force myself to eat, but I'll have to find a way, won't I? Chloe can't find out the entire truth, no matter what. It's not about being honest with my best friend, it's about her life. John may have made me orgasm, but he hasn't completely clouded my head. I understand just how fucked up he is and I don't want to put my best friend in danger. I've already probably put Cameron and Gabe in danger.

"Why did you leave the party?" Chloe asks. "I don't know girl, you seem shaken."

She sticks her hands in her pockets and scrunches her brows like she's expecting me to lie about what happened last night. That means I have to make my lie believable and make sure it includes as much of the truth as possible.

"Something happened in Cam's room that freaked me out. I ran. Left everything and then…"

"What happened?" Chloe asks, her voice taking on the high-pitched trill I desperately wanted to avoid. I don't need her worry about this. While I'm here, in Buell Hall, I'm a normal college student at a normal private university and I don't have to think about what I witnessed John Vicari do or what he did to me in his bedroom. While I'm here, I definitely don't want to think about Gabe.

Despite my desire to push what Gabe did to the furthest corners of my mind, the truth pushes against my chest, filling me with too much air. I have to tell her something.

"Gabe climbed into bed and tried to have sex with me."

Chloe stops walking, and her face turns red. "He did what?"

Her voice is already on fire.

"Keep your voice down," I hiss. It's bad enough John wants to kill Gabe for touching me, I don't need Chloe getting involved.

"Did you explain this to Cameron?" she asks. "What did he say? Please tell me that asshole isn't running around campus a free man after what he did to you."

My throat tightens in a knot. What does Chloe expect to happen to Gabe? It's not a crime to climb into bed with a woman, especially not if that bed is in your own room and if you can easily claim it was a mistake. The thing no one tells you before you become a victim of rape or attempted rape is that there's no way for you to avoid blame. It's easy for us to tell each other that we shouldn't blame the victim, but it'll happen anyway. Someone out there will blame you for what happened.

Today that person isn't Chloe. She wraps her arms around and pulls me against her chest with uncomfortable ferocity. Her affection feels weird after the weekend I've had but after a few seconds I lean into her very normal hug and squeeze her back.

"I'm so sorry," she says. She probably already guessed that Cameron was a total asshole about it considering my silence.

"Cameron is such a selfish dick. Is this why you broke up?" she asks, piecing everything everything together before I give her all the details.

"Yeah."

"That still doesn't explain where you've been," Chloe asks, separating from our hug and giving me a suspicious once-over. There's still no way I can tell her about John without her freaking out, so I have to avoid giving her more information than she needs.

"A friend picked me up. He doesn't go to Columbia."

"He?"

"It's a long story."

"Did you sleep with him?" She whispers. My stomach lurches and I hate that I have to lie again.

"No," I tell her, shaking my head. "He's just a friend."

I DON'T KNOW what the fuck John Vicari is to me, but he definitely isn't my friend.

"WANT to go to the library after class?" Chloe asks. Her request directly defies John's orders to wait for him after class, but I don't want to obey John. I want to hang out with my best friend who can provide real comfort to me after the weekend I've had. John was a mistake–obviously. I don't feel the need to run back to him.

If/when he finds me, which I'm sure he will, I'll just explain that his secret is safe and he'll have to leave me alone. What's he going to do, kidnap me from my university?

"Sure," I tell Chloe, again smiling to seem normal. "I have a ton of homework left from this weekend."

It'll take John at least an hour to track me down. By then, maybe I can make a good excuse to Chloe to leave. I guess I'm trusting he won't kill me for going to the library. He can't be that crazy. I hope.

Chloe asks me more questions about the weekend as we walk along the paths towards the dining hall. It's getting colder and for the first time, I notice how vulnerable we are just walking to the dining hall—two women alone. My chest tightens as I struggle to hide my growing anxiety from Chloe who notices my body tense and my facial expression match.

"Are you okay?" she asks.

I nod and I'm about to answer that I'm fine when I look up toward the dining hall again and see that I am absolutely not fine. I didn't think there was a strong chance of running into either of them, but running into both Cameron and his room-mate at once turns my tension and anxiety into outright panic.

They tell you about fight or flight, but they don't tell you about freezing, an extremely common response to trauma and the unfortunate effect their presence has on me. Chloe hooks her arm around mine, pulling me protectively against her body.

"Alexis," she whispers. "It's going to be okay. Come on, we'll walk right past them and we won't say a fucking word. I might spit. But we don't have to talk to them."

I can't even unfreeze enough to tell Chloe not to spit on Cameron who would be all too happy to sue over something that completely petty. They're getting closer and Chloe tugs on my arm again. "Alexis. Come on. Aren't you hungry?"

She's trying to help. But it doesn't. Nothing helps me move except making out the shapes of both of their faces much closer and the realization hitting me that if I don't just get away from them, I'll lose my shit. I move with out-of-control trembling in my limbs, only finding stability in Chloe's grasp. As we take a few steps forward, a jolt of adrenaline surges through me and I can breathe. I can breathe and I can focus on just getting past them with my heart racing out of control.

I won't give Cameron or Gabe the satisfaction of seeing me

run from them, but I sure as hell feel the burst of hormones pleading with me to disappear.

"I've got you, girl," Chloe whispers. I steel myself for the horrible moment I'll actually have to walk past them and assure myself that neither of them would dare say a word to me. Cameron takes his baseball cap off a few feet ahead of us and ruffles his fingers through his hair. I swear he's smirking. *No, Alexis. You're just freaking the fuck out.*

I don't want to look at Gabe, but I can't help it. When Cameron readjusts his cap, he looks right at me and he touches his dick through his sweatpants. Or scratches it. I don't know which. Gabe touches his fucking dick while staring straight at me. He knows what the fuck he's doing. Nausea nearly over-powers me but I have the strength to walk past them without reacting until one little word.

Slut.

The word flies out of Cameron's mouth, which probably explains my reaction. I wouldn't have dared react the same way toward Gabe, the man who pinned me to Cameron's bed and threatened to rape me. I don't know what the fuck made me react the way I did. Maybe it was the adrenaline. I stop walking and Chloe stops too, but she's too late to stop me from reacting. I move too fast.

"What the fuck did you just say to me?" I yell at Cameron.

He stops talking and turns around, giving me a cocky little smirk that blinds me with rage. I hit him. I know I hit him really hard because there's blood all over my fists and even if I don't remember the next few minutes, my body aches with all the signs of what happened. After the first punch to Cameron's face, the next thing I remember is Chloe screaming, "Call 911!"

"Don't you fucking dare, Chloe!" Cameron snarls. "I'm not calling the cops because a fucking girl hit me."

"I think she broke your nose," Chloe shrieks at him. "Oh my God, Alexis… Are you okay?"

I don't know where Gabe went, but he must have been there

and he must have dragged Cameron off. I'm on the ground when Chloe crouches next to me and waves her hand in front of my face.

"There's blood everywhere! Alexis! Alexis, can you hear me?"

I inhale and all that fear and adrenaline—all that shit leaves my body and I sit up feeling fucking crazy. I know I'm smiling like a maniac because Chloe looks like she wants to institutionalize me.

"I'm fine," I tell her, trying not to laugh out loud and confirm my status as a crazy person. "I promise. I needed to do that."

"He could have killed you," Chloe said. "You broke his nose and… Alexis… are you crazy?"

"Help me up, please…"

He must have fought back at least a little because my stomach hurts like Cameron tried to shove me off. I nearly touch my pants with my gross, bloody hands but when I finally look down at them, I understand Chloe's concern.

"Ew," I mutter. "Fuck."

WE GET CLEANED up in the dining hall bathroom and don't get caught and no one asks questions about the blood. After a year at Columbia, everyone here fancies themselves a New York City person which means not reacting in the slightest when you see something strange taking place in public. New Yorkers keep it moving.

Chloe shakes her head at me throughout dinner, reviewing all the ways Cameron could have hurt me.

"He could have kidnapped you," she says after running out of potentially horrific scenarios to warn me about. "Think about that."

Ha. She doesn't know that I'm technically already kidnapped. I have to go home tonight to John and despite how desperate I am to avoid him… I can't. All I can do is put him off.

"I still want to study later," I tell Chloe. "I doubt Cameron will show up to the library with a broken nose."

"Word probably spread around campus that a girl broke his nose. Score one for feminism."

I don't have the heart to tell Chloe that punching our shitty exes in the face probably ranks pretty low on the feminist agenda. My hand hurts too much for that because I'm not exactly a street fighter. After dinner, we head over to the library together and I pretend that it's not suicide to ignore John.

I JUST WANT one more hour of feeling normal before I have to return to him. That's it. One fucking hour.

* * *

Chapter 10
Hurt Sammy
John

I don't want to be at the casino when I know she's miles away on the fucking Upper West Side doing God knows what. What about that rapist, huh? What about that ex-boyfriend? How the fuck am I supposed to think about work with this shit going on? I need to know exactly what the fuck she's doing right now.

"Meg, I need a glass of tequila with lime. Get it here yesterday." I growl at my newest hire.

"Yes, boss."

Sammy's been out of the hospital, and he's heard the news. They don't have a body (of course they don't have a body) but he's been in the mob long enough to know what the fuck happened.

We don't pussyfoot with rats the way the Italians do. Our country's too fucking big and it's too fucking easy for rats to get out of their traps. It's not like I enjoyed what I did. It's not like I would enjoy it if it were Sammy I had to kill. Or Lucky. But I would fucking do it because I trust the man in charge.

I trust my father.

But tonight, I have to do the shit that makes the mob feel like hell. I have to talk to a man whose son I killed, a man I grew up with like a brother, and hope he doesn't kill me or one of mine to avenge his son's death.

I can fucking feel Sammy enter the room before I see him. The darkness coats the golden casino walls and my back tightens. My instincts tell me to put my hand on my pistol but... it's Sammy. I dunno. Kid spent his teen years in and out of prison and not because of our stuff—because of his stuff.

Sammy slides into the stool next to me and the bar falls quiet. I hate how much attention we attract these days. Those Murray fucks put a spotlight on our family and the shit we've had to do hasn't exactly attracted the best attention.

"Tell me you had a good fucking reason," Sammy snarls. I don't need an explanation or a dramatic preamble from him. That's not how we communicate. We were thick as thieves. The Buffalo mob took out Sammy's dad when he was fourteen and since then, we've been tight as fuck.

Thick as fucking thieves, the two of us.

How can I face him after what I did? How can I keep justifying this fucking shit? Is there ever a good enough reason to do the shit that we do? We do it because if we don't, it's our ass on the fucking line and no one wants to be the guy on the wrong end of a gun. Not even me.

"My father's orders. The Murray shit has gone too far. They used our money to fuck with Padraig's boys. Do you know what that could fucking do, Sammy? That could start a war. They hate Italians. They call *us* the n-word."

I don't like saying the word or talking about shit like that. I need Sammy to understand that his son nearly had us all wiped out like fucking cockroaches because he gave information and money to the wrong people. You can't survive in the mob like that.

"Were you at least man enough to do it yourself?" Sammy asks. His face is red with tears and grief. I hate that I'm the one who put this fucking hole in his heart. I hope Lucky doesn't have to see him like this either. The last thing I need is that asshole going off the deep end with his own grief when I need him to stop going off the deep end with mine.

If I didn't have Alexis, maybe the horror of what I did would have kept me up all night and made me put a bullet in my fucking head.

"Of course I was," I whisper. "I would want you to do the same for me."

"You don't want to be in my position," Sammy answers forcefully. The waitress returns with my tequila but I don't get my hands on it before Sammy grabs the cup and pours the entire thing down his throat. Christ.

"Protect what you love, John," Sammy murmurs. An instinctive chill runs down my forearm.

"What do you mean by that, cousin Sammy?"

We're family. I did what I did because his son broke those bonds. Our bonds are still strong. I hope he knows that.

"I mean… You never know how long you have with what you love. So fucking protect it."

"Yeah. I will."

"He had a girl," Sammy says. "He had a girl. What happened to her? Does she know? She's not part of the life."

"I don't know shit about a girl. I swear."

"So you didn't kill her?" Sammy asks.

I shake my head. Nope. No girl. Lucky wouldn't have killed a woman either. There's only one girl on my mind from that night and she is… the thing I have to protect. I order two more glasses of tequila because Sammy probably needs another one so he can leave here without snapping my neck and I need one because that big motherfucker drank mine.

Sammy wipes his eyes and stares into the empty glass.

"I need to find that girl."

"Do whatever you want. Don't let me stop you."

"I wasn't asking permission, John."

"You know I love you, right?"

Sammy looks up briefly. "Yeah, man. Whatever. I fucking love you, too. But I'll never get over this. For the rest of my fucking life, I'll never get over this."

The waitress gets back with the tequila, but Sammy's gone by then. That's what I get from him tonight—his grief, his rage, his subtle request that I leave him the fuck alone to sort his shit out.

We grew up together, and this is the shit I have to do to him. It's fucked up, and it fucks me up. I finish both glasses of tequila and by then I notice that I'm fucking late to pick up Alexis. And drunk. And I need to fire that waitress for taking fucking forever with the tequila.

Fuck. Fuck. Fuck.

I call her phone, but she doesn't pick up. Shit. My first response is to panic. My second is to call Lucky because he's the only person in the life even the slightest bit sober this time of night. He picks up after one ring.

"Yes?"

"I need you," I say to my brother, who pauses far too long before responding.

"Work?"

My heart races. I shouldn't get Lucky involved in this, but I can't help it.

"Personal."

"What happened? Sammy called."

Already?

"I need you to go to Columbia University and find a girl for me. I need her…"

"What the fuck are you talking about, John? You sound drunk. Althea, Chiara and I are having a game night and-

"Fucking hell, Lucky… I'm drunk and I'm desperate and there's a girl I fucking care about out there."

"You don't know any women."

It'll come to him, eventually.

Lucky continues once the realization hits him. "Are you

talking about the girl from that night? Where did you leave her? Fuck, you'd better hope she didn't go to the cops."

He hangs up and I don't know what the fuck that means, but I have just enough presence of mind to get a taxi to my place in Bayside and wait for my brother. I love Lucky. I trust Lucky. He'll bring her to me safe…

I'm too drunk for my own good and I hate that I let myself get so out of control. I need her.

Chapter 11
Say No To John
Alexis

Chloe hasn't noticed how nervous I am, but my foot tapping and pencil chewing gets on her nerves. I can tell. I want to slow down, but I can't. John will lose his mind. This is a mistake. Three hours have passed since we were supposed to meet and with my phone switched off, I don't know how many times he's called me or how pissed off he is. Chloe slumps over her laptop.

"Remind me why I took anthropology?"

"Because you said it would be an easy A," I reminder her. Chloe made that comment several hundred times.

Chloe groans. "It's not easy and Goldman keeps giving my papers B-. What's the point of the minus? He's trying to kill me."

"You still have a 3.8. No one at this school has a 3.8."

Seriously. The academics at Columbia destroy your self-esteem. We aren't ranked the fourth most rigorous university in America for nothing. At least Chloe studies the humanities. I'm the complete idiot who chose to study biology, take all the pre-med classes, and accomplish a minor in African Studies because I want to get into medical school and make a real difference as a doctor in the black community. Unfortunately, with my

Columbia grades and this failed pop quiz to add to the pile, I don't know what medical school will accept me. That's next year's problem…

It's crazy how little you think about medical school when you're trapped in a crazy man's apartment and he has his tongue between his legs. I shiver thinking about John and try to push him out of my head for good. I can't have fond memories of John. He's not a good person. Yes, he showed me more caring and understanding about "the incident" than my idiot ex-boyfriend, but that doesn't make him better.

He's a killer.

Chloe scoffs. "You have a 3.9. That's crazy. You're like a genius, Alexis. Don't worry about your grades at all."

I appreciate Chloe's compliments, but I study hard for my grades and I'm lucky to have natural talents in science and biology. Chloe just needs to find her talents and stop trying to force herself into these weird boxes. And her grades are fine.

"Maybe you should quit anthropology and try something completely different."

Chloe rolls her eyes. "You know my parents are the highest paid forensic anthropologists in America. They'll kill themselves if I don't study the same thing."

I think Chloe's parents would love her no matter what she studied, but I don't want us to argue about anything. As my panic increases, I wonder if I put her in danger by defying John with her. What if he walks into this library and kills both of us? As the thought enters my head, I try to come up with a reason we should leave.

"I still have three pages left," Chloe says. "You go ahead… Unless you need me to walk you to the dorm. I don't want us to run into them again."

I shake my head. "I'll be fine."

I don't know if I should go back to my dorm and run away while I can. My head swims with irrational thoughts and dumb ideas. I don't feel like myself, but I know I need to get out of the library and figure out what to do next. I can't give up my spot at Columbia, I can't voluntarily move in with John, I can't go to the police. Maybe I need a city walk to clear my head but how the fuck can I take a city walk when walking to the library makes me jump at every sound.

I hate the men who did this to me. I hate Gabe, John, Cameron… all of them.

Once I'm a few hundred feet outside of the library, I glance around to make sure the streets are cleared and there's no chance of running into John or any of the other people I need to get the fuck away from. In my dorm, I can call John and beg him to let me stay here. Everything will be fine. The path seems clear, and I put my hood up, walking to the dorm as fast as I can.

Be fearless, Alexis.

I must be completely crazy to walk outside alone, especially after what happened with Gabe and Cam, but at least I punched that motherfucker in the face and if either of them dare to talk to me, or treat me like shit again, I'll do it again. I can handle myself.

When I get confident that I'm alone, I let my guard down and that proves to be a complete mistake. Before I even realize I'm in trouble, a large forearm wraps around my torso and a man that must be around twice my size lifts me off the ground. I scream bloody murder. Despite my attempts to rationalize my safety and calm myself, my body remains ready for an assault and the scream comes out of me far beyond my control.

I shriek and try to fight, but the man sets me down.

"Fuck," he says. "Sorry. I didn't think you would scream."

I push him and try to run away, but his arm shoots out, and he grabs me, pulling me back against him.

"If you run, I'll have to pick you up again. Please, I'm doing my brother a favor. I didn't mean to scare you."

I stop moving because he has my arm twisted and gripped against his body so I can't move. He smells like really strong cologne and even if he's not as attractive as John, he still cuts a striking figure. He's definitely John's brother, there's no mistaking that. They look alike, with similar crops of thick brown hair.

"I won't run," I say to him, trying to hide my trembling and doing a terrible job of seeming brave. It's not my fault. This man stands at nearly John's height with sharp features and an unsmiling face that could strike terror into almost anyone.

"I won't let go of you until you swear."

"I swear."

He lets go of me. "I'm Lucky Vicari. John sent me. Believe me, I don't want to be here, but I think we can agree it's for the best if you go with me without a fight."

I shake myself off, but Lucky's right. He could probably snap my neck without a second thought, and I don't want to risk it at all.

"Okay. Fine. Where's John? He's late."

"You ignored his calls. And my calls. You're lucky he's too drunk to come get you himself."

"Drunk? Why is he drunk?"

Lucky scowls and I regret asking him. I don't know him and he's not like John, I can sense that much coming off of him. He doesn't have any reason not to hurt me and if it were him and not John who found me in the alley, there's no telling what John's brother would have done to me. My tongue feels dry and heavy in my mouth. I can't take in a breath of air.

"John is a complicated person," Lucky says. "Which is why, I suppose, he got himself all involved with you."

"You disapprove. Clearly."

"Walk with me," Lucky says. "The less time I spend on the Upper West Side, the better."

"Please tell me we're taking the train…" I mutter, because I desperately want to be somewhere Lucky can't talk to me, or where I'll feel the descent of awkward silence between us.

"No luck, kid," Lucky grumbles. "Trust me, I don't look forward to a late night drive back to Queens. My brother should have left you alone. He should have... done anything else but disrupt your life or your innocence."

I don't feel like I have permission to respond to his comment. I hold my tongue and bundle myself up against the cold. Lucky walks in step with me and close enough that if I try to bolt, he could easily grab me and drag me off to his SUV without a second thought. Upsetting him seems like a very stupid idea.

We get to Lucky's SUV and the drive is just as painfully awkward as I could have predicted. Lucky stumbles over discussing the *Islanders'* scores, his daughter Chiara's recent lacrosse championship, and his wife's insistence on remodeling his kitchen. I try to keep up, but it's so awkward that I just want to jump out the window. When we get to Queens, Lucky is red in the face and stammering awkwardly to keep the conversation going.

"You don't have to do this," I mutter, releasing him from this awkward contract.

"I'm sorry for what my brother has done. If he hurts you—

"He hasn't," I assure him quickly. The last thing I want to do is accidentally start a mafia war. I can handle John and right now, I'm tired of handling Lucky. It's like he feels guilty for kidnapping me from my university campus, but I don't give a shit about his guilt. I'm back here in Bayside, back outside John's apartment where he ripped me from my life and then dragged me into his bed for the most confusing night I've had in my life.

"If you need anything, go to Westhampton. Althea's pregnant again and she's home more often. She'll help if you need anything."

"I'm fine. I can handle your brother."

Lucky grunts. I don't know what that means, but I'm too terrified of him to respond in any way that might upset him. So far, letting him talk throughout the drive worked out great for me.

Lucky smirks and shrugs as we walk up the stairs together to John's place. I don't look forward to seeing John drunk and I don't look forward to what revenge he could enact on me for daring to defy his instructions, staying at the library late with Chloe and forcing him to send his brother out to get me. He can't possibly react well to that.

"I'll leave you at the door," Lucky says. "He instructed me to bring you here, not to interact with him. I gotta go home to Althea."

His thick, Long Island accent makes him sound so wholesome and family oriented that I can almost forget he was there the night John ended another man's life. Lucky leaves me at John's door. I knock, even if it feels weird to knock on the door to my prison. If John expects me back here every night, this place is as good as my prison cell. It's not a bad apartment, it's just not where I want to be.

I hear John shuffling over to the door and swearing loudly to himself. He must've stubbed his toe or something. My body tenses, but when he opens the door, I relax. I don't know why I expected him to look like a deformed ghoul, just because he's been drinking. When I see him in the doorway, a strange sense of relief floods me and I have to fight the strange urge to wrap my arms around him. There's nothing about John that should make me feel relieved, or safe, but the feeling hits me hard.

"You're safe," he says, finally allowing me to smell how drunk he is. He's tequila drunk too, which makes me nervous. "Thank fucking God."

"Of course I'm safe."

"You're fucking late," John swears. "Come in. It's cold."

"Maybe it's because you're shirtless."

I don't know why I blurt that out. I was in complete denial about noticing John's bared muscular chest, but how the hell can any sane heterosexual woman ignore a body like that. It doesn't matter how much of a fucked up criminal he is, John's body defies reason. He doesn't have an ounce of body fat on him, just thick rippling muscles like he takes out all his tensions on a slab of raw meat like Rocky Balboa. He has a few scars, lots of tattoos, and blue eyes that bore into me when I close his apartment door behind me.

Holy fucking tequila. His entire apartment reeks, and John is barefoot in just a pair of black trousers. Again, no shirt.

"Nothing to do with being shirtless, cupcake," he slurs. "I'm fucked. I'm fucked up, and I just fucked with a man I called my brother. I just don't see the fucking point. Where's Lucky? Is he still fucking outside?"

I've never hurt a man squeeze so many eff-words into a single sentence. John could definitely win some type of world record for swearing. I hate that his blatant disregard for any social convention with swearing sends a thrill straight through me. He doesn't have to give a fuck what anyone thinks because he has something a young black female college student could never get her hands on–real power.

"No. He left."

John's eyes won't leave me and I suddenly feel nervous and disobedient, an uncomfortable combination while standing beneath his intense gaze. Those eyes are impossible to ignore. I look straight at him and fuck, it's a horrible time to notice how gorgeous his face is too. This is pure fucking torment.

I squeeze my thighs together as I remember how horrifying and pleasurable it was to have his full muscular weight on top of me as he spread me apart with an unreasonably large cock.

"Good," John whispers. "You fucked up today, Alexis. I think you know that."

"I needed a break," I say to him, as honestly as I can manage. "I've been through hell and I owed Chloe more than a bullshit excuse and another disappearance."

"I don't know if I give a fuck," John replies flatly. He runs his tongue over his lips. It's both threatening and oddly sexy. What the fuck is wrong with me? This is the absolute worst time for my attraction to John to root in place. Maybe he was right about his messed up idea to sleep with me.

I can't look at him without imagining his big dick jutting

proudly from his torso and I can't forget the way he felt thrusting between my legs. I've never been so full and I don't imagine they make too many men with a body or a cock like John Vicari's.

"I'm sorry," I tell him, fully aware that I don't sound sorry at all. "I have a life, John. I didn't go to the cops. I didn't get into trouble."

John scowls and grabs my hand. There are visible cuts from when I punched Cam and my messed up outfit and bedraggled hair don't exactly give the impression that I've had a peaceful night. John runs his fingers over the cuts until I wince and yelp from his rough fingers touching a sensitive open cut on my knuckles.

"Oh?" he murmurs. "You didn't have those when you left."

"I fell."

"Onto your fist?" John murmurs, closing my fist and then running his thumb against the cuts on all my knuckles. I wince again.

I cleaned myself up, but I couldn't exactly get rid of all the evidence.

"I'm fine, John. I'm here, listening to your damn instructions, so just let me get to sleep. I have class in the morning and I don't want to stand here listening to a drunk guy lecture me on how to behave."

John raises a vicious eyebrow that seems impossibly thick. It's not fair that he has nice hair and eyebrows too. Seriously.

"You're very brave," he whispers, his palm closing around my fists. I grit my teeth to stop myself from wincing again. He knows he's hurting me and he wants to hurt me for lying to him, but I refuse to give in to John's attempts to get me to confess.

"Yeah. Maybe."

John grins, releasing my palms. "Brave, but stupid to disobey me. I can't let you get away with that, Alexis."

It's not like I think I can get away with talking to him however I want to. I know the man I'm dealing with is dangerous, but even a rat in a trap at least considers chewing its own tail off to get out of his (or her) sticky situation.

"What are you going to do, John?"

I sound stronger than I feel.

"It's your punishment," John says. "So I want you on your knees. Immediately."

I run my tongue over my lips. It's clear what he wants, but I don't want to succumb to him so quickly. I'm not the only one who screwed up here.

"You weren't even there to get me," I snap at him. "According to your brother, you were face deep in tequila, getting too drunk to give a crap about me. So if you think I deserve punishment, what the fuck do you think you deserve."

Fire lights in John's eyes. I'm pushing my luck with him and testing his ability to resist the dark force inside him I witnessed the night he killed that man.

John's response shocks me. He lets go of my hand and runs his tongue along the inside of his lower lip slow and steady.

"I'm fuckin' sorry," he says. "I should have been there. I'm going through some shit."

I allow myself to feel relieved too quickly.

"Okay," I tell him. "Then we're even."

John grins. "I still need you on your knees, cupcake."

I've started to have the most infuriating physical responses each time John calls me cupcake. I'm not a pet name type of girl, but his Long Island accent and the fiercely devoted tone he uses to call me his cupcake make me virtually weak at the knees. I'm not the type of girl to get weak at the knees for a killer.

"John... please."

"You can buy yourself time," he says. "I can get a beer and you can tell me who the fuck you cracked in the face."

"Beer is the last thing you need," I snap at him, tempted to drop to my knees just to stop John from getting even more drunk than he is already. Even without more liquor in him, I can see his face getting redder and he's stumbling and slurring more than when I entered the door. I'm a college student – I've seen enough drunk guys to know that he doesn't need a damn beer.

"You are not drinking a beer," I snap at him. "And I hit my stupid ex-boyfriend, who I don't want to talk to you about since you're the reason we broke up."

John smiles and I strongly consider punching him in the face. He doesn't even bother trying to hide how fucking happy he is that I punched my ex-boyfriend in the face. He seems especially pleased when I blame him for the breakup.

"My dick broke you up, technically."

"Shut the fuck up, John."

John laughs. "You aren't afraid of anything, are you?"

"I'm not afraid of you. Not while you're like this."

He's stumbling around too much for me to fear him the same way I did the night we met. He seems kinder, like a guy you could meet at a bar and hit it off with.

"You should be afraid," John says threateningly. I don't want to believe that he could hurt me, but I know it's naïve to assume that he wouldn't. He's probably done worse things than I can even imagine.

"Whatever, John."

He's drunk, and he's not in the right frame of mind. That's why he puts his hand around my waist, I tell myself, although I know John only puts his arm around my waist because he wants something from me. It's not entirely because he's drunk. He wants what we did before even if he ought to know by now it's a terrible idea.

"We can't keep doing this," I whisper as his palm curves over my ass possessively. I'm a college student. I need to study, not spend my nights in Queens on my knees for a gangster or whatever the hell John is.

"We must," he whispers. "It's the only way we stay loyal to each other. It's the only way men and women can stay loyal to each other."

"You have a fucked up way of looking at the world, John."

Saying his name makes me feel like I have more power over him than I actually do. He snaps to attention when I say his name, his blue eyes visibly focusing on me. There's no good explanation I have for wanting to be the center of John's attention. When he's distracted, he broods too much, and he's a nightmare to deal with. When he's looking at me, he can't seem to remember that I'm pissing him off or a problem he'll have to deal with eventually – without using his dick.

"No," John says, shaking his head. "I see the world just fine. Once we stop having sex, the bond between us dies. I don't make the rules. The only way this shit works out is... we keep that bond alive."

I'm so close that I can smell the mixers he had with the tequila. I can smell the aftershave he must have used this morning because the smell is oh-so-faint and his thick chestnut stubble already spreads out over his face. He's handsome. His palm closes around my hips and John's throat bobs with anticipation of something.

I can't tell what he's thinking and I don't know why that thrills me. Cameron was never a mystery to me. He was the Columbia All-American fratty white boy that I was just thrilled I kissed. Sitting in the glow of Cameron's light was always predictable but not as safe as I apparently thought.

John's breathing slows down and the way my body seems to calm him ironically makes me very nervous. It's like he's getting something he wants from me and I'm too naïve and young to know exactly what it is. Everything about John is a total mystery and unlike with Cameron, he's fucking unpredictable. I let my guard down around Cameron and Gabe nearly hurt me.

My senses could never completely dull around John. Never, considering what I've seen.

"I don't want to tonight," I whisper as John leans forward, pressing his nose to my neck. He doesn't kiss me yet, but I know what's coming and I know that resisting him could end badly.

"Why not?" he murmurs, allowing his warm breath to tease my neck, but still no kissing.

I feel so fucking dirty for wanting him. I know everything about it is totally fucked up and wrong, but I can't stop myself from craving his touch and his tongue and the monster between his legs.

I just can't tonight. I have to say 'no' to him.

Chapter 12
A**holes Make The Best Lovers
John

She's a smart fucking girl, so Alexis must know that I can smell her resistance to me tonight. My first panicked and possessive thought is that she saw her boyfriend on campus and that she fucked him and the reason she doesn't want me tonight is because she has another man's creamy load dripping between those tawny thighs. My stomach lurches with disgust at the thought.

"That's not what I want to hear."

"Can't we just talk?" Alexis says. She has a voice that brings me to my knees.

"We can do both."

That's what this is about? Chick stuff? Will it make her feel better to fuck the drunk villain with the shifty stare and the laundry list of crimes under his belt if she knows he had childhood fucking trauma or whatever? It's not like there was anything traumatizing about growing up in the mob.

I always knew we had power. I grew up wielding that power recklessly and ruthlessly. There was never any John Vicari the victim. Sometimes the truth doesn't make as good a story, but it's the fucking truth, so what are you gonna do about it?

I press my lips to her neck this time, teasing her with what she knows she fucking wants. I don't give a fuck what her mouth says, she smells like sex and she smells like what I need after a long fucking day of ruining the oldest relationship I've ever had.

She moans when I kiss her, and my cock wants to leap out of my pants. She makes this incredibly fucking hard on me. I can't control myself when everything out of her mouth is pure sex.

"Shhh," I whisper. "Moan too loud, I won't stop myself."

"I want to talk," she whimpers as I cruelly run my tongue over her neck. She tastes like sweat and some cheap college girl perfume. Remind me to get the girl some fucking Gucci.

"Then talk," I whisper, pressing my nose to her neck and taking in the scent of that college girl perfume. "Did you see your boyfriend today?"

"I don't have a boyfriend anymore."

Good answer, but not the answer I'm looking for.

"Not what I asked, cupcake."

"I saw my ex," she admits, carefully omitting his name as if I won't notice. I don't need her to omit his name for me because I already know the motherfucker. It's easy to find out which Cameron out of the sea of Cameron-named-douche-bags was the one who had his fingers in my honey pot. That'll be a problem for another day. Right now we're getting to the truth, something Alexis had better straighten her relationship with immediately.

"Good," I whisper. "The truth."

Finally, we're getting somewhere. She wants to keep her secrets and I want to crack Alexis open for my safety and hers. Dad will lose his fucking mind when he gets back. What the fuck will I do about that?

I run my fingers over her knuckles again. I bet she didn't get those knuckles bruised up from taking a crack at a fucking mirror.

"What happened when you saw him? Did you hurt him? More importantly… did he hurt you?"

"You can't kill him, John," she says seriously. Every time she says my name, my cock jumps in my pants. I don't have any fucking control of how my body reacts to her. Doesn't she understand how hard it is for me? She walks in the fucking door and I turn into a damn animal. All I want is to feel her lips around my cock and I can't think straight until I empty my dick..

I run my tongue along the front of my mouth, struggling to find the patience to get through this without hurting her. I can't hurt her for real because once I do that, I break the trust between us for good. Once she stops feeling safe with me, I fucked up for good.

"I want to kill him," I tell her. "For being a stupid fuck. But especially for hurting you like this."

I take her bruised fists and hold them up. Alexis scowls, naturally. God forbid a man take a fucking interest in her life and the bullshit she gets up to when she ought to be studying or some other college girl shit.

She attempts to pull her hands away from me, but I can't let her do that. I squeeze her wrists and keep her hand up.

"He did this, didn't he?"

"I did that," Alexis hisses fiercely. "I punched him because I'm not weak and I might have a natural sense of fear, but I'm not a coward."

"I don't think you're a coward," I tell her and fuck, I mean that. She's the bravest person I know for standing up to that dick, for coming here, for being dumb enough to defy me with her nerdy escape to the library. She's lucky I sent my brother and not my cousin. That might not have gone well.

"Great," she hisses. "I don't care about your approval."

She brings a smile to my face.

"I don't need you to care about anything except pleasing my cock tonight."

"You're drunk and I told you I don't want to have sex."

"Right," I whisper, touching her cheek. "You want to talk. Tell me about this boyfriend."

I hold her so closely against me that she can definitely feel my cock pressing against her leg, which means she can feel just how impatient I am to have her.

"I never said I wanted to talk about Cameron and he's not my boyfriend."

"Hm," I murmur. "Do you have *another* boyfriend?"

Alexis rolls her eyes and scowls at me more intensely. "You think I got a new boyfriend in the three hours after my classes I escaped your extreme control?"

"Perhaps. Women are very resourceful."

"Fuck you, John," she whispers. Again, I love her fucking voice.

"So no boyfriend?"

I don't want to hear that they patched things up. She's mine and she always will be.

"No."

"Good," I murmur, kissing her neck again. "You have something more important than a boyfriend. You have a lover. You have a protector. You have a man who will die for you as long as you remain… bonded."

"You have fucked up ideas about relationships."

"My idea of a relationship doesn't include leaving my woman in bed for another man to fuck."

She slaps me, and I probably deserve it. I'm drunk and getting too cruel with her. I can't expect her to want me or to love me if I treat her like this. I can't taunt her or let her see my jealousy up close. I can't help it. Once I fucked her, I wanted her more. I want her more than ever now.

Even if she hits me very hard, I don't let go of her. I let my face sting and then I keep looking at her, staring at the frown lines on her face and feeling her tremble in my grasp.

"You are such an asshole."

"I'm your lover. Of course I'm an asshole. Assholes make the best lovers."

I kiss her neck again and suck on her flesh until she moans. Despite her protests, Alexis can't help herself. She's a woman and just like other women, she has soft spots and sweet spots and I can kiss each one until she produces the most perfect moan. I pull her against my torso as she moans and quickly tries to stifle it.

As she bites her lower lip, I give her a nice red hickey on her caramel neck. When I pull away from her, she gasps for breath and gives me a judgmental expression. I could leave marks on her all night long if she let me. Fuck, I could do it even if she didn't elt me.

"You have a serious problem."

"You watched me kill someone. Yeah, I got a problem."

"And you're a bad person," she continues. Fuck, is she gonna list all my fucking problems?

"Yeah," I whisper, kissing her tenderly on the forehead. My tender instinct surprises me, but I don't suppress it.

"Then why couldn't I get you off my mind today?" she whispers, shutting her eyes and admitting something that I had to have fucking known.

I kiss her forehead again. "Because I fucked you really well."

"Shut up," she pleads with me. "Just shut up. You can't keep me here forever like some type of sex slave."

"Slave?" I murmur. "If you were my slave, you wouldn't get to cum. You're better than a slave, Alexis. You choose obedience to me. Every fucking thing is your choice."

She nods slowly, and I move my hands away from her.

"Good," I whisper. "If you want to talk, we can talk, but I need your lips on my cock first."

"Are you serious?" she says, not bothering to hide her impatience and her frustration. I suspect she's not resistant to sucking my cock, she's just envious that I get to cum first. She can't hide from me. That's why I fucked her – so neither of us could hide from the other again.

"Yeah," I tell her. "I've waited all fucking day for your lips. You're the best head I ever had, cupcake."

Alexis bites her lower lip and drops her gaze from me. I don't want her to be shy. I want her lips open so I can put my cock deep into her perfect fucking mouth. She's everything I want in a fucking woman.

"I need something from you."

"Yeah."

"Promise you won't hurt anyone in my life. I know they messed with me and hurt me but… you can't hurt anyone, John. It'll come straight back to me."

"Understood. Now get on your knees."

Alexis sighs and then drops to her knees. I love the sound of her knees thudding on the floor of my apartment. My cock nearly bursts out of my pants once she gets on the ground and I protrude my hips forward rudely. Alexis makes a frustrated sound but her palm immediately jumps to my pants. Fuck. Her palms are warm and my dick squirms in my pants, eager to let go.

"You're acting like you need a daily blowjob."

"I need a daily blowjob from *you*," I tell her. "Your lips are special."

I mean the compliment. Alexis gets my dick out of my pants, but as she grabs my shaft, she hesitates before opening her mouth. I jut my hips forward impatiently and Alexis' grasp on my shaft tightens. I groan as she slides her hands slowly up my shaft. It's fucking torture.

"Fuck, Alexis…"

"If I was really brave, I would tease you all night," Alexis whispers. "Instead, I'll give you what you want, John."

"Yes…"

She leans forward, and as her tongue sticks out to touch the head of my cock. I nearly explode. Her mouth is warm and fucking perfect. I move my hips forward and Alexis grunts as I impatiently thrust a couple inches into her mouth. It's enough to stretch her lips and quiet her, but getting my cock deep in her mouth will definitely take more time. She has tight lips and a warm, perfect mouth that I desperately want to fill with my cum.

Alexis grunts and makes a gurgling sound, so I thrust my hips forward to drive my cock a few inches deeper into her mouth. I can feel her tongue wriggling desperately beneath my shaft attempting to make more room for my dick in her tight hot mouth. Tears stream unconsciously from Alexis' eyes and she gags on my cock as she grabs my hips and pulls my dick into the back of her throat.

I cum immediately. The tip of my cock touches the back of her throat and the tightness around my dick forces me to the edge of an intense orgasm. A thick pump of cum spurts into her mouth. Alexis grunts and I push my hips forward, filling the back of her throat with an extremely large load of my seed. I quickly withdraw my dick and Alexis sucks in a sharp inhalation of air through her nose and then swallows before coughing and nearly collapsing forward. Fuck, my dick nearly suffocated her.

I hold her up and crouch down, kissing Alexis' sloppy, teary face. I push my tongue into her mouth as I kiss her and then we rise to our feet together, falling into a tight embrace. I need to feel her close to me.

Alexis collapses on my chest, and then voluntarily wraps her arms around me. Her head presses against my chest and she coughs a little more, her chest shuddering as she holds me. I think she's only holding me because I'm there and not because there's anything special between us, but I think she's special to me. I don't know why, but it's the only explanation I can come up with for my obsession with her.

I kiss her on the forehead.

"No sex tonight," I whisper. "What if I took you out on a real date?"

Alexis tilts her head to the side in confusion. "What do you consider a real date?"

"Bowling. Islanders game. Movie night in Manhattan."

Alexis pulls away from my chest and for the first time in a while, she has a smile on her face. She's got the cutest fucking smile, and she makes me feel all warm and mushy, which grosses me out a little, but it also feels good to have fucking feelings for a change. I thought I'd stopped feeling a long time ago. When I locked eyes with that terrified woman in an Upper West Side alley… I felt something.

I couldn't let that feeling go. I still can't.

"HOW ABOUT A REAL date where you help me study for my midterm exam tomorrow?"

"I'm not a good student," I tell her honestly. "If it weren't for Lucky, I probably couldn't sign my name."

Alexis rolls her eyes. "You don't seem like a dumbass."

"Never said I was a dumbass. I just wasn't good with words and stuff."

Alexis shakes her head. "I think you were just a troublemaker."

I grin. "Probably."

"It doesn't matter. All you have to do is quiz me and we can't stop until I'm sure I can get an A+."

"How long will that take?"

"All night, John. We'll be up all damn night."

"Can I at least get a coffee?" I grumble.

"This isn't a coffee kind of night. It's a Red Bull night."

I've never had a Red Bull without liquor, but right now I would do just about anything Alexis asked if I thought I could get any closer to sleeping with her. There's nothing noble about the way I want her and I don't think there ever has been.

"Do I have Red Bull?"

"If you don't, you'd better get some. I'm not letting you mess with my grades this semester."

"You witnessed a murder a few days ago and you're worried about your grades?"

Alexis glowers at me. "I didn't kill anyone. Now are you going to help me study or not?"

"You're fucking serious. You'd rather study than have…"

"Yes," Alexis interrupts. "Believe it or not, your dick isn't some magic instrument that strips me of my common sense."

I smile. Sure it is, cupcake, otherwise you would ask me to study alone. If Alexis wants to spend time with me, all she has to do is ask. Then again, maybe it's easier if both of us pretend we don't feel a fucking thing for each other, because we really shouldn't. She's a girl I met in an alley and I'm a killer – a fucking butcher. I've done so much shit I'm not proud of, I could fill a book the size of the Bible.

One day, I'll have to say goodbye to Alexis and I only fucking pray it's not too soon. There's been too much darkness in my world for me to hang in there without her. She's my proof that light exists. She's my proof that somewhere, there are people who don't know a fucking thing about the mob and they're safe and comfortable and they deserve to stay that way.

I don't have to go far for the Red Bull and when I get back to my apartment, Alexis has all her notebooks, papers, markers, highlighters and pens spread out over my small dining room table.

"Are you planning a fuckin' invasion?" I grumble as I slam the six-pack of Red Bull on my kitchen counter. Alexis ignores my question and gestures towards the Red Bull. I am twisted in fucking knots over this chick, I swear.

She opens a Red Bull and I grab one because I guess tonight instead of getting laid, I'm fucking studying.

"Can we at least make this fun?" I grumble.

"How can this be fun?" Alexis snaps, giving me a sharp look that reminds me of my first-grade teacher. She's a serious dork, and that kinda turns me on.

"Each question you get right, I get a blowjob."

"That sounds fun for you," Alexis huffs, grabbing flash cards out of my hand, shuffling them and handing them back to me. "It's one night, John. This exam is important. Are you going to quiz me, or not?"

"Fine. I'll quiz you."

It's like she put a fucking spell on me. She struggles through the flashcards at first, but after an hour, she gets the hang of it and she recites the scribbled paragraphs on the back nearly precisely.

"Think you're gonna ace this," I tell her, enjoying how fucking pretty she looks with a giddy and caffeinated expression on her face.

"I had too much Red Bull," she says. "I want to go through them one more time just in case."

I groan. "Isn't there something else you'd rather do?"

Alexis leans forward, her dark-brown eyes gleaming. She's gorgeous enough to make me regret not going to college. If there were girls this pretty in my life, maybe I would have been too distracted to kill so many fucking people at my father's orders. I reach over the table and take her hand. I'm close. I'm so close to getting her tonight.

"Of course there's something I'd rather do," Alexis says suggestively. "I do it every night before a big exam… But I normally study for ninety minutes first, take my break and then stay up all night until four a.m., nap for an hour and get ready."

Christ. She is one heck of a nerd. On the bright side, I am so getting a blowjob.

"I see… What do you do on this break?"

I have a hundred dirty things I could do with her on this break.

"Watch my favorite rom-com," Alexis continues. "Do you have *Netflix*?"

"Are you fucking kidding?"

My cock hurts.

"Do you want to help me ace this exam, or not?"

I want to push her against the wall and enter her until she screams. I want to push my tongue between her legs until she drives her fingers through my hair and yells my name loud enough for the neighbors to hear. What I really fucking want is to lick her cum off her inner thighs while she begs for more.

"Whatever you want, cupcake."

I got fucking Netflix, so that works out okay. Alexis jumps from the table and rushes over to my couch. My place ain't enormous, I don't like having too much, but I have a nice living room and Alexis curls right up on the loveseat. There's panicked throb in my chest as I sit next to her. She doesn't move her body against me at first. I worry that she won't and then Alexis nudges my arms and moves against me.

She wants to cuddle? With me? I almost can't believe it. I feel like a dog in a fucking shelter. It's been so long since a woman wanted anything like this with me. I'm too beastly and rough, too fucked up for anyone. Except her…

I lean over and gaze at Alexis, wondering if she's changing something in me that can't be changed back.

"What's your favorite rom-com?"

"Guess."

"The Godfather."

Alexis wrinkles her nose. "That movie is not romantic."

"I don't know any chick flicks."

"Well, my favorite is Girls Trip so get ready to laugh your ass off."

She gives me this funny look and I can't fucking help myself. I have to kiss her. I take Alexis' cheek and draw her face to mine. I'm treating her like a girlfriend. I shouldn't do that. I know how much I risk if I let myself feel for her, but there's a part of me that wants the life I thought I could never have – the family. The girl.

I kiss her slowly at first, like I'm nervous and like it's my first time because tonight feels like the first time I've felt like this – at least I haven't felt like this in years. I take in her scent and push my lips against hers. Her lips are like soft pillows and as I spread them apart, thrusting my tongue into her mouth, Alexis responds with a soft, barely audible moan. Fuck.

A movie… we're watching a movie…

* * *

Chapter 13
The Death
Alexis

e should watch the movie instead of clutching at each other and kissing like teens at prom. Better yet, I should be studying instead of kissing a killer in his living room and imagining all the places I want to feel his dick.

I can still taste John in my mouth and I want more. I definitely never kissed anyone as good looking as John before and the thrill pulls me away from any sensible thinking. *I can still pass this exam with a 90%, right?*

As I hold on to his thick, tattooed biceps, I let myself feel and enjoy just how thick and muscular his arms are. He's strong. He's safe. He might be completely fucked up, but I know John would never hurt me.

I don't think he could hurt anyone who was truly weak. His fingers sink into my hair and I don't even stop him from kissing me, which is completely stupid and irresponsible of me. How the hell can I expect to keep my head on straight with John's fingers in my hair and his scent all over me.

Cameron never made me feel like an animal when he kissed me. John makes me feel like I'm in touch with a primal part of myself that other guys made me afraid to share with them. He's just so… sensual. Even with arms the size of tree trunks, he's so gentle when he holds me that I can move in his arms and nuzzle against him. John's warm, firm chest makes me forget everything about the outside world.

We're ourselves with each other, which is fucking weird, because we're from different planets. John seems to think my world of college exams and planning for my future is completely alien. He's always known this would be his life, I guess. I can only guess because he never talks about his feelings. He never shares. He just shows me how he feels with unnaturally talented lips.

John tilts my neck to the side, controlling my head movement with his grasp on my hair. I shiver as he exposing my neck and then runs a thick, possessive tongue over the length of my neck before he mutters, "Mine… You're mine…"

I can't avoid shivering more and then pushing my body against his for more of the tempting, forbidden warmth that John's firm chest offers. I want him naked. I hate the thought popping into my head because I really thought I could pop a movie on and fall asleep to avoid this, but there's no avoiding John's magnetism, especially not in his apartment's limited square footage.

John doesn't give me any room to respond to him before he sucks on my neck harder, adding another hickey to my neck. I wriggle out of his grasp and as I break free, he kisses me on the lips again. This kiss freezes me in place because it's more intense and desperate than the others. The exchange of emotion forces me to jerk back from him and John's grasp on my waist tightens, reminding me that despite his gentleness with me, he's very fucking strong.

"Don't go," he murmurs. "Please. I'll be real with you, Alexis. It's not just about sex. That night… You were helpless. You made me fucking feel something and I haven't stopped feeling it. The more I touch you… the stronger it gets. What the fuck is that feeling, cupcake? Hm?"

The Death

I don't think he wants me to answer, even if he phrases it as a question. I want to call it animal lust, but John's kisses don't feel unpleasant or cloying. He knows how to make me want to kiss him. John brushes his thumb over my lips slowly.

"I don't want to go."

"Good," John whispers. "Because I'm really fucking hard and I can't stand it. I can't fucking stand what you do to me."

"I don't feel sorry for you," I whisper back to him.

"You shouldn't," He whispers. "I deserve what you do to me. This feeling… It's fucking torture and there's a part of me that loves it."

John slides the sleeve of my sweater off over my shoulder. He kisses my shoulder and I shudder once I feel his lips, my strength giving way to the sheer pleasure of having a powerful man hold me and kiss me and make me feel like nothing matters except my heart. John gets my sweater off and then my pants before he slides his face between my legs and slowly moves my underwear aside with his index finger.

As John's face gets closer to my wetness, heat rushes through me and I nearly clamp my thighs together to find John stopping my thighs with his palms.

"I need to eat first, babe," He whispers. Babe. That's a first and unlike "cupcake", the word makes me gush buckets. John presses his tongue between my legs and once he touches my clit with those slow, smooth circles, I can't avoid a climax for long. John uses his lips and tongue on me until I can't hold myself back. I do the same thing when I cum. I grab John's hair and desperately try to reduce the intensity of my climaxing, but he grips my thighs and sucks my pussy lips more passionately until I finish and gush my juices into his mouth.

John grunts and sucks on my pussy lips as my juices dribble out. John's body quickly hovers over mine and his weight presses me into his couch. I squeeze his biceps again, his strength sending a surge of something exciting and primal through me. A strong, sexy Italian man has me pinned to his couch and he won't let me leave until we make love, fuck, whatever you want to call it. I get to cum dozens of times and think about nothing.

"You are so fucking hot," John whispers. "Not just pretty. Not just cute. You're a fucking knock out."

He runs his hands over my hips and the parts of me I feel most self-conscious about before his palm curves over my boobs. I run my tongue over my lips and bite down on my lower lip to avoid moaning as John teases my boobs.

"I could play with those gorgeous black tits all night," John whispers. "I love your dark nipples, babe. So. Fucking. Pretty."

He eases his dick out of his pants and my reaction surprises me. I reach between John's legs and my hands wrap instinctively around his thick cock. John grunts as I touch him.

"Fuck," he whispers. "Your hands feel good around my dick."

I move my hands over John's shaft, enjoying the weight of his dick in my hands and how beautifully thick his dick feels in my hand. John lets me touch him for a few more seconds before he sighs and says. "I really don't want to use a condom."

"Don't," I whisper. "We'll worry about it later."

I know my emotions are getting the better of me, but I can't help myself. There's a sexy Italian man on top of me and I have his perfect cock in my hand, inches away from my entrance. I want him more than I've ever wanted anyone. I press the bare head of John's dick against my entrance. I know it's a bad idea, but I can't stop myself. John eases his hips forward and my body resists him at first before he thrusts harder inside me. As John pierces my entrance, I cry out loudly and John holds me against him as he enters me with one stroke, burying himself inside me to the hilt.

"You feel fucking good," he whispers. "So fucking good."

We move together on the couch until John slides his hand between my legs and uses his fingers to make me cum faster while he thrusts into me. John feels so fucking good to me that it doesn't take long for me to climax and then climax again even when he stops rubbing my clit slowly.

He kisses and sucks on my neck as he thrusts into me slowly, whispering dirty words that make me cum repeatedly. When John's muscular body tenses against mine, I want to feel his cum inside me so fucking badly it hurts. This is not how I meant to spend my night studying, but I'm the one who draws John's body closer and I'm the one who whispers into his ear, "Cum inside me. Please…"

John explodes. The thick spurts of cum throb in the base of my abdomen, and my hips buck upwards to meet his grasp. He holds me tightly as he empties buckets of his seed between my legs. The euphoria is too intense for this to even feel like a terrible decision. I just want to feel more of John's body and more of his cum. I thrust my hips up to meet him and then wrap my legs irresponsibly around his torso.

"MORE," I whisper. "Please…"

"Fuck no," he whispers. "We're watching that rom-com. Then you're gonna ace that fucking exam."

I HOOK my legs around John's torso. "No. Not yet," I say as firmly as I can muster. He chuckles and then moves his hips inside me so I moan.

"Okay," he whispers. "Whatever you fucking want."

WE MAKE love until the Red Bull wears off. I hope all this sex doesn't ruin my exam performance. We study as much as possible, but I pass out on John's lap at 4 a.m. He fell asleep first, which made me feel less weird about curling up against him.

He's also awake first and the gross smell of his cigarette wakes me up. He let me sleep *way* too late.

"John!" I call out to him.

He doesn't answer. When I walk into the kitchen just wearing his t-shirt and a thong, coughing dramatically, he doesn't bother putting it out.

"Your ass looks hot," he says. "Ready for class?"

"How have you been up for hours?" I grumble, yawning and wishing I could give his chipper ass a good smack. "You're going to make me late."

"Business calls," he says. "I was watching the time anyway. Come on, cupcake. I gotta get you to that exam. You got nothing to worry about."

"I'm exhausted," I yawn. John sets his cigarette down and comes over to wrap my arms around me. Weird. He's a killer, not my boyfriend. I don't hug him back and John kisses me on the forehead. That's it… I wriggle away.

"What are you doing?" I murmur, wiping off the kiss and searching for the scent of coffee I detect in John's kitchen. He can't expect me to get through this exam without more caffeine. I suppose there are probably more of those Red Bull cans left…

John slides me a mug already filled with piping hot coffee across the kitchen island counter as he answers my question. "I'm kissing you and taking you to class."

"You're making this weird by acting romantic. You and I are not romantic. We are entangled. We are confused. We are exhausted."

"You have five minutes," John says, ignoring everything sensible that came out of my mouth and grabbing his car keys off the hook. "I'll wait in the car."

I guess we aren't talking about feelings this morning. Despite my desire to keep John in the kitchen so I can chew him out, he's right about how little time I have to get ready for my exam. I throw some clothes on, toss the necessary books in my bag and chug my coffee before I meet John in his warm car downstairs.

"You look like an A student this morning."

I think this is his idea of being comforting and supportive. I want to respond positively to him, especially because of last night, but in the cold illuminating daylight, I can't lie to myself about what type of person John Vicari is.

"We can't talk feelings," I say sharply. "It's game time."

John drops me off two blocks from campus after I negotiate with him throughout the entire drive. It takes forever to get into the city and I swear it would have been much smarter to take the train. I meet Chloe at the drop off point and she stares into John's car with confusion as he drops me off. John waves at her, but because I'm already out of the car when he does it, I can't give him a sharp reprimand.

Chloe turns to face me and I expect her to give me a lecture about John and pepper me with questions, but her expression falls completely.

"Is something wrong?"

"You didn't hear?" she says. "You need a new phone, Alexis."

"What happened?" I ask her, a sudden lump forming in my throat. I can tell it's bad before Chloe says anything. I couldn't have predicted just how bad it would be. Chloe takes a really deep breath.

"They found Gabe this morning in Central Park. He was... near the Glen Span Arch... He's dead."

The silence feels less like silence and more like what happens after a really loud noise blows your hearing for a while.

"Gabe? As in... Cameron's roommate?"

The words don't sound like they're coming out of my mouth. The thoughts and ideas sound like they belong to someone else, because I'm mostly stammering something incoherent and Chloe's holding my hands and shaking her head as tears stream down her cheeks.

"I know he was an asshole to you, but someone murdered him. There are these photos going around but—

"I don't want to see them," I say sharply. Chloe squeezes my hand with understanding. I can at least appreciate her understanding even if I can't calm down the way she wants me to.

"I haven't seen them," she says. "But I heard they're pulling people out of class to ask questions. If you need a lawyer, I can call my dad. He has lots of connections in DC."

"I don't need a lawyer," I whisper, but a part of me wonders if it's just wishful thinking. What if Cameron thinks I have something to do with this? What if I do have something to do with this?

John…

"Come on," Chloe says, linking arms with mine. "Let's see if we can get the counselor to give you time away from class."

* * *

Chapter 14
A Devious Plot
John

When I get her ass safely on the Upper West Side, I flagrantly violate every traffic law to get back to Lucky's office. Dad's back. We have three hours until his flight lands and probably even less time before he calls us to a meeting. I need my brother's help.

I can hear my brother swearing on the phone before I reach his office door. Great. This shit finally got to his head, huh? I don't bother knocking before opening the door.

"What the fuck do you want?" Lucky grunts, knocking a stack of papers and binders off his desk.

"Hello, fuck nut. Dad's flight lands today. Sammy wants to kill both of us and we have rogue fucking Zagarella bozos who could rip this family apart."

"Sounds like its dad's fucking problem."

Lucky grabs a flask of what looks like green tea and takes a big sip before wrinkling his face.

"This shit is disgusting."

"It looks like diarrhea."

"She calls it matcha," Lucky sneers, smacking his lips and muttering Althea's name under his breath.

"Focus, fuck nut," I snap my fingers aggressively in front of Lucky's face. "What the fuck are we supposed to do about our fucking father coming back, huh? I didn't tell him about Chiara."

"Good," Lucky snarls. "I'm sending her and Althea to Nashville for the next week until we settle shit up here. If you care about anyone, you would be smart to send them away. Being dad's favorite won't stop him from putting a bullet in anyone's head."

"Don't you think I fucking know that?"

Lucky's getting a little bolder with dad's return. I can't blame him. It's not like I'm not tense.

"We did what he fucking asked," Lucky snarls. "What did he expect? We killed Sammy's son. This shit won't be sunshine and roses."

"It's Sammy. He'd never do nothing to fuck with us."

Lucky scoffs. "You wouldn't feel the same if you had a kid or a fucking family."

"I understand what it's like to lose people," I snap back. I don't need Lucky lecturing me when he spent the first decade of his daughter's life never knowing she fucking existed. My hands curl into fists, but I pull myself from the edge before I blow up at Lucky and turn our sibling snipes into a full-blown fist fight.

"We need to make restitution to Sammy. That's the bottom line."

"You think dad will agree to that? He just spent the past year fucked up in Florence or wherever the fuck he's been. You know our father…"

Lucky sets the green tea down on his desk. He knows I'm right.

"He's our father," Lucky says. "He's not just our father. He's the boss. We obey every fucking thing he asks us to do. That's our job. Our job ain't asking questions. John…"

My brother gives me a funny look.

"Yes, Luca."

A Devious Plot

I'm the one who started calling him Lucky. It was our thing first, and then it became his thing. He needed all the luck he could get, that one. For most of our lives, he was smaller, weaker, utterly dependent on me. So much has fucking changed since we were kids. We don't trail after older cousin Sammy anymore. We have power Sammy always knew we would have. We were always princes on Long Island, destined for this power — power over life and death. Power we wielded against a man we called a brother.

"Why did you come here?"

"I need to protect Alexis," I answer him. That's partially honest. Lucky runs his hand over his stubble.

"You don't need my permission to hide your women. I didn't seek your permission to look after mine."

His voice is serious. Our conversation has changed, hasn't it? We aren't just Vicari killers, but brothers, and we're talking about something real.

"We're family," I tell Lucky. "But we're getting to that age where we want to start our own families."

"Sammy had a family, and we took that from him," Lucky says. "We both know that could happen to us."

His statement twists with several meanings that I don't need more words to decipher. We have families that anyone could take away. That our father could take away. We obeyed his orders without questioning, but killing Sammy's kid wasn't fucking easy and it's been hard to sleep since I did it. If I didn't have Alexis, I don't know what the fuck I would do.

"We have a duty to our family."

Lucky pauses far too long before answering. "Which one?"

"There are some things you do that you can't take back," I mumble. I wish I had liquor. I don't know how the fuck Lucky does this without something in his body to stop this inhuman numbness from taking over. I need to feel and I need to remember that I can feel. It's fucking easy to forget that you can feel when you live how we do. We're fucking monsters when we need to be and when dad comes back…

"Yeah," Lucky says. "We've killed a hundred fucking times each but some deaths come back to you, don't they?"

"Yeah."

"Why did you come here, John?" Lucky asks.

"BECAUSE I WANTED to see how you were doing," I answer, again giving him a half-truth that sends hot shame through me. We grew up together, us and Sammy, and we know each other better than anyone in the fucking world knows any of us.

"And?" Lucky asks. "Because I can count on one hand the number of times you've come here instead of summoning me. I don't keep cameras in my office, no one but you and Althea know I have this tiny place. So I'm asking you, John… Why?"

"DAD," John whispers. "We have to deal with dad."

"Deal with?"

"Don't make me fucking say it."

"Is that what you and Sammy talked about?"

"No," John says. "But if we do it… we have to take care of the dudes loyal to him. We have to prepare to ruin our fucking lives, start a war in Long Island and grieve the man who gave us our lives."

"Yeah," Lucky murmurs. "It's heavy. But…"

He pauses for so fucking long that I don't think he's going to finish his sentence.

"But what?"

Lucky rakes his fingers through his hair and shakes his head, like he can banish the circumstances that brought us here to this secret office meeting where we're talking about shit that could get both of us absolutely fucking annihilated. Once we walk out of this room, either of us could flip and fuck the other over. This is the riskiest thing I've done in my fucking life...

"But Chiara," Lucky murmurs, his daughter's name heavy on his tongue. "She's mine and our father... he could..."

"Not anymore."

"We shouldn't talk about this," Lucky says.

"I'll call you."

"We never had this conversation," Lucky answers.

I LEAVE Lucky's office and grab a quick bite at a pizza joint close to the casino before heading down there to check on the girls and the managers before we open for the night. It's been too long since I've come down here, but there's still a tight ship without me.

One hour before our dad's flight lands, I get a text from an unknown number with the address to the Trump Hotel in Manhattan and a time. Doesn't take a genius to figure out the text is from my father. I wish Alexis would keep in touch using that burner phone I got her, but there's nothing from her. It's probably for the best that I don't hear from her until our agreed upon time. She promised to stay in the library until I came to get her...

I can't show any signs of nerves when I see my father for the first time. He'll know I'm hiding something if there's even a whiff of it on my clothes and if there's one thing Signor Vicari does not fucking like, it's a secret. He prefers keeping secrets, not having them kept from him. I don't bother asking Lucky if he got an invitation to the meeting. It doesn't fucking matter. If we have to deal with our father, it won't be tonight. The head of the Vicari family won't just vanish.

I park a few blocks down from the Trump Hotel and walk without a weapon into the lobby so I get there at exactly the time my father requested. His bodyguards, Michael Ludovici and

Isaac Molinaro approach me the moment I enter the lobby and don't hold back from patting me down right there. The hotel staff know better than to look too closely and I know better than to show up to a meeting with my father carrying a weapon.

"How's my old man?" I ask Michael and Isaac, who I've known since they were kids, even if they're closed to Sammy's age than mine. My smile betrays none of my concerns about meeting with my father, especially not to bozos like Michael and Isaac. They don't have the rank to question me anyway.

"Your father had one hell of a trip, kid. Those Doukas fucks ran our business partners out of the country, pushed up against us in Florence and… you know what? Alfonso will want to tell you himself."

Isaac doesn't speak. He's never been as communicative as Michael. Can't blame him. The less you fucking say, the fewer people can use against you. Plus, he's older. The older you get, the easier it is to understand why there are only young men in the mob — young men and crazy motherfuckers.

"I'll talk to him. Did he come back alone?"

Isaac snorts and makes a face before quickly regaining his composure. He doesn't have to talk for me to have my answer. My father isn't alone. Great. I hope he has a business partner up there and not a woman, but he's Alfonso Vicari, boss of the Long Island mob and he knows that he doesn't answer to a fucking soul.

It's just sometimes I wonder whether he's doing it for the right reasons, you know? I fucking wonder sometimes if our dad has a fucking reason for all the shit we've done. All this fucking fighting, this entire fucking war over business and territory… why the fuck can't we stop?

· · ·

Isaac and Michael sandwich me between testosterone filled biceps as we walk upstairs to my father's room on the top floor. He never cheaps out on his suites here and he doesn't seem bothered by how fucking overpriced this place is. His favorite fucking spot in Manhattan...

I got all the money in the world I need, but I can't imagine leaving my little place in Bayside unless... Well, I could move for Alexis. I would move to fucking Kazakhstan if Alexis gave me a fucking reason to be there. I have to stop myself from thinking about her because knowing my dad, he would read my fucking mind and that would be a bigger problem than I'm ready to deal with.

Hopefully, we can deal with this shit before it becomes a problem.

Despite all the shit in my head, I don't feel nervous when we open the door to my father's hotel room. I've had enough adrenaline pumping through my veins that this is fucking nothing compared to other shit I've been through. My father gets up from his seat at the bar when I walk into the room and spreads his arms wide. His companion still sits at the bar.

It's been a long fucking time since I've met a real Florentine Ludovici, but I recognize this one by her striking red hair and her ocean colored eyes. She seems young. Very young. I sincerely hope my father plans to announce that he adopted this child. The girl, who must be a little older than a girl, sips what looks like white wine, but she doesn't look up from her glass and she doesn't leave the bar. I don't acknowledge her.

My father hugs me and I try to smell hints of what he wants on him. Tobacco. He's in a good mood, or he wouldn't have smoked his good cigars. He smells like liquor, which means he probably drank on the flight because there aren't any liquor bottles open here — just wine. He also smells like he hasn't taken a shower, but he at least put in the effort to shave his face.

He doesn't have bad news.

"What did these fuckers tell you downstairs, huh? What's

with the sour look John. I'm home. Ready to deal with the fucking Murray cockroaches, Sammy Zagarella's mouthing off and all the shit that I put on your fucking back. Smile, Johnny. I'm going to handle everything."

YEAH.

THAT'S MY FUCKING WORRY, dad.

* * *

Chapter 15
My Ride Or Die
Alexis

After class, I walk towards the library to meet up with Chloe. She at least has notes from the morning class I missed while I was in the counselor's office. I don't bother mentioning my previous history with Gabe other than his relationship with Cameron. He's dead — what's the point in bringing up the fact that he assaulted me? It's not like he'll ever see a day in court.

I'm not happy he's dead. I'm definitely shaken up about it, but not for the reasons the counselor suspects.

At least she gives me the morning off to process everything that happened, but I hate the thought of being a mental patient and I don't want to risk having some school counselor dredge up the murky mess of what happened the night of Cameron's party. If I have to get into the details of that night, I don't know how I can avoid mentioning John. The notion enters my head that maybe John did this... but could he have acted so quickly?

He's a killer, Alexis. Of course he could have done this. Still, I keep my mouth shut in the counselor's office.

I don't know what scares me more — counseling, the police or betraying John. Probably betraying John would be the worst of the three, but I'm not eager to spend all day in the counselor's office turning crayons into nubs either. I'll go crazy if I take more than the morning away from classes. It's bad enough I got a C on my last pop quiz.

I request permission to head to my afternoon classes, massively grateful that I don't run into Cameron or any of his other friends. A part of me wants to talk to Cameron about what happened and see how he's holding up, but my heart turns to ice when I remember how he sneered at me. Gabe's dead, that's true, but he'll have to rely on his crew of party animals to carry him through this one.

Even without running into Cameron or any of his boat shoe wearing goons, being on campus is painfully awkward with the constant whispers, stares and flagrant comments made within earshot. Everyone heard the news about Gabe and the story has blown up not just on the local news, but major new stations too. Everyone keeps saying that Columbia will be crawling with journalists too.

On my walk to the library after classes, I hear two girls gossiping and theorizing like the real-life murder of one of their classmates is an intriguing true crime podcast.

"I bet it was a student," the shorter girl says with glee. "Or maybe it was revenge..."

"Who the hell would kill someone for revenge when you could just get them cancelled?" her friend replies.

I want to act inconspicuous, so I keep my step behind them and try to ignore what they're saying. They continue theorizing loudly.

Apparently, half of campus blames Gabe's death on a drug deal gone wrong but the other half, including the girls in front of me think the theory is racist and students are only saying it because Gabe's Latino.

He did it, didn't he? I've been trying to suppress my instincts all day, but I can't account for every minute I spent with John. He must have done this and if John did this, it's only a matter of time before the police come knocking on my door and before this all falls apart. I practically sprint upstairs to Chloe's study room once I get to the library and she immediately notices how out of breath I am when I open our study room door.

"Was someone following you?" She asks in utter panic. "Don't tell me it was Cameron again. I heard he wasn't at school today. Alexis, talk!"

I would talk if Chloe would breathe between syllables. I wait for her to stop freaking out before I answer.

"It's fine," I gasp out. "I just ran here." I slam my backpack on the desk. The weight off my shoulders feels incredible but my heart keeps jumping into my throat as I gasp for breath.

"Why?" Chloe can't understand why anyone would voluntarily run anywhere.

My heart is already racing at a fever pitch. Telling Chloe my big dark secret can't possibly make this worse. It feels like something is about to jump out of me and it's this secret, or the contents of my stomach. She's my best friend, and she's a wild child at heart... she'll understand. Right?

"Alexis!" Chloe hisses. "Talk to me. Why did you run here? Who do we need to kill?"

She gives me her serious strict best friend look which she reserves for very special moments like this one.

"I've been keeping a huge secret and I think I need to get away from Columbia. For good. I need to run away."

"Why? Where would we go? Are we going to your friend's house?"

I've been telling Chloe that I'm staying with "a friend" but John definitely isn't my friend and I'm definitely not staying with him. Not anymore. He promised me he wouldn't hurt anyone in my life and he broke that promise.

He's just as dangerous as I expected, if not more and if he would lie about this... If he could kill Gabe and look me in the eye like he loved me after breaking his promise to me... he's capable of worse. I witnessed him killing someone else and if he decides he's tired of trusting me, he'll kill me too.

But how the hell can I tell my best friend that I made a huge fucking mistake? Obviously, I have to leave out the part where he gave me the best orgasms of my life. Those were clearly manipulative orgasms and they can't be trusted at all.

"Promise not to call the cops, Chloe. Call the cops, we both die."

"Jesus, Alexis. Why are you acting so dramatic? You're scaring the crap out of me."

She puts her pen down and gives me a terrified look like she's ready to dart for the door. It's probably not a bad instinct.

"I have to leave."

"Why?"

"Because…" I say to my best friend, trying to stop my shaking hands. "I think I know who killed Gabe and I think it had something to do with him hurting me."

"Go to the cops," Chloe blurts out. Just her mentioning the cops makes me want to throw up.

"No!" I hiss, glancing nervously at my watch as if mentioning the cops could make John materialize three hours early. He's never early and last time, he didn't even come get me himself. We don't have much to worry about, but I need to act now before we have a big tattooed mobster to worry about.

"Why not?"

"Because. I think the guy who killed Gabe is in the mob."

Chloe snorts. And then she laughs. Okay, this definitely isn't the reaction I expected.

"The mob isn't real," she says. "Alexis. I thought you were serious."

I can't explain what I saw to Chloe, but I have to at least get her to see that what I saw was very real.

"Can you just trust me?"

"Okay," Chloe says. "But you have to say something that makes sense."

"We cannot go to the police." I have to reiterate this because I don't want anything bad to happen to Chloe just because I couldn't keep my mouth shut. She finally looks worried, like she actually believes what I'm saying. Good.

"Do you actually know who killed Gabe?" she says, her face wrinkled with concern.

"I think so. And he's dangerous. I can't let him find me."

"Who is he?" Chloe seems to catch herself and then she just shakes her head. "Never mind. Where do you want to go? Whatever happens, I'm coming with you."

"I can't make you miss classes because I need to run away from some crazy asshole. Absolutely not. I just want you to know that I'm going and that I love you and—"

"I can't just give you money and send you on your way," Chloe says, immediately packing her things. Fuck. I didn't want her to come with me, but before I can protest any further, Chloe has her backpack on and she doesn't look like she has any intentions of letting me out of her sight.

"I'm ready," Chloe says firmly. "Let's do this, girl. We need a plan to get out of the Upper West Side undetected."

There's no way in hell we can do anything undetected. We just have to hope that we're faster than John or whoever the fuck he might send for me. Chloe and I leave the Burke Library on the corner of Broadway and 120th. Chloe's black hair blows out of her face with a huge gust of trash scented city wind.

She glances around furtively, but the streets are empty. It's dark out though, and I'm not confident we're alone. My heart jumps into my throat as I imagine the night I first saw John kill. How fucking stupid can I be to think that he wouldn't kill again? Chloe slips her hand in mine.

"We should call an Uber," she says. "He won't be able to track an Uber."

I don't know what the fuck John is capable of. I just know we have to move fast or we'll be in trouble. Chloe pulls her phone out before I can fully agree to her Uber plan, but I don't have a better plan so I let her go for it.

"We're looking for a black Jeep Wrangler," she says after I hear a few excitable dings from her cell phone.

"How long?" I ask, tapping my foot nervously on the sidewalk, avoiding a wad of gum as I chew on my lower lip and swivel my head in every direction at the slightest noise. We just have our backpacks and the clothes on our backs. Where could we possibly run to when we get in the Uber?

"Three minutes," Chloe responds confidently. "We're going to my friend's apartment in East Village. She goes to NYU. No one will guess we're in the Lower East Side. No one."

It's not exactly a foolproof plan since it requires staying in the radius of Manhattan, but it's better than staying here and letting John find me. He could be on a murderous rampage for all I know. That man who pretended like he cared about me and pretended that he would listen to me was a complete fraud.

"Okay. Three minutes. We can handle that."

In what feels like several years longer than three minutes, a black Jeep Wrangler pulls up to the curb. We run up to our Uber, but I recognize the Uber driver. I've never seen him before, but the family resemblance is so striking that I grab Chloe's forearm and my fingers dig into her like claws.

I want to scream out, "Run!" but I don't have enough time to react. There's the moment of recognition and then there's a gun. It gleams off the street lamp and Chloe screams. We both freeze because there's a grown man holding a gun in our face and he looks like he's ready to kill.

The man opens the front door to his Jeep and steps out, keeping the gun trained on both of us, swiveling chaotically from my face to Chloe's. My bladder feels like it wants me to let go but I fight every urge in my body not to wet myself. He grabs Chloe's hand and shoves her towards the backseat.

"Get in the fucking car or I'll shoot your friend in the face."

There are no other cars. Nowhere to run. Something tells me John didn't send this man. He didn't send the first one with a gun.

"I'm Sammy," he says to me, forcing me to make eye contact with his grisly face. He looks like a Marvel movie villain all cut up and bruised, plus he just doesn't look all the way there. "We're going for a ride, princess. I owe my cousin John a fucking favor."

"He didn't send you, though?"

"Get in the car. We'll talk when I'm ready."

He leads me at gunpoint to the passenger seat and forces me in. Chloe has her phone out, which proves to be a bad move. Sammy reaches back and grabs it, tossing it in front of the Jeep. Once he has me locked into the passenger side, Sammy slides into the driver's seat and sets the gun on the dashboard.

"Reach for that gun, princess and I promise, I'll kill us all."

"Where are you taking us?" I whisper, because I have to ask and because I think I know the answer.

"I told you," he says calmly. "I owe John a favor."

He's going to kill us. I know it. I sense it from the way he won't look at us properly and from the deadened expression on his face. Sammy looks like John Vicari in more ways than one. He has the same look on his face that John had on the night I watched him kill.

THIS IS IT—THE last night of my life and the worst part is, I hurt my best friend too. I'll do anything to save her life, even if it means sacrificing mine.

* * *

Chapter 16
Where The Fuck Is My Girl?
John

I head to the corner where I planned to meet her, and she's gone. I see the crushed cell phone on the ground and instantly, alarm bells go off. After parking on the curb, I rush out to grab the phone, ignoring confused stares from students walking home from the library. Where were those motherfuckers when Alexis was here?

Despite being crushed, I can make out the picture on the screen. It's Alexis, and a young pretty Asian girl with her arm around her. My stomach tightens. I call Alexis' phone for the fifteenth fucking time and she doesn't pick up. I call Lucky.

"I'm playing online chess with my daughter. This had better be an emergency."

"Dad must've found out about her. She's gone."

"What do you mean she's gone? Who? Your college girl?"

My college girl has a name, but Lucky knows that. He just has this magical ability to piss me the fuck off. I stick my tongue in front of my mouth to stop myself from telling him off.

"We're in deep fucking shit. I hope you have your daughter and Althea far the fuck away from this 'cause if dad got her already–

"He doesn't know about her. He can't," Lucky says far too

fucking confidently for my liking. Does he have a crystal fucking ball that can see into our wack job father's head?

"How the fuck can you be so sure?" I want to slap Lucky in the fucking face. With our father back in Long Island, I don't have the power that I used to. I might still outrank my older brother, but with Alfonso fucking Vicari back in town, there's always someone bigger he can get to have his back. It's not the power I miss – it's the safety. Since I looked my father in the fucking eye, it's like that safety we built could all fall apart.

He wants to start a war. He doesn't give a fuck who he kills or who he has to kill to get what he wants. We killed our own fucking family, and he's not even upset about it.

We're the monsters who listened to him. The monsters who did it. But maybe that can be the last time. Maybe Enrico Zagarella can be the last person we kill. There are other ways to get what you want without causing so much pain.

"I met with him," Lucky says. "I tested him. Trust me, if he knew, I would have found out."

"Now you can fucking play mind games with dad?"

"I didn't play mind games. I was smart. There's a difference. He doesn't know. Maybe your college girl ran off. I can't imagine she wants anything to do with a screwed up asshole like you."

"Like you're one to talk."

Lucky grunts. "Every day I have to convince Althea I'm worth it. Every fucking day."

I would do the same for Alexis if she would just give me a chance. Maybe she ran off, but there's a crushed cell phone on the ground and my gut instinct tells me she's gone.

"Look around for her," Lucky says. "You can't find her, I'll come help you look. She can't have gone far. She's a college student. She's probably hiding out in the East Village with the NYU kids."

"How the fuck would you know that?"

"While you were doing dad's job, I was doing what you're

doing, chasing down civilians. Good luck. Chiara's kicking my ass. I need to get my head back in the game."

My brother hangs up on me and I spend half an hour driving around the Upper West Side and another two hours searching on foot and illegally entering buildings on the university campus. She's nowhere and my dad doesn't have her so I have to accept an unfortunate truth – a truth that hurts.

She ran.

And right now, she may be with the police, she might be halfway across the country or halfway across the world, but that girl is fucking gone. She could be with her boyfriend too. What was his name? Cameron? Maybe I should pay that motherfucker a visit and see if he knows where Alexis is.

Cameron. How many motherfuckers named Cameron can there be at this fucking school?

The answer is apparently fifteen. I have a cousin who knows a guy who knows a guy who gets me access to precious fucking Cameron's full name and his current address – a place not too far from where I met Alexis. It's near Bleeker and I don't want to go there again, but if it's my only chance at finding Alexis, I'll have to do it.

I'm not in control once I make it out there. I can't stop the memories of that night with Lucky from rushing back. I turned my brain off to the sounds of my cousin begging for life and then just like that, we ended his existence. We tell ourselves it was mercy because at least he got family to do it and he wasn't tossed off a pier or nothing like that, we were very respectful. But he's still dead and I'm still a fucking monster for killing Sammy's son.

You always have to question your loyalties out here and tonight, I'm questioning mine. What happens to me if I lose Alexis? How the fuck can I keep doing this if I lose her. She never deserved any of this. She's the only fucking thing in my life that's remotely connected to a sense of innocence. I need her safe.

John

I knock on Cameron's door. It's almost four in the fucking morning, so there's no way this dick is anywhere else, right? I ring the doorbell and bang on the door again. Some other blond asshole answers the door.

"Hey man. What's going on?"

"I'm looking for your buddy, Cameron."

"He's upstairs."

"Go get him."

"Alright, man. Chill. You're waking the house up. Kyle has an exam today. I'll be down in a minute. You a friend of Cameron's?"

"I'm… his dealer."

"Cool."

College kids are incredibly fucking stupid. It doesn't matter the college, they're all fucking idiots. This particular idiot leaves me at the front door and I have time to finish a cigarette before Cameron slides the front door open. One look in that bastard's face and it doesn't even matter if he has Alexis here. I want to kill him.

I promised her I wouldn't.

"Hey um… I'm sorry, who are you?"

"I need to ask you a few questions," I tell him, dragging him by the collar out of the house and shutting the door quickly. It'll be easier for me to handle what I need to handle on the streets. Cameron looks like he's never had anyone touch him or rough him up like this and I don't mind that one bit. I push him against the door and he yelps.

"Hey, man! Chill out. What the fuck? I don't fucking know you, man."

He's whining so much that I take my hands off him. Maybe the tough-looking athlete doesn't need my kind of tough talk. I'll go easy on him.

"Tell me where the fuck Alexis is or I'll shove your balls so far up your ass that they'll sprout out your fucking mouth."

Cameron barely stifles a yelp. "Who the fuck are you? I'm

calling the police, man. Alexis isn't here and you don't know her, so—aahhhhhhh!"

I change my mind about going easy on him and twist Cameron's forearm, pinning him to the door with as much strength as I can muster. He squeals like he's getting fucked in the ass with a cactus and he struggles far more than he needs to since I ain't even hurting him, just keeping him against the door to make sure he answers my fucking questions.

"Chill the fuck out," I growl at him. "Tell me where Alexis is and cut the fucking bullshit."

"Alexis dumped me!" Cameron yells. "That slut fucked my roommate and now he's dead, I don't have a girlfriend and some fucking asshole is showing up at my place to——ahhhhhhhhh!"

That time I wanted to hurt him, but I push the idiot jock too far and he flips the fuck out. He's struggling so hard that he'll hurt himself. I try to tell him as much, but he doesn't fucking listen and the only sound to pierce over our yelling at each other is a loud crack. The kid turns white as a fucking sheet and I let go of his hand. No need for me to hold him back now…

His wrist hangs limp, and he screams loudly. Very fucking loudly. Cameron grabs his wrist which only makes the situation worse as the shots of pain runs straight through him and forces him to realize that his wrist is incredibly fucking broken.

Dead. Did this asshole just tell me that his roommate was dead? I shove him against the door and he yelps again, even if I only push his chest.

"What the fuck did you just say? Dead? Your roommate's dead?"

Is that the asshole who touched Alexis? I don't know how the fuck I'm going to leave this dick alive here, but my promise to Alexis has to be stronger than my desire to put several bullets in this motherfucker's head just for calling her a slut.

"Yes," Cameron squeaks out. "Yeah, my roommate's dead and you just broke my fucking wrist so can I catch a fucking break, man?"

He reaches for the door handle with his good hand and I smack it so fucking hard, the jock's eyes nearly pop out of his fucking head. What the hell did Alexis ever see in this stupid motherfucker? But a dead roommate... That's different. Did Alexis do something incredibly fucking dumb?

"What happened to your roommate?"

"Someone killed him," Cameron says and for a second, I see a hint of fucking empathy on the kid's face. Maybe he's just a run-of-the-mill asshole, not utterly irredeemable. Fuck, if that kid's going to hell, I'm well ahead of him.

"Who killed him?"

"How the fuck would I know?" Cameron whimpers, holding onto his wrist, which has already turned three different shades of red and purple. There's swelling and the whole situation looks pretty fucking bad.

"If you hadn't struggled so much, that wouldn't have happened."

"Who the fuck are you?" He whimpers, examining his wrist and giving nervous glances towards the door handle. This dick has to understand that he leaves when I say he leaves.

"I'm a friend of Alexis."

Cameron's face turns redder than it did when he snapped his fucking wrist. Suspicion gives way to outrage as he feeds his own suspicions.

"Are you fucking kidding me? She was fucking you too?"

Don't do anything stupid, John. You need to focus on finding her.

"I'm not here to answer your fucking questions kid. When's the last time you saw her?"

"Before Gabe died," Cameron says, sadness returning to his voice again. "She was a bitch to both of us and she wants everyone to think he's a bad guy, but he wasn't."

I'm not here to assess the motherfucker's morality. Doesn't matter what I wanted, karma caught up with him already. I just hope my spunky college girl didn't have a fucking thing to do with this mess. I can keep my ass out of jail, but if she hurt this guy, I don't know how much I'll be able to protect her.

Maybe she's already spoken to the cops.

"The cops come talk to you about your roommate?"

"The cops don't give a fuck," Cameron spits, his sadness mixing with genuine anger and a little defeat. "He's a Latino scholarship kid from the wrong part of New York. They made up their minds about him when they found him dead in Central Park."

Central Park. When the fuck could this have happened? I've had eyes on Alexis' every move. Unless she's much sneakier than I thought, she couldn't have done this.

"You smoke?" I ask the kid, because he seems pretty fucking stressed out and I could use a smoke myself.

"No," Cameron whines. "It's early and I have to go to the nurse."

"You'll be fine, kid. You'll be even better if you tell me where Alexis is."

"If you're so close, why don't you know?"

The temptation to squeeze his broken wrist in a vice grip until he cracks strengthens significantly.

"ANSWER MY FUCKING QUESTION. Tell me where she is. Tell me what you know. I'm fighting the temptation to break more of your fucking bones."

The kid looks beat up as it is. Alexis must have broken his nose when she cracked him in the face. My heart swells with pride. *She's fucking special, that girl.*

"I don't know where the fuck she is!" Cameron whines. God, he's such a little bitch. I want to make him pay for that, but I need to stay focused. I need to find my girl.

This kid doesn't know anything. Fuck. I need my brother's help...

John

* * *

Chapter 17
What Sammy Wants
Alexis

We've been in Sammy Zagarella's captivity for two weeks. These have been two painful weeks where I have no connection to the outside world. I haven't called my mom, I haven't spoken to my dean or my advisor, I've dropped off the face of the earth and I don't have a clue what's happening on the outside world.

We are missing persons, True Crime cases, murder victims waiting to happen. I don't know much about our captor and he hardly interacts with us directly in any way I would consider sane, but I know that he's going to kill us because he's told us so several times. He yells at us and at the voices in his head and every minute we spend with him, I fear he's going to snap and end both of us.

Chloe can tell that I'm awake, even if I'm trying to be subtle and go unnoticed. She groans and rolls over.

"Please tell me this is a nightmare," she whispers. She says this every morning, but every morning our nightmare continues. I can't blame her for having a daily ritual in this grim situation. I have daily rituals of my own. I check the windows every morning, pretending the thick black burglar bars on the windows don't exist and pretending that I can recognize any of the thickly wooded landscape outside.

We're nowhere near the Upper West Side, that much I know.

I also check the door to the bedroom every morning and find it locked. Sammy has it bolted too—I know his name now, not like that makes a difference. Sammy Zagarella will kill both of us. I can't say exactly when he'll finally snap and do it, but the man isn't all the way there.

"I wish it was a nightmare," I whisper to Chloe. She snakes her hands beneath the thin microfiber blanket that barely keeps both of us warm. I hold her hand and try to stifle my own tears. Chloe cries every day too, but I can't bring myself to cry. I don't want to give Sammy the satisfaction of bringing out tears from me. John will come. I want to get out of this on my own, but John will be here. He won't abandon me.

He hasn't.

Sammy knocks on the door three times like he does every morning around this time. Chloe groans and hides under the covers.

"I'm not having breakfast with him," she whispers. I can handle Sammy when he's not yelling or hearing voices, but Chloe detests getting anywhere near him at all. I can't blame her.

"We have to eat," I whisper. "He's fucking crazy, we can't piss him off by turning him down."

"He's going to kill us anyway," Chloe hisses.

Sammy knocks three times again, this time even more impatiently than before. Fuck. I'm cold and I don't want to leave the thin microfiber blanket because even the shitty insufficient blanket is better than nothing. Wherever we are, it's fucking cold…

I approach the door and knock back three times. Sammy opens the door a crack.

"Breakfast. Is Chloe calm?" he asks.

He seems relatively sane this morning. There are signs of

sanity that I can look for. He shaved, he's wearing a clean shirt, and he doesn't smell like alcohol. He looks like he got a few hours of sleep which is a rare occurrence for him. He looks just sane enough for me to push back against his insanely stupid question. What reason on this damn planet would Chloe have to be calm?

"How calm do you expect her to be?"

I try to keep it together with Sammy so I don't piss him off, but I can't stop myself from snapping sometimes.

"Hm," Sammy grunts.

"We need another blanket. It's cold."

"Get up and I'll get what you need. Big snowstorm coming through today," he grunts.

A snowstorm? Great. We must be somewhere really cold, and we must have already missed our finals. This is such bullshit. I know it's very dorky, but the thought of having to repeat a semester at Columbia almost makes me sicker than having to put up with Sammy. He doesn't have a bad personality, but he's clearly unstable.

He's taller and larger than John, and not very lean at all. Sammy's pure muscle and visibly fucked up from scars and black eyes. He's been in several recent fights judging by the purple bruises and recently healed cuts with scar tissue still scabbing over. He's terrifying and beastly in a way John isn't. They're related, but John's side of the family clearly got all the looks.

"Chloe doesn't want to get out of bed," I tell him firmly. If he tries to attack her, I'll defend her. Chloe was ready to ride for me, so I'm ready to ride for her.

Sammy seems insistent today, but not violent. He replies firmly without raising his voice, "She needs to eat."

"Yeah, she does. She also needs to go to her history classes and back to her dorm."

"I'm not having you girls go to the cops," Sammy grunts. "If she wants to wait until lunch, that's fine with me."

His annoyed tone returns. Whatever. As long as he doesn't

start screaming and threatening to blow a hole in our heads, I can deal with him.

I glance back at Chloe, who can clearly hear our conversation. Fuck, there's no getting through to her. She's found one way she can protest, but I'd rather pick Sammy's brain and search for a potential escape than curl up in bed and give up. Sammy sighs.

"Are you staying with her?"

I'm not too proud to eat.

"No," I tell him. "I'll have some breakfast."

Sammy grunts again and opens the door wider. I step out of the bedroom to an equally cold house. When I instinctively wrap my arms around my shoulders, Sammy grunts that he'll get me a hoodie. He heads into a bedroom that I presume is his (I've never entered it) and returns with a bright blue *New York Islanders* hoodie. Seriously? I give him the best withering look I can muster as I take the hoodie from him.

"Sorry," Sammy grunts. Weird motherfucker. He apologizes for giving me an ugly hoodie but doesn't have a problem with kidnapping me or my friend. I can tell he thinks this is humane, but it isn't. I slip the hoodie on and dutifully follow Sammy to breakfast. By now, Chloe and I know what we can and can't get away with under Sammy's rule.

Once I'm in the kitchen, I sit at the small wooden table and Sammy brings over oatmeal with fruit chopped up in it, bacon on the side and more fresh fruit. For a fucking psychopath, he eats healthy. Sammy sets down a bowl of the same with a protein shake next to it and joins me at the table. He has to pull the chair all the way out to fit his long, enormous legs. He's easily twice my size, but he does better in the mornings than the evenings. At night, I almost look forward to him locking us up.

"John knows you're missing," he grunts. "So does all of New York."

He never talks about what he did or why we're here. Normally, he reviews football or hockey scores, sports news and petty events. He talks about elections and politics – not John.

"He knows I've got you but… none of 'em know about this place."

"Thanks for the update."

I don't mean to sound sarcastic, but I can't just sit there quietly while Sammy calmly discusses the fact that he kidnapped two Columbia students.

"I can't have you or that girl running to the cops," Sammy grunts. "This wouldn't have happened if John hadn't killed my son. So if you need someone to blame, blame him."

John killed his son. Those four words make my stomach turn, but I can't buy into Sammy's view of the world. John made his choices, but Sammy made his too.

"John didn't make you kidnap me."

Sammy's sea-green eyes flash to mine and he looks amused, not threatened. I'm okay with that.

"No," Sammy says. "He didn't. But he deserves worse than what I've done to him."

"I don't understand how you consider yourselves a family," I grumble. "All you do is hurt people and hurt each other. Where's the glamor in that?"

Sammy's answer surprises me. "They were born into this life. They can't help it."

They. He's not just talking about John. He does this often, where he assumes I know who or what the fuck he's talking about with no context. He talks a lot, which is different from John, and it seems in my best interests to let him talk so I can learn something that might help me get the fuck out of here.

"Are you defending the men who killed your son?" I ask him.

"I might've done the same if Alfonso asked me. Their father is the most powerful man in New York. There ain't a fucking governor or politician in that city who Alfonso doesn't approve of. He has more money and power than any man should."

"Yet he's nowhere to be seen."

So why bother listening to him? Sammy gives me a sharp look, like he thinks I'm crazy for even questioning Alfonso's power. How can he be one of the most powerful men in New York and I've never heard of him? Maybe there are parts of John's life that I'll never understand.

Sammy grunts. "True power is quiet. You're in college, you should know that. Don't they teach you anything fucking useful at these fancy schools?"

I don't appreciate him telling me off about college when he's the reason I'm not in my biology lecture right now, so I scowl and ignore him for a few minutes while I eat some of the oatmeal. It's not satisfying enough, but it's either Sammy's healthy foods or nothing, so I make do.

"What's wrong with her?" Sammy grunts eventually. "What's so different today?"

"We're regular college students. We're freaked out about tuition, classes and other normal things. We don't want to be here and we don't want you to kill us. It's depressing to be forced away from our old lives."

"Who said anything about killing you?"

"We've seen your face. We could go to the police. You have to kill us."

Sammy laughs. "I won't kill you. And I don't give a fuck about prison. I've been there before and before the end of my life, I'll be back behind bars again. I'm punishing my cousin, but I'm not as fucked up as he is."

"Then what's the point? You're traumatizing us and you're ruining our lives."

Sammy grunts again. I'm getting tired of his annoying ass grunting. "This isn't trauma. Trust me."

He's an asshole. I stop talking and finish eating. Sammy clears my plate and then returns with coffee. I don't want to let him win me over with coffee, but he's very sparing with his drugs and he only gives us coffee when he wants something.

"Will vanilla flavoring wake your friend up?"

"I doubt it."

"If it makes you feel better," Sammy grumbles. "This will all be over soon."

Oddly enough, that doesn't make me feel better. Sammy says he won't hurt us in the morning but at nights… everything changes at night. He becomes a different person. He drinks too much and then he starts talking and rambling and becomes a more monstrous version of the already terrifying person sitting in front of me.

"Where are we?" I ask him. He never answers me, but I hope today will be different. Maybe I'm in luck.

"Adirondacks."

"Could you get more specific?"

"No. But when the snow blows through… we'll lose power. I have to leave for a few hours and I don't need either of you getting into trouble."

I DON'T WANT to go through what we went through the last time Sammy left us with this warning. I glance away from him and nod. Trouble. What kind of trouble could we possibly get into over four hours away from New York City? We have no car, no wallets or cell phones and absolutely no chance of escape. I still don't even know what Sammy wants.

Chapter 18
The Road Trip
John

Lucky returns to my place at midnight with a case of beer for me. At least he knows how to get into my good graces. We've spent the last two weeks making up for dad's absence. He demands our presence every night and acts like he's making up for lost time.

We have more important shit to deal with.

"So. I have good news and bad news."

Lucky says this every night, but it's never the news I really want to hear. I'd better crack open a beer before I let this motherfucker ruin my night. I sip over half the beer before Lucky says a fucking word. That means the bad news is really fucking bad.

"Dad asked about Sammy."

"Did you tell him the truth?"

We can't tell dad the truth without fucking ourselves over. Telling dad the truth would mean burying ourselves in deep shit that we ain't ready to get out of yet. We need more time and we need dad off the case.

"No, I didn't. It doesn't matter. He thinks Sammy's hiding out with two prostitutes in some fucking hellhole called Speculator, New York and he thinks they're Sammy's... you know. Girlfriends."

"Two prostitutes?"

"Yeah. It's them."

Shit. Dad knows and if he doesn't know, he'll find out soon.

"What the fuck is the good news?"

"He gave us the order to kill Sammy and all his remaining descendants."

Does Lucky understand the fucking meaning of good news?

"What the fuck?"

Lucky keeps talking like he doesn't have a lot of fucking explaining to do.

"He's sending one of the Ludovici brothers up there to take Sammy out with a sniper rifle tomorrow. He wants us to follow up."

"Do you understand good news?"

I put my hand on my thigh. Even if I don't have my pistol there, I wish I did because I would definitely consider pointing it at my idiot fucking brother. Lucky grins.

"You don't understand. We have Sammy's address. We get there first. We get them out of there and… we don't have to wait long. The kid has two weeks to get Sammy. That gives us two weeks to figure out how to—

Lucky's still not brave enough to say it out loud. I'm too fucked up to avoid it. I have to get used to what we're going to do. I have to prepare myself for the reality of what will happen when I become the boss of the Vicari mob.

"Kill dad," I whisper. "Two weeks to figure out how to kill the man who brought us into the world."

Lucky nods. "Yeah. Like I said. Good news and bad news."

"Why the fuck did you bring beer?"

"Because, motherfucker, I'm driving."

I DON'T RELAX until we get out of the city, but maybe that was a mistake. Lucky turns on the radio and we get the weather report for Route 90 where we're headed. Too far upstate, just the type of place Sammy would put a fucking safe house. He ought to know there are no secrets in the mob, especially not from dad. All secrets come out eventually. It's why we need to strike fast.

We have enough guns in the back to waste a small town, but we both hope we can get through this with a single shot. We both agree we can't let Marco Ludovici go, but it brings us no pleasure to kill him. Soon, we'll handle things for the last time…

Another hour passes and our driving conditions worsen considerably. They must've had a hell of a lot of snow up here.

"Fuck, Albany," Lucky grunts after we get around the city traffic and venture deeper into the back country, the shitty part of New York with too many rednecks and not enough noise or bagel shops. Unlike Sammy, I hate the fucking country.

I've polished off all the beer and taken a few naps, but it's been weeks since I've seen Alexis and I don't know what the fuck we'll find up there. Lucky glances over at me once we get off the interstate and onto the winding state highways that take you to the middle-of-fucking-nowhere.

"Forty-five minutes. Think he'll be there?"

"It's ten in the morning and it's snowing like fucking crazy," I grumble.

We can barely make out ten feet of the road in front of us and the snow just keeps coming down. I swear this part of the country is fucking miserable.

"I didn't hear that he hurt them. They're fine. That should make you feel better."

"He doesn't have to cut off a finger to hurt them. They're women."

"Sammy's not the type," Lucky promises me. I know he's just trying to make me feel better, but it's easy for him to act like this when Chiara, Althea and his unborn child are safe and far the fuck away from here.

"He might not been the type, but he's been here for two weeks and when's the last fucking time Sammy had a girlfriend?"

"He wouldn't do that," Lucky promises me. "He knows how much she means to you."

"But what does he want? It's been weeks and he's been far off the fucking grid. What does he want?"

"I dunno. We need to stop for gas. And lunch."

Lucky's appetite has always been one of the most fucking annoying things about him. He acts like he'll fucking die if he misses any of his meals.

"Lunch? How much fucking lunch do you need?"

"I already missed breakfast for you," Lucky grumbles. "We're stopping for lunch."

We stop for lunch and gas. I don't kill Lucky, but I seriously want to until we get back in the car and get further from civilization. My attention heightens when I see the sign that Speculator is ten miles away. I keep my hand on my pistol and Lucky notices quickly.

"Can you get your hand off your fucking gun? You're making me nervous."

"How fucking stupid would I have to be to kill you?"

"Relax. Alexis is fine and whatever the fuck is going on with Sammy… we have a way to make it up to him."

"He could kill them and he could kill both of us."

Lucky smirks. "I never thought I'd see you in love again."

"I'm not in love. Don't be a fucking idiot. She's a college girl, and she's my responsibility. That's all."

"Was it your responsibility to keep her locked in your apartment for weeks? You could have sent her off to Stanford or University of Florida, or anywhere a thousand fucking miles away from here. But you kept her."

"She was scared after what she saw. How the fuck could I do that?"

"You care," Lucky insists. "Admit it."

"You're asking me to admit the worst thing you can admit in the mob."

"Bullshit," Lucky grumbles. "It should have been about family. We've forgotten what the fuck cosa nostra is about."

"Remember grandpa?" I whisper. Our grandfather, the man who created Alfonso would have been so disappointed at what our father became. An old world Sicilian with old world Catholic values, there was a time when the Vicari name was synonymous with bringing peace to the city. Our father changed that.

"You think too much," Lucky mutters. "Tonight, we need to act. Whatever you need, John... I'll do. You're my brother. Understand?"

"I understand."

THE SNOW COMES DOWN HARDER the closer we get to Speculator. This is the land that God fucking forgot. I'm nervous and I've started smoking, which bothers Lucky. I can tell even if he doesn't say anything. I crack the window, but I'm already getting nervous that I'm running out of fucking smokes. Three more. That's all I have left and I don't know when the next fucking gas station is.

"You're choking me to death," Lucky finally groans.

The brown flash in front of the car changes everything before either of us can react. The car lurches forward as Lucky slams on the brakes and sends both of us flying forward. We hit the deer anyway. Lucky swears, and the car swerves out of control across the country road, slamming into the guardrail. The brown flash lies in a crumpled heap in the middle of the road, but seems to be only stunned. He gets up and runs off. Fuck. He probably won't make it, but at least he won't die out here.

We might not be able to say the same.

The front of the car is totally smashed. My head aches like fucking crazy. Lucky's airbag inflated, mine didn't. The bastard is totally passed out and the snow just keeps coming down. We aren't in the middle of the road anymore, but it won't be long before our car gets completely fucking covered in snow.

John

I push Lucky's shoulder to get him up. My breath comes out of my mouth in a white cloud. The radio reads the weather report, but it's fuzzy and hard to make out the words. We must be close to Speculator, but not close enough that walking will be anything fucking pleasant.

"Wake the fuck up."

I push against his shoulder. Lucky groans. There's blood on his head and pouring out of his nose, but it doesn't matter. We need to get out of here. It's too cold. There's gonna be too much snow and the car… Well, fuck the car. It's no good anymore and we don't need it. We need to move before anyone finds us out here with a car full of guns and our fucking pants down.

"Luca fucking Vicari, wake the fuck up."

I elbow him hard and Luca coughs. Good. Coughing is better than nothing. I gather up as many guns as I can, shaking his shoulders intermittently. He's waking up, but he doesn't sound good.

"Luca, we gotta move. We gotta fucking move."

My hands are already red by the time I get my elbow wedged against the door. It won't open. The car's too crushed and I can't get out. I'll have to break the window. I slam the stock into the window once. Twice. It doesn't work. I take out my pistol and with shaking hands, get a bullet in the chamber. Lucky grunts an audible word.

"We're going to go deaf, you fucking—

I blow a hole through the window and neither of us can hear the end of my brother's sentence, But at least he's awake. He groans as he slides the seat back.

"What the fuck happened?"

"You hit a deer, then you hit your head."

"Yeah. Where are we?"

This is a bad time for Lucky to lose all his fucking brain cells.

"I don't know," I grunt. "You're the one with the GPS."

Lucky groans and I smash the window so I can get out. I toss the guns out of the window and work my body out, picking glass out of my coat once I land on the snow. We're the only mother-fuckers dumb enough to drive around here, but we can guarantee a plow will come through soon to get the snow. Eventually. The crash pinned the driver's side of the car to the guardrail and Lucky's side got even more fucked up than mine. I can get the back door open and pull him out through there. Hopefully, the motherfucker can walk on his own. He twists himself out of his seat and crawls out of the car as I pull the back door open.

Lucky holds up the small rectangular GPS unit.

"Ready for a ten-mile hike?"

"With over 50 lbs of weapons? What the fuck could go wrong with that."

"We need to take the plates off the car," Lucky growls. "Throw them off as long as we can."

"No," I whisper. "We don't know who could find this. A small town cop could trace the car with the VIN number. We need to burn it."

Lucky nods. There's still blood on his face and he's shivering. He needs gloves and we need to get moving.

"I'll start the fire. Start walking."

LUCKY TAKES HALF the guns and starts towards the woods. Probably better for us to stay off the road. This ain't the first car I've torched, but I don't particularly enjoy the process in the winter. I have to take my coat off to get my undershirt. I pop the gas tank open and snake the rolled-up shirt into the tank, soaking it with gasoline. I open the back seat of the car and toss the shirt into the back.

Once the fumes get into the air, the whole thing will blow. I just have to light it. I rip the sleeve off my first long-sleeved layer and drip use it like a shitty fucking fuse to set the whole thing on fire. The fire starts small at first, but in a matter of time, the whole thing will blow and attract more attention than either of us need. I start off behind Lucky. The snow is much deeper in the forest and it won't take long before we work up a huge sweat, but until then, I'm freezing my fucking ass off out here.

"Ten miles. Think we can get there before it gets dark?"

"No," Lucky grunts. "It gets dark too early and my head hurts. I don't know if I can make it all the way…"

"You'd better get it together, brother. I'm not leaving your ass behind. Ever."

Chapter 19
Crazy Sammy
Alexis

"**I**'M GOING TO KILL YOU. I'M GOING TO FUCKING KILL YOU."

Sammy keeps screaming that outside our room. To himself. I lock myself and Chloe in the bedroom, because he normally gets this way after dark. The snowstorm must be messing with his head. There must be at least three feet already and it's only been coming down a couple of hours. The snow out here isn't like anything I've seen.

The thought might be cruel, but it occurs to me that Sammy's mental break might provide the perfect opportunity for escape if the man rambling and screaming to himself didn't have an arsenal of weapons at his disposal. Chloe's out of bed and pacing now. Despite skipping breakfast earlier, she found her appetite for lunch and once the snow started, her cynical mood appears to have been replaced with more fire for escape than I've ever seen from her before.

"This is bullshit," she hisses. "He has no right to punish you for some bullshit that isn't even your fault. This is where toxic masculinity leads."

"Maybe he'll calm down and fall asleep."

"Great. And we'll have to tiptoe past a sleeping bear and

venture out into deep snow where he can easily follow our tracks. We don't know where we are. We don't know where we're going…"

"There has to be a police station somewhere. As long as we can find a cop or a trucker, we can get out of here."

I can see that Chloe wants to believe we can get out of here. She's scared. She's coming up with all the ways that this can go wrong not because she doesn't think we can get out — she wants to make sure we do it and we do it right.

Sammy howls again and begins breaking dishes in the kitchen.

"YOU DON'T UNDERSTAND," he yells at nobody in particular. Chloe gives me a terrified look.

"He's lost his fucking mind," she hisses. "And you're saying his brother is a totally normal guy?"

"His cousin," I mutter, somewhat desperate to think that John doesn't have any of Sammy's insanity flowing through his veins. There are a few minutes of silence which we're careful not to mistake for safety.

"He locked us in, anyway," Chloe says. "We would have to break down this door without him noticing."

"Or convince him to open it and overpower him."

"He could literally fit both of us in one of his shoes," Chloe says.

"We have the element of surprise. I'll tell him you're sick and you whack him over the head with something."

"With what?"

WE DEBATE HITTING Sammy over the head with something for several more minutes and settle on the small porcelain lamp on the bedside table as our weapon of choice. Chloe insists on being the one to hit him over the head. I make her promise that she can hit him hard enough to knock him out. If we fail, we will have essentially just woken up an angry bear.

It takes another two hours for us to go fifteen minutes straight without hearing one of Sammy's screams. He can't seem to go longer than that without yelling at the demons in his head. He may not be a bad guy. He may just need some help, but it's hard as hell to feel sympathy for the man who ripped us off campus at gunpoint and kept us captive in the woods.

I pound on the door. "Sammy! Sammy, we have an emergency!"

I try to sound as high-pitched and dramatic to snap him out of his sleep or whatever delirious state he's in right now. I scream as loudly as I can again. Chloe wraps the thick black cord from the lamp around her hands and holds it over her head, ready to smash it into Sammy once he opens the door. She hides herself on the other side of the frame as I slam my hand into the door as hard as possible again.

I hear grunting and then Sammy's footsteps. Chloe's breathing gets louder and the color fades from her face.

"You've got this," I mouth to her without making any noises. We have the element of surprise. We've got this. Sammy thrusts the door open aggressively, forgetting that he has a chain lock on the other side. He undoes the chain lock and thrusts the door open again. Chloe grunts and slams the lamp down on Sammy's head as hard as she can. I hear a crack and then Sammy slowly crumples, not without latching his hand around my forearm and dragging me onto the ground with him.

I scream as the giant man's body lands on top of mine. He's heavy as fuck and Sammy's weight crushes my chest. I gasp and Chloe hits him over the back of the head again.

"CHLOE!" I gasp. I don't want her to kill him. There's no blood, so I assume he's alive, even if technically I don't know. Chloe apologizes and drops the lamp before trying to move Sammy off me. We work together and eventually roll Sammy onto his back. He doesn't move. I hurriedly scramble away from him and Chloe runs to the other side of the room with me. We clutch each other's hands and seem to be waiting for Sammy to suddenly jerk awake.

"We did it," Chloe whispers. "We knocked him out."

"Did you really hit him that hard?"

"I didn't think so but… we don't have time. We need to run," Chloe says, taking my hand and dragging me towards the door. I didn't realize just how frozen in place I was, but once Chloe drags me along, I follow her. We have to step over Sammy to get through the door and my body trembles as we jump over him. He doesn't wake up.

"We should get a gun," I whisper. Chloe stops outside of the room and gives me a serious look.

"No guns," She says. "We are in much more danger if we have a gun. We don't know what we're doing."

"The second he wakes up, he'll get a gun. We need to figure it out."

"No. Guns."

I don't have time to argue with Chloe. We at least agree that we need to get out of here quickly. Chloe searches for ways for us to bundle up and handle the outdoors. She has a couple pairs of boots and a few jackets.

"We don't know a damn thing about where we are. How are we going to find the cops?"

"We have to try."

We dress up in all the warm clothes, but as we run to the front door, we hear Sammy give an audible groan from the other room. I grab the handle on the door and twist the lock. I yank the door. Fuck, there's another lock. My hands are shaking as I reach for the bolt.

"Hurry," Chloe hisses. I get the door open. Sammy's feet plant on the ground. We have to run. Chloe and I burst outside and try to run to the road. The snow is deep and my legs feel instantly cold. If we stop moving, we'll freeze to death out there.

Once we're a few feet out of the house, I can see the highway.

We can make it, especially if Sammy has to take time to get a gun and especially if that blow to the head weakened him in any way.

"There's the road."

Chloe races ahead, and I struggle through the snow to catch up with her. It's cold, but we keep going. As we get closer and closer, I hear a voice that sounds like it's getting closer.

"ALEXIS. ALEXIS."

"That sounds like Sammy," Chloe yells. "We have to run!"

We run as fast as we can towards the highway and then we hear a loud gunshot cracking overhead. Chloe screams.

"Get down on the ground!" I yell at her, slamming my body to the ground instinctively and covering my head. As I face plant in the snow, my entire body shivers. I'm shaking too much to look over at Chloe, but I call her name loudly.

"I'm fine!" she yells. I hear boots in the snow. One pair. Two pairs… I don't know anymore. There are a lot of fucking people and I don't know if we're in trouble, or if Sammy's in trouble.

"Put the gun down, John."

That's Sammy. He sounds pissed off, and he slurs his words. I hear Chloe's breathing and footsteps in the snow. Then a coyote howls somewhere far off. Maybe it's a wolf. It's not like I would be able to tell the difference.

When I hear John, I want to get off the ground, but my instincts tell me that there are still guns out and if I move, this will all come crashing down around us.

"Don't make me fucking kill you, Sammy."

"You move, I kill the Asian chick."

Chloe cries out. I don't blame her. I hear Lucky's voice. John's not alone. Thank God.

"Don't fuck with us, Sammy. We're not here to kill you. We just want the girls back and we want to talk."

"Did Uncle Al send you?"

"No," John says. "We fucking told you. We're not here to kill you."

"Why the fuck would I believe you?" Sammy says. "You killed my fucking son. You watched my son die and one of these bitches here must've witnessed it."

"Call her a bitch and I'll crack you a fucking shot," John snarls. "I swear, Sammy. I don't want to fight. I want to make a deal."

"If you want a deal, put the guns down."

"Fine," John says. I hear a loud thud in the snow.

"Those can't be your only weapons."

"Doesn't fucking matter," John says. "Dad sent a Ludovici to kill you, but he won't be here for a while. We have time to talk this out."

"Chloe, Alexis, get up," Sammy says. "I won't hurt you even if you didn't pay me the same courtesy."

"You don't look hurt," Lucky grunts. Chloe moves first, but I don't know how. I almost don't believe that Sammy won't hurt us until John reaches his hand down for me. His busted up fists and beat up hands reach down for mine and when I touch him, a surge of warmth floods me that almost makes me forget we're standing outside in a blizzard with hardly any clothes on.

Once I get to my feet, I look directly at John's face and see the purest emotion I've ever seen from him. My knees are nearly weak from the way he looks at me. He doesn't hesitate. He moves his hand to the base of my chin and drags my face towards his. John's lips plant firmly against mine and he kisses me right there in the snow in front of his brother, cousin and Chloe.

As his lips touch mine, John's hands drop to my waist and he pulls me firmly against him, kissing me for a very long time. He holds my lower lip between his teeth and then sucks slowly on my lower lip, sending a shiver through me as he pulls away. Those blue eyes still don't leave me. There's not very much light out, but there's enough for me to see John's eyes and how much he cares.

"I am so fucking happy you're safe," he whispers. "I'm never letting you out of my sight again."

"Are you fucking serious, John?" Sammy growls. "My head hurts. Can we head inside if you bastards insist on ruining my night?"

Chloe and I exchange glances. Should we tell them that Sammy's not all the way there?

Chloe handles that problem easily. "You all should know he talks to himself and he's a bit crazy."

Sammy's face darkens. "I'm fine. I'm completely fine."

He holds the side of his head and shakes it a little. John and Lucky exchange glances. I have to trust that John can handle this one for me. He puts his arm around my shoulder and Lucky points towards the house.

"We'll have to leave this house tomorrow," Lucky says. "But let's go in and enjoy your secret cabin while we can."

Chapter 20
Getting Her Naked
John

We only have tonight — this one special night between us before it all goes to shit. Dad won't take long to catch on to our first betrayal and it'll take his mind even less time to travel from the first betrayal to the next. At least I have her. Here. She doesn't want to sleep in the bedroom Sammy kept her in and she doesn't want to sleep in the house with Sammy. I can't blame her. Lucky takes Sammy out for the night to assess his mental situation and hopefully get him drugged up or drunk enough to go the fuck to sleep.

I set up one of the guest bedrooms that Sammy left untouched, but Alexis still steps into the room tentatively before spinning around hastily to beg me not to lock the door. I can't stand seeing the terror on her face. It breaks my fucking heart to see her like this.

"What did he do to you, princess?" I whisper. "You can tell me."

Alexis shudders and looks away from me. I can tell she doesn't want to talk about this but I need to make sure that my cousin didn't stoop so low as to rape her or manhandle her in any other way.

"He tried not to hurt us, but he's crazy, John. Whatever happened to him, he's lost his mind and I won't sleep under the same roof as him."

"You might have to until we get back to the city."

"I've already missed two weeks of school. That's way more than any sane Columbia student can catch up from. Your cousin cost me an entire semester of tuition. Thanks."

"I'm just happy you're alive."

It's true. I want her to come running to my arms. I want her to throw herself on me and thank me for saving her life — but that's not Alexis. And I doubt I deserve that much praise. I just want to hold her. Expressing my pleasure at her survival awakens her attention.

"Did you just express a feeling, John?"

"I worried sick about you. I haven't slept since I… since I lost you."

Alexis takes a nervous step closer to me. Yes. I want her closer. I can't wait. I close the gap between us because I can't stand it anymore. I grab Alexis' face and kiss her again, just as deeply as I kissed her outside. There's no fucking point in waiting and there's even less of a point in pretending that I don't desperately want this. I rake my fingers through her hair and pull her close.

"You didn't lose me," she whispers.

"I know," I murmur. "But I got too fucking close. I…"

My throat catches because it has been way too many fucking years since I've said these words and even longer since I meant them.

"I love you, Alexis."

I have to say her name because I don't want there to be any mistakes, any confusion at all that she's the one I fucking love more than anything and anyone under the sun. I know I should give her time to respond, but I can't stop myself from kissing her again and showing her with my lips exactly how I fucking feel.

"I love you," I murmur again.

I almost lost her without saying it. That can't ever happen —
especially considering the crazy shit I'm about to do.

"John…" she whispers, pressing her fingers to my chest. Can
she feel how fucking hard my heart beats? She makes me more
nervous than a damn gun to my head.

"Uh huh?"

"I love you too. But I feel so… guilty."

"Hm."

"And…" she whispers. "You killed Gabe."

She makes the accusation with such conviction that it knocks
the wind out of me. I might be a killer, but I'm not a fucking
butcher. I wouldn't kill a man in cold blood with no reason.
Fucking with my girl ain't enough of a reason to kill a man. It
might be enough to beat him up, shake him loose of a few
hundred-dollar bills but…

Alexis feels my hesitation and searches my face for answers
she'll never find. Over the years, I've learned not to allow my
face to betray me. I might have scars, a flicker of anger, a tiny
expression here or there that someone who knows me very well
might read. But this… she can't tell if I killed him and it kills me
because I want her to trust me. From the beginning, I've wanted
her trust because fuck, if I can prove I'm human to someone as
pure as Alexis Carter, maybe there's hope for me.

Maybe… I just have one more job — the last job to clean up
our streets and bring peace to our people for a long, long time.

"John?" She asks, a hint of panic in her voice. How can I
expect her to think differently about me? What the fuck do I
expect her to think of a man she saw blow his family member's
brains out?

"I didn't kill Gabe. I swear. I didn't kill that kid."

She doesn't recoil, and she doesn't yank her hand away from
my chest, which makes me feel like despite all odds, I have a
fucking chance to win her back and keep her in Queens or wherever the fuck she wants to go. Maybe I have a chance at a life
beyond that apartment. A family of my own. I can't have a family

of my own until I make a few fucking changes in my current family.

"I want to believe you," she whispers.

"Because you know it's true. I will confess every fucking one of my sins to you, Alexis. I will, if that's what you need."

She moves so close to me, I can feel her breasts pressing against my torso. She's warm and soft, and her curves in all the right places distract me from the very somber mission of proving my fucking love to her. Alexis sighs and moves her hands over my chest, touching the outline of my muscles through my clothes. Yes. Her hands feel so fucking good.

Alexis has hands that make a man want to tell the truth. Her softness unravels me.

"Yes," she says. "Maybe it is what I need. Because... I want to love you, John. I really want to but... how can I trust men after everything? Even after this?"

She gazes up at me with enormous brown eyes that reflect pebbles of white light and seem so infinitely dark as I gaze into them. I want to fall into those black holes and never escape. After all this time, after all these women, it's a little brown-skinned thing like her that makes me nervous and uncentered.

"You can trust me, because I'll confess," I whisper, kissing her cheek and then her neck. "I'll never hide who I am from you. I will be the man I promised you to be the first day I met you. I will always come after you. I will never abandon you. For as long as we both shall live..."

She giggles at the last part and possibly because I rest my nose in the crook of her neck and allow my lips to kiss the exact spot of her skin they fall on. Alexis rakes her fingers through my hair to push my head away. The ticklish sensation of her fingertips on my scalp stiffens my cock instantly and I growl as I push back against her hand to kiss her neck again.

Alexis giggles and then shoves me away harder.

"Stop it," she whispers. "You aren't getting any of that until you confess."

"Cruelty," I whisper back half-heartedly. There's nothing cruel about getting to kiss her now. Any contact with her after this much time apart feels like a fucking blessing. I could spend all night only kissing her if that were all she wanted. Alexis pushes back against my head and this time I relent. I can't avoid this forever and I love her.

"Where to begin with a confession?" I whisper. "It would be much easier to forget all about it and fall asleep with you in my arms."

"Nice try."

"Hm."

"How did you get like this, John?"

Like this. It's obvious what she means. She wants to know what tragic fucking backstory made me like this. Not every monster gets forced in tragedy. My father loved me, in his own way. He taught me how to kill. He started with animals — those made me cry — and then he slowly desensitized me to violence. He wanted me prepared to live in the world as it was, not as he wanted it to be.

I try explaining this to Alexis and she gazes on in horror, as if I were describing some kind of horrific abuse.

"He made you throw your pet hamster in a grinder," she says. "John…"

"He was there the way most fathers weren't," I mutter, although I feel foolish and exposed before her. It helps that she doesn't stop touching me. It helps even more when she kisses my forehead. She must be an angel to return the affections of someone so beastly, deformed physically by scars and tattoos, deformed emotionally by a life of death.

"Most kids had dads who couldn't survive our world. They got whacked, they lost everything. Dad made sure we had it all. He made sure we became the kings of Long Island."

Alexis doesn't look terribly impressed.

"He made you kill people," she says, but she phrases it halfway like a question.

"Yes."

"Since when?"

The answer makes me deeply uncomfortable, but it's also the truth.

"I can't exactly remember. I remember the first one but... not all the others. I was too good at it. I was too good at burying everything and I worked all my life for my father's trust. All my life."

I feel my chest tightening and my voice must have risen because Alexis moves her hands, clutching mine and she squeezes them.

"John, stop," she whispers. My hands shake. I have to kill him. I don't want to kill my father, but if I want peace — I must.

"No. You wanted a confession, it's what you get."

"You're shaking."

"I'm fine."

Alexis tiptoes and kisses me. She stops the shaking and then she stops me from fucking thinking by running those long fingers through my hair and then pulling my face against hers as she kisses me desperately. Oh, God... how the fuck did I live without her.

"I love you."

"I love you back," she whispers. She jumps into my arms and I catch her, pulling her body tightly against mine and holding her in place against me. I squeeze her against me and Alexis' thighs grip my torso as she holds on.

"I am only halfway done confessing, cupcake."

"Don't care," she whispers. "We only have one night for this and we have a lifetime for your confessions.

A lifetime.

"A LIFETIME?"

"Quiet," Alexis whispers. "Just... don't let go."

"I won't," I murmur, stumbling back a few steps and then

flipping Alexis around so it's her back against the wall and not mine.

This time, I mean it. I don't want to let her go.

"I can't wait to get you naked," I whisper. "So I am definitely not letting you out of my sight until I make that happen."

* * *

Chapter 21
Melted Panties
Alexis

John's physique could melt the panties off anyone, but I'm even weaker because of my feelings for him. My plans to extract dark confessions out of my tattooed, filthy-tongued mobster are absolutely failing all because of a few kisses from those perfect, Italian lips. I'm weak, but I feel like it's okay to be weak when I'm with him.

He shoves his hips into me and I feel John's gigantic dick pressing into my crotch. This isn't the ideal situation for maintaining my self-control. John holds me in place with his hips and slowly eases my arms over my head, pinning them there with ease. I thrust against John's grasp, but he abolishes my need for self-control by tightening his grasp and thrusting me hard against the wall.

"There is no fucking way you're getting away, princess," he growls, in a deep, gravely voice. I buck my hips against him, testing him again and failing to provoke anything in John Vicari but an impish smile.

"Never again," he whispers. "You are never getting away from me again, you hear that?"

He moves in close to me so his lips brush against my ears and he sends a shiver straight through me that makes me fucking greedy for his touch. I let him kiss me and tighten my thighs grip around him, which forces John to touch my thighs, spreading his palms and then appreciating every inch of my flesh with one hand as his other keeps my hands tight above my head.

"I love having you pinned against the wall," he growls. "But I'd much prefer eating your pretty ass pussy in bed. It has been way too fucking long."

John doesn't give me half a second before he drags me over to the bed like a caveman. I squeal as he slams me down and then he kisses me like he's trying to lick me clean. There's a lot of tongue and soft lips and I feel so young and dumb and so perfectly in love as John kisses me and teases me. How can a man who I know is fucking dangerous feel like such a puppy in bed? His lips tickle me to the point of laughter and when I finally try to push him away, he forces my thighs apart and drives me into the point of silence.

John kisses my inner thigh. I whimper as he kisses outside my clothes and desperately want him to strip me naked. I want to forget that I spent weeks in a bed with my crying best friend and I just want to remember this flash of happiness that burst through all that pain – John.

"I fucking love your thighs," he grunts before stripping my pants off. Those lips contact my skin and I arch my back to give John greater access to my thighs. I love John's lips on my thighs. He runs his curved fingers over one thigh while kissing the other and then he switches before nibbling slowly along my inner thighs, inching closer to my underwear.

John slows down as he closes in on my panties. When his fingers slide beneath the fabric, I gasp and John chuckles with delight.

"You are so fucking wet," he murmurs, kissing the top of my mound as he moves my underwear off. "You smell so fucking good."

Once he peels my underwear off, John wastes no time sliding his tongue between my legs. I moan the instant his tongue touches my clit. I'm fucking weak in his arms and I don't want to keep hating myself for how easily I unravel with him. His large biceps easily hold my thighs up as he spreads me apart with beastly arms and an even more beastly tongue.

"You taste delicious," John murmurs. "Fucking delicious."

His tongue laps slowly around my clit in slow circles and John's touch builds me up to quick arousal. He growls and runs his tongue along the inside of my slit before returning his attention to my clit again. I push my hips against John's lips, using my body to beg him to make me cum.

"Don't stop," I moan, pushing my hips up to John's lips and he grips my ass, dragging me to his mouth and sucking on my lower lips until I finally feel an orgasm welling in me. I gasp and plead with John for him to slow down, but no words come out. I grab onto a thicket of his chocolate brown hair and keep his face pressed against my wetness as I cum.

John's tongue pushes deep inside me as I climax, forcing me to cum harder. A warm gush of desire pulses through me, but John doesn't seem to give a crap about getting his face completely covered by my cum. I whimper and try to push his head away so I don't get more juices on him, but John uses his finger to push my juices inside me as he keeps licking my clit.

"I can't take it…" I whimper.

John growls and pushes his finger deeper. I cry out again. He chuckles and returns his lips to my pussy again. Ugh, John. I whimper again and John keeps licking my clit until I climax again. I moan and then John finally lets go of me.

"Delicious," he whispers, pulling his face away from me. "My delicious girl."

"Your delicious girl?" I'm floating in an orgasmic haze and can barely understand anything coming out of John's mouth.

"My girlfriend. My wife."

"Your wife? Don't you need a priest to make that happen? Not to mention a proposal."

"Ain't this a proposal," John whispers, taking his tongue and running it along the length of my thigh. Oh, fuck. His tongue makes me gush again, and John chuckles because he absolutely delights in his effect on me.

"No."

"I'm joking," He whispers. "I'll propose all you want, cupcake. I have some shit to take care of first."

He wipes his face off my thigh. I shudder and try to push him off, but John insists on coating me in my own sticky juices. Ugh.

John chuckles and lays his head on my thigh. It's a quiet, intimate act and not the sort I'm used to from John. He missed me. And he finally missed me enough to fucking show it. I move a little and John clutches my thigh.

"I'm not exactly done confessing," John murmurs. "Once I get you outta here... I gotta do something bad, Alexis. I need you to trust me. I need you to believe that I didn't kill Gabe. I need you..."

Men have wanted me throughout my life, but they've never needed me and they've especially never needed me like this. For something real. John kisses my thighs and I want to trust him. I want to believe this was all a misunderstanding. But if John didn't kill Gabe... who did?

My fingers sink into John's hair as we lie there. We aren't done, I can feel that, but I don't mind the opportunity to catch my breath.

"I trust you," I tell him. "I believe you."

John nods. "I'm going to take over the Long Island mob."

THOSE WEREN'T the words I expected to spill out of his mouth. I freeze in John's arms, wanting to enjoy his grasp, but I'm smart enough not to take the words coming out of John's mouth lightly.

"What?"

It's not exactly the most intelligent response, but it's all that comes out of my mouth. John holds my face and stares into my eyes with more intensity than I've seen from him in the longest time. His fingers feel rough and worn on my face, but I love how good it feels when John touches me.

"I'm about to do something fucking crazy and I need you to trust me to keep you safe."

"Let me guess. I'll have to leave New York."

"Yes."

"John…"

"I care about your education… but Sammy already fucked that. I can't let you lose your life."

"Where the hell can you send me where I'll be safe? From what I've seen, you people control everything. You have eyes everywhere."

His hand drops to my shoulder and I see how nervous he is, which makes me nervous as hell. Does John know what he's doing? And if something can scare John enough for me to see it on his face… what does that mean for me?

He kisses the spot on my shoulder where his hand touches, and that makes me feel better. He strokes my shoulder slowly. "Sammy's a fucking idiot and he's lost his mind. When I hide you, no one will find you."

John has a very convincing voice and even more convincing lips. I squirm a little and he pulls me closer.

"No one," he growls. "But I'll give you a choice. And something else."

John pulls away from me and I hate the cold spot he leaves behind. He only sits up to reach into his pants pocket and removes a golden crucifix on a chain. John takes my hand and puts the crucifix in my hand, closing my hand around it.

"What's that?"

"The preview to the engagement ring."

"A crucifix?"

He knows I'm not Catholic right? I don't even know if John considers himself Catholic. He kills people, so I doubt he's *very* religious. The chain and the crucifix feel heavy, but I've never seen John wear this—at least not that I can remember.

"My grandfather gave it to me before he died. He claims the pope blessed it and that it will keep us safe. I keep it in my pocket and now it's yours. No matter where you are, cupcake, you will have my protection."

"Why do you sound like you're sending me to Timbuktu?"

John grins and finally lets go of my hand. My heart pounds. He's holding something back from me, even while trying to be totally honest. I need him to stop. If John wants me to trust him, he needs to do the same for me. I lean forward and kiss him. I rarely kiss him first and John notices.

"Not Timbuktu," he says. "Maybe worse. Florida."

"Florida?!"

"I thought you might like to hide out somewhere warm."

"Dropping out of college to party in Florida is not my style."

"Then study," John says, lying down next to me in bed again as I clutch the golden crucifix in my hand. He kisses my forehead. "Do whatever the fuck you want and stay safe."

"Okay."

"Also… I'm sending your friend. I don't trust her not to go to the cops and I need her out of the way right now."

I want to argue that he should give Chloe a choice, but fighting with John probably won't go anywhere right now and he seems determined — and again, I trust him. If he thinks sending us away will keep us alive…

"What about Gabe?"

"The dead kid?"

He says it so harshly that it only gives me another reminder that John is messed up in the head and maybe trusting him isn't the best idea. John notices the disturbance on my face and bites his lip.

"Yeah. Gabe."

"He's not my priority, babe. This time, we gotta trust the cops."

I fold my arms. I don't think John killed Gabe, but he has the power to find out who did and to find out if whoever killed Gabe might come after Cameron. Judging from his expression now, he won't budge. Again.

"Let's hope whoever killed Gabe doesn't come after me."

John grows fierce again. "That's not gonna happen babe. Not gonna fucking happen."

He pulls my body against his again and kisses me like he means it. I can't escape, not like I would want to. He has the most delicious lips and I hold John's face, raking my fingers through the dark brown stubble as I pull him close to me. John tries to pull away, but I'm the one who doesn't let him get away. I suck on John's lower lip until he makes a low growl in the back of his throat.

"Careful…"

Absolutely not. We have one night here and there isn't a single part of me that wants to be careful with John. I push him onto his back and straddle him. John chuckles at my blatant disobedience and tightens his grasp on my hips.

I press my hands against John's broad, muscular chest, easing the base of my palms into his thick muscles as I lean forward to kiss him. John groans again as our lips make contact. Yes. I love when he gets all vocal with me. Getting a beast like John to make soft moans of pleasure brings me greater joy than he can imagine.

"You minx…" he grunts. "I am so fucking hard."

I grind my hips into John, getting him stiffer. His cock thickens and seems to acquire more girth too as I rub my body against him. John's fingers dig into my hips more and he pulls me against him for more kissing. My toes drag along his thighs as I straddle him and John's palms eventually move from my hips to my ass. We're getting closer. I wriggle my hips more and John chuckles.

"Take my pants off," he says. "You don't have to be patient."

I struggle not to rip John's pants off. It's not like captivity makes you horny or anything, but the rush of hormones and emotions when you finally escape captivity make you both lustful and reckless. I have this new appreciation for every inch of John's chiseled body I thought I would never see again.

Once I have John naked from the waist down, he runs his fingers between my legs and covers my mound with his hand. I grind my hips so my wetness splits around John's fingers and I soak his hands with my desire. I continue moving my hips so I can at least stimulate myself from John's rough fingers, but he's clearly teasing me.

"John…" I whimper. He grins.

"I love watching you get all hot," he whispers. "Before I put my cock in you… I need your mouth. I don't need you getting greedy."

"How am I greedy?" I grumble, rubbing myself even more against John's fingers. I moan loudly as I get him to touch the sweetest, most sensitive part of my clit.

"I made you cum buckets and I haven't felt your lips around my dick."

"Is that what you consider an injustice?" I respond, trying not to sound whiny, but failing miserably as I attempt to fuck myself on John's hand. He pulls his hand away and my wetness lands on his bare crotch with a wet thwacking sound. John licks my juices off his fingers patiently while I dig my nails into his chest.

"John…" I grumble.

"Mouth on cock, cupcake. Hurry it up."

I consider a well-placed slap, but John has the proudest, most excited grin on his face when I bend my lips to his chest and the smile gets bigger as I trail my way down the thicket of chest hair, scars and black ink tattoos. As my lips head to John's dick, it stands even more proudly at attention. Holy fuck, that thing is big.

"Problem?" John grunts impatiently. No, John. There's never

a problem fitting your enormous pole that stretches my mouth wide inside me. Never any problem at all…

To avoid more of John's impatience, my tongue sticks out slowly and I lick the head of John's growing cock. The enormous thing pulses in my hand, which can barely wrap around the entire shaft. He has the biggest and thickest dick I've ever seen and watching his flesh redden and veins bulge out in my dark brown hands fills me with lust that defies description.

I don't fucking know why his big, sexy white dick fascinates and allures me, but now is the wrong time to think of it. John shifts his hips impatiently and I wrap as much of my mouth as I can around his entire head. John groans and his cock turns even more rigid. Holy fuck.

My mouth stretches to capacity again. I press my palms into our tiny temporary bed so I can balance my weight and take more of John's impressive cock between my lips. I emit an unconscious choking noise, yet struggle against it to fit more of John's inches inside me. As I gag, he groans with pleasure and my motivation to pleasure him increases. I push against the bed and then force more of him down my throat.

I will myself not to gag and then I feel a gush of warmth that surprises me with its immediacy and quantity. John, with no warning at all, bursts with desire and his milky eruption fills my mouth. I gag with less control this time instinctively swallow the thick load of John's cum. His cock is too big for me to remove my lips from the shaft, so once I swallow the first load of John's cum, he erupts with another one, more intense than the first.

Now, I have room to breathe, but John's cum spills into my mouth faster and it's harder to swallow this time, so his sperm leaks from my mouth and I feel humiliated that it dribbles down my chest and I'm totally covered in. John sits up, his wet and recently emptied cock flipping over with satisfaction onto his thighs.

I'm a teary-eyed mess from my efforts. John props himself up on his elbows and gazes at me like I'm fucking beautiful — not a mess with cum covering her mouth and chest — but a princess who stepped out of a fairy tale.

"I should clean you up," he grunts, leaning forward and wiping the cum off my face with his bare hands. I shudder from the contact and half expect John to shoo me off to the bathroom across the hall to get clean. Instead, he leaps out of bed and as I crudely attempt to clean my face up, he scoops me up and carries me towards the door.

"John! Chloe could see us. Or Lucky could come back."

John gets his face dangerously close to mine, and presses his forehead to mine.

"I don't care," he says. "I'm taking my girl into the shower and… whatever happens, happens."

I KNOW I'll remember this night forever, because we'll either have forever or this will be one of the best. John sneaks me across the hall into the bathroom and I don't even know how we don't get caught because we aren't quiet and we're both mostly naked messes.

Once we're in the bathroom, John shuts the door behind him and then exhales.

"Sammy has shitty taste in safe houses."

"I suppose yours is much better?"

"You'll find out."

John doesn't explain himself, which by now, I expect from him. He sets me gently in the shower and turns the water on. I squeal as a splash of cold water hits me. John chuckles, which pisses me off because he totally did that on purpose. I splash him and he jumps into the shower with his t-shirt on.

"John!"

He grabs me around the waist and holds me tightly before dragging us both beneath the water. We strip what remains of our clothing off and toss them into a gross, wet pile outside the shower. Who cares about gross when we have each other? It doesn't take much water or scrubbing to clean my face from cum and other evidence of our entanglements.

Once I'm clean, we stand naked in the shower, kissing and touching beneath the flood of warm water. Kissing John here feels so good that I almost don't want to stop the kissing. My body has other plans for me. A gush of desire spreads between my legs and I move closer to John, pushing my hips against him greedily.

His hands move down the length of my thighs and then he slides his hands over my mound, spreading my lower lips and rubbing my clit slowly with his fingers. Finally. I moan greedily and ease my body closer to his, wanting so much more than John's fingers or lips between my legs. I did what he asked. I exhibited perfect patience. Now, he's the one I want.

John turns me around to face the wall and runs his fingers between my legs again. I whimper as he massages my clit and stop the second his dick presses against my entrance with a warm thud. John can never fit his cock inside me with one smooth thrusting motion.

He grabs onto my hips with both hands and attempts to ease the head of his dick inside me. My tightness resists him at first, but then he pushes again with a grunt and I scream because John's dick gets too far, too fast and I feel a thud deep inside me like the head of his dick just touched the deepest parts of my pussy. Holy fuck.

John holds my hips to keep my pussy on his cock and he pulls me against him so I'm squealing with the mixture of pain and intense pressure.

"You are so fucking tight," he grunts. "I am going to cum right inside that perfect ass pussy."

John holds nothing back. Still holding onto me, he withdraws his dick and pushes into me so slowly that it feels like his cock is giving me the best orgasm of my life. I moan again, bracing myself against the wet wall of the shower. John leans his body against mine, so the force of his weight pushes me into the wall and his cock drives into me deeply.

My hips move against him and John makes a low growl in the back of his throat that makes me want more from him. I want to cum on his dick before John empties himself inside me again. He pushes hair away from my neck, letting my wet hair stick to my back, and then he kisses me as he drives inside me. My pussy tightens and John reacts by holding onto my butt cheeks and pushing himself into me deeper.

"You are very fucking tight," he grunts. "I love it."

"Please…"

"Don't worry, cupcake. I'll have your cum all over my dick."

He sucks on my neck as he pumps into me, and I explode all over John. My tightness unravels and a gush of juices floods my thighs. I cum hard as John holds me. He rubs my clit slowly with a purposeful thumb and makes me cum again without thrusting. I plead his name for some relief, but John promised me climaxes, and he intends to deliver.

He lifts me off the ground, forcing me to submit to his will as I press against the shower wall. John keeps his lips planted on my neck as he fucks me to another orgasm and then he sets me on the ground when I'm a withering mess in his arms. John sucks on my earlobe and then flips me around so I'm facing him when he's done. I am a fucking unraveled mess.

"If anything happens to me, you get to Boston, find a man named Darragh Murray and give him that necklace. He'll help you."

"Nothing's going to happen to you, John."

He touches my cheek and pulls my face to him for yet another kiss. I can't stand those kisses. I can't. They make me feel like John's trying to say goodbye, and I can't accept that.

"It might," he whispers. "I'm trying to take over the fucking mob. It's dangerous business."

"Just promise me you'll live, John."

"Promise me you'll run if I don't."

"No," I whisper. "Because you're coming back to me and you're going to promise me right now…"

* * *

Chapter 22
Sammy's Pregnant Girl
John

She doesn't talk to me for most of the night when I refuse to promise my survival. I only make promises I know I can keep. She's safe, and that's what matters—and she's far away from any of my father's hired hands. We've been running for three weeks. I can't keep in regular contact with Alexis and it hurts. Lucky got Sammy on medication, but he hardly moves when he's not on his surveillance shift.

While we hide out in the Pocono mountains, readying ourselves to head back to New York and finish our dirty fucking business, we have no word on what the fuck is happening in the city, but we've lost two of our people and possibly more, depending on who dad thinks we're loyal to.

The Zagarella side of our family sides with us, and that will be very fucking helpful when it's time to go back to the city. Geno has our father's ear and he's back in Long Island, working for us. We have more help too. The Irish fucks in Boston who run the city are more than happy to help us if it means a stronger truce, more business partnerships and an end to all the mob violence in both cities.

We can rule and keep peace if we get rid of the men who resort too quickly to violence.

John

Dad came from another time when life was way more fucking cheap. I don't know how he made it as far as he did without recognizing how precious life is. I guess he didn't have a woman like Alexis to teach him about love, the fucking light in this world. I guess having kids wasn't enough for him.

I wish I could give Alexis kids – whenever she wanted them. But I don't know if that's in the cards for us. We'll just have each other, maybe adopt. Have a dream wedding. We can move out of my bachelor pad and into a place that Alexis wants with a giant bed with fluffy sheets and blankets. We'll have it all once I get out of this. If you get out of this, you idiot.

Lucky's phone rings, and he sighs before picking up. We're waiting to hear from Aiden Murray and it's been so long that we both have to worry. It's not Aiden this time.

"Geno?" Lucky says. "Do you have him? What the fuck is going on?"

Lucky's shoulders relax, which probably means we're getting somewhere, even if he's hearing from Geno and not Aiden. Lucky puts his phone on speaker phone and Geno's voice comes crackling on the other end of the line. I can hear city noises in the background – ambulances, horns honking, and folks screaming in the background.

"Aiden and I are heading over there now. He brought backup. Darragh. A couple others. We have a meeting at the casino."

Lucky and I exchange glances and shift uncomfortably. Why the fuck would dad want to use my business for this meeting? Whose idea was this? There are cameras everywhere and Lucky's security team. Maybe that's why. Still, it's our turf and since dad knows we've fucked off and he doesn't know why, choosing our turf either means he's certain he can avoid any backlash or… he has no idea what's coming.

"You need to keep them there," Lucky says. "Leave around two in the morning. Get him drunk and take him to Aiden's hotel. That's the best route."

Geno agrees and swears to fuck that the Irish won't screw us over. We've promised them help in tracking down their rogue cousins and in keeping peace between our cities. I don't know the Murray brothers well, but we have good reason to work together – money, future investments.

Given the news, we have to get out of here now. Sammy's medication levels him out and he's eager to get the fuck out of here. None of us really want to talk about what we're going to do tonight, but the air is thick. If we fuck this up, we're all dead. Once we have the Jeep packed up, Sammy leans against it, waiting for me to finish up a cigarette.

Lucky leans against the car, scowling and most likely contemplating his wife and child, tucked safely away, but never completely safe unless we succeed tonight. It's almost too heavy and being here, I miss the fuck out of Alexis.

Whenever she's away from me, my heart hurts. Every part of me hurts and not even a cigarette can kill the low-level heartbreak I feel being away from her. Will more power give me what I need to keep her safe? I don't want to go through all of this just to become my father – cruel. Unkind.

Sammy paces in front of both of us.

"Do you know what the fuck we're getting into?"

"Hell," I growl back. "Now are you in?"

"We're all in," Lucky says. "We all have a lot to lose. Or we've already lost it."

This doesn't seem to faze Sammy, or stop him from his pacing. He has his hands on his hips now. Sammy doesn't show his nerves like this and there's no way in hell killing Alfonso Vicari has him this… unwound.

"Sammy, what the fuck? Are you good?"

Lucky smirks, because he probably realized a while ago it was only a matter of time before Sammy's pacing got the fucking better of me.

"No," Sammy growls. "I spoke with my sister… she thinks your father has someone important to me."

"Who the fuck is important to you?" Lucky blurts out. It's

not exactly the way that I would have phrased it, but it's a good question. Sammy doesn't do romance–just one nights stands with women who work for him or just… women. Sammy has never had problems with women or getting them into his bed, but caring about women isn't Sammy's skill set. He's a slayer, not a lover.

Sammy turns red and growls, "Why? So you can kill them too?"

"Cut the shit, Sammy," I snarl at him. "If there's information we need to know before we do this shit, we need it now."

"Your father might have my grandchild."

Lucky gives me a look – a "don't fuck this up by overreacting" look. Sammy can't have a fucking grandchild. He's in his early forties and his son died. I killed his son myself and if he had a grandchild. I pull out another cigarette. Lucky whistles and points to the front seat of the car. Now we have to argue about this on the road and I have to piss Lucky off by smoking. Lucky drives. I'm in the passenger seat. Sammy kicks his feet up in the back. He puts his feet up and I tear into him.

"How the fuck does your son have a kid I don't know about?"

Sammy grunts. "I'm not exactly in a great state of mind."

"That's not a fucking answer, Sammy. I let it go when you took my girl but I'm done with the fucking secrets. I'm not doing this shit so you or any other fucker can get my guard down and take my place. I don't want to become my father, but I swear to fuck, I will."

Lucky glares, which means he takes my extremely calm statement as an overreaction, but I'm dead fucking serious. Sammy sighs and clears his throat.

"It's not my deception. Enrico had a girlfriend. He didn't want to tell me about her, I guess but… she's pregnant. She tried to find out what happened to him and found Giovanna. My sister wanted to help her but… the girl is gone and Giovanna thinks Alfonso took her."

His sister, Giovanna, has no involvement with the mob. It's

probably best that Giovanna was the first person to find out, but my father must have eyes on her too.

"So he has the pregnant girlfriend?"

"Yes," Sammy says. "And I don't know where or how pregnant or what the fuck I'm gonna do about it. Enrico was in no place to get a girl pregnant."

"He should have told you," Lucky says.

"The girl's black. He knows how I feel about that kind of thing…"

Lucky and I exchange glances again. It's not an argument worth getting into because Sammy is "old school" and he's always made his opinion clear. The girls are gorgeous, but they aren't worth the trouble. He's against mixing races, mixing cultures, mixing things until they're too fucking complicated. Sammy has too many fucking rules and this one… this rule could cost him.

"Didn't we meet her?" Lucky mutters, turning the Jeep down the highway. I search my brain for memories of a girl I saw with Enrico, but I don't recall one. Lucky launches into his description of her and maybe I remember, maybe I don't. He claims the girl lived close to the Upper West Side, had long straightened hair that fell down to her shoulders. Enrico's girl apparently has medium-brown skin, like coffee with the slightest touch of heavy cream, and a full figure. Sammy coughs when Lucky brings it up – probably because of my cigarette.

"You know her," Sammy says. "Problem is, we don't know where the fuck she is."

"Soon, Sammy. Soon."

Maybe finding this girl will atone for what we did. Maybe killing my father will. Maybe things will never be the same between us, but tonight, we're taking steps to make our wrongs right, bring peace to New York and make it safe to have a family again, to fall in love with whom the fuck we want.

Lucky gets us to the city twenty minutes earlier than we promised. Now, we wait for my father, Aiden and Geno to pass on the correct streets. I take one shot and if I miss, Sammy takes the second. Lucky's the fastest driver, so he's the one in the driver's seat this time. Plus, I'm too fucking shaky to drive. I don't want to admit it, but all the nicotine in the world can't make it easy for me to kill my father.

I have to do my duty to keep the city safe but... this act brings me no pleasure. Once the job is done, we'll be free. Alexis, babe... I'll do whatever the fuck it takes to fight for you. I promise.

Chapter 23
A Dark Secret
Alexis

Chloe's mental health has improved with more time outside of New York City. She doesn't want to go back to Columbia, and I can't blame her. We have a pool here in Florida – an enormous pool with two levels and waterfalls. Chloe knocks on my door aggressively, the way she does every morning.

"Breakfast is here!"

We have a credit card and instructions never to leave the house or show our faces to delivery people. Chloe has taken to a non-stop stream of restaurant food, but my stomach bulges from our Indian food binge the night before.

"I hope you ordered salad."

"Um… if by salad you mean Mexican breakfast. Yup."

I roll out of bed and walk to the door. It's amazing how much luxurious surroundings have helped me feel less traumatized. Considering the average apartment John had in Bayside, I'm shocked at how unbothered he seems about paying for a safe house that's a freaking mansion. I need fluffy slippers for my feet to survive the cold tiles, but then I bound over to the door to meet Chloe's smiling face. She's been smiling for four days straight when I meet her in the morning, which means a marked improvement in her mood.

"Mexican breakfast!" Chloe says. "You excited?"

"Um… yes. Since when are you Miss Peppy?"

"Since I woke up and remembered your terrifying boyfriend left us a fucking pool. It's going to be 87 degrees today and we need to soak. Not to mention tan."

"I thought we were planning to go to a new college for next year."

Chloe rolls her eyes and shakes the plastic bag in front of my eyes. "Earth to Alexis… we have food and a pool. We can talk about college after."

She's probably right. Chloe semi-patiently waits for me to get ready. I throw on a little royal blue bikini and a white kaftan over it along with royal blue Tory Burch flip flops that match my outfit. Chloe approves. She has a matching bikini in lime green and she throws on a very cute hot pink kaftan over it. Unlimited shopping means we now have crazy and expensive wardrobes that John outright demanded we spoil ourselves with. I feel like a regular Columbia student, not a scholarship kid now. John let me email my parents before we came here, so they think I'm doing a semester abroad. I don't want to worry them with anything close to the truth.

Chloe and I have breakfast poolside, which gets us warm enough to want a refreshing dip in the pool after. Each time we enter the pool, I think about John. I bet he isn't anywhere as comfortable as this and that makes me sad. He's not a bad person. Maybe he's done some bad things, but he's also done… this. After everything Chloe and I went through with Sammy, he's trying to make up for it and he's trying to keep us safe.

"Did you call John last night?" Chloe asks me, swimming over to my spot in the pool. I shake my head. It's the first night he hasn't called me at exactly 8:05 p.m. and that worries me. I know he told me that phone calls weren't guaranteed, but not hearing from him makes me think something horrible happened.

"Nope. Let's hope he's okay."

Chloe rolls her eyes. "He's a badass. He calmed down that psycho and he's giving us health and healing in this mansion, a refund on our college tuition and he says he's going to pay for our tuition at the next school we choose. How the hell did you meet this guy again?"

Chloe winks. She knows I won't ever tell her all the details.

"I wonder what happened to Gabe…" I mutter.

Chloe wrinkles her nose. "Why? We're in a pool away from all the bullshit that happened in New York."

"We have to go back to New York."

"Whatever," Chloe says. "We might be going back to New York, but we can avoid the Upper West Side. I met a guy who never left SoHo. I swear to God."

I give Chloe a weird look. It's not a flex to have never left six by nine blocks of square footage, but she has a point that we don't have to go back to Columbia, physically or mentally. That's probably for the best.

"Yeah… maybe Gabe really did get caught up in something drug related."

"We don't need to talk about him," Chloe says sharply. She seems to react to her own sharp reaction. Chloe dips her head under the water and goosebumps break out over my skin. Pay attention, Alexis. That's what the goosebumps say and whatever instincts I've picked up hanging around John are telling me to pay attention. Chloe knows something about Gabe.

I don't know how I didn't notice instantly. She acted normally. But then again, I watched John kill someone in cold blood and when he's not holding a gun, he acts normal too. Chloe shakes her hair out and grins at me. "Are you hungry again?"

"No. I want to know why you're acting weird about Gabe."

I can't tell if Chloe's turning red or if it's just the sun finally spreading some color across her cheeks. She combs her fingers through her black hair and twists her hair up into a tight knot that she ties without a hairband. It's all deflection. All distraction. Chloe shrugs.

"I just don't know why you want to talk about something so gross when we're in Florida and you have a boyfriend who could probably beat up the biggest guys on our campus."

"It's a mystery."

"He tried to rape you," Chloe shoots back. "I don't give a fuck who killed him."

"He tried. He didn't succeed. And he's dead anyway, so he can't hurt me. I want to know who thought they could get away with killing a Columbia student…"

I also want to know who did it. If John didn't kill the man who tried to rape me, who the hell did?

Before I can press Chloe, my burner phone rings. It's the only way I have of contacting John, so I launch myself out of the pool and grab the phone before grabbing a towel. With wet ass fingers, unlocking the phone and actually answering takes a few extra seconds, but I practically yell John's name when I pick up.

"Hey, cupcake," he says in his smooth Long Island accent when he picks up the phone. Holy fuck, I missed that voice. It's too bad we can't have our nightly ritual right now. That voice does incredible things to me.

"Hey. How are you? What's going on?"

"Missed you last night."

My heart thumps. "I missed you too."

John clears his throat. "You're coming home, baby. Shit ain't perfect over here, but the city is safe and more importantly… it's mine."

"What do you mean? Did you…"

"Yes," John whispers, his voice betraying an emotion he desperately tries to hide from me. "Yes. We did."

"I'm sorry."

"No," John protests forcefully. "You are safe. That's what's important."

A Dark Secret

. . .

JOHN ARRIVES in Florida alone and with a haircut. I notice the haircut before anything else, but there are far more changes to John's appearance. Chloe and I greet him at the door to the house and she makes excited squealing sounds as I run up to John and launch myself into his arms.

"I fucking missed you, princess."

Chloe shrieks with the excitement you would expect at a dramatic plot twist – not a fated kiss. I don't care that she's watching. Chloe and I have shared so much the past few months that kissing in front of her is the least of my concerns. John's large arms wrap around me and I let myself sink into the strength of his large, perfect biceps. I hold on to his sexy arms and let him lift me up and spin me around.

I wrap my arms around John and grab his cheeks as I kiss him. He has the softest face that feels incredible beneath my fingers and the closer I get to him, the more I want to kiss him deeper. And deeper. I press my tongue into John's mouth and his body tenses at the shocking invasion from my tongue. He chuckles and kisses back. As our tongues tease each other, I push my hips against John and lose myself in the kiss.

He has to pry my thighs away from his chiseled torso.

"You have never kissed me like that," John says. I can't take my eyes off him. He's alive. He's more handsome than ever and those dark circles that seemed to be permanently beneath John's eyes are gone.

"I'd better start then," I whisper. "In case we don't have forever."

John gives me a reassuring peck.

"We have forever."

Chloe claps her hands and squeals. "I am living!"

John gives her a nervous look, sets me down and clears his throat. "Hi, Chloe. My apologies for the display. Are you ready to leave?"

"Um… no!" Chloe says. "But please tell us we can use this place for spring break."

I shoot Chloe a disapproving look, but John nods and agrees. "Sure thing. This place is yours, Alexis. You needed somewhere if anything happened to me."

"Um… what do you mean it's mine?"

"I bought it for you. Vacation home. Now come…"

I can't tell if John is joking or not, but he seems serious. He enters our house and seems impressed with how neat we kept the place. I could never live in a place like this and trash it. No way. Chloe and I kept a cleaning schedule and the mansion always smells like cleaning products.

John orders food and eats with us, making conversation about normal things. Every time I make eye contact with Chloe, she gives me two thumbs up. Considering what happened to us with Sammy, I'm shocked she approves of John. Mansions and swimming pools go a long way in Chloe's world.

Over lunch, we tell John our final plans. Chloe's leaving NYC for Rutgers in the fall. I considered returning to Columbia, but I don't think I can do it. There are too many bad memories there and I don't think I'll feel safe until I know exactly what happened to Gabe. Joining Chloe in New Jersey was very tempting, but I couldn't leave the city and I don't want to leave John. I don't think he needs me, but he wants me and I want him.

The chemistry between us can't be the only deciding factor. I have to think about my future and what I want. Now, more than ever, I want to help people. John seems to find it fascinating that I want to be a doctor and encouraged me to keep working hard to get there. So, I'm heading to NYU in the fall and John is absolutely thrilled that I won't force him to move into a bigger home.

He's too much of a city rat, in my opinion, and if we have kids, I'd prefer they were closer to their cousins. John doesn't seem to think there are kids in our future, but I don't know. I'm open to anything as long as we get to be together. He shows me and Chloe our future apartment in East Village and it's a dream.

There are three bedrooms, so it's much bigger than his place in Bayside. John wants me to have an office so I can study and a guest bedroom so Chloe and stay over when she visits.

His girl. I'm his girl. I almost don't want to believe it. We're going to have a future together and everything's going to be okay.

RETURNING to New York is harder than I expect. Chloe doesn't want to leave me before the semester starts, so John helped her sublet a place in Brooklyn until she moves to New Jersey. She has a job out in Brooklyn at a vegan café and a second job bartending at a gay bar in East Village. I don't settle back into New York as easily.

I still have questions about Gabe but mostly because of Chloe's reaction. She knows something and I want to know what she's keeping from me. John thinks I need to let it go, but I can't. If the mob had nothing to do with Gabe's death, someone did. I know he hurt me and it's not like I've forgiven him but… I still want to know what happened.

I pester John for the tenth time, conveniently blackmailing him by standing in black lingerie in front of the football game until he agreed to listen. He's going to help me keep tabs on Chloe to see if she does anything suspicious. I know I shouldn't spy on my friend but… what if she can't tell me because she's in trouble? What if someone is blackmailing her? If the mob has taught me anything, there are a million horrible things that could happen and I'm done letting bad shit happen to me without taking control.

AFTER THREE DAYS of putting John on the case, he finally returns to our apartment with useful information and an extremely serious expression on his face that tells me he doesn't want me to get involved in this at all.

"I've had a guy watching Chloe," he says. "She's meeting up with your boyfriend Cameron tonight."

"How did you get that information?"

"You don't need to know."

That's John for you. Ever since taking control of what he calls his "family business" he issues commands like nobody's business. I roll my eyes and his expression softens.

"Listen, cupcake. She's meeting him tonight and you can go down there and confront them or whatever the fuck you gotta do. I met that girl and she's not a killer."

"You don't seem the least bit concerned. Can I at least borrow a gun?"

"Absolutely fucking not. If you get in hot water, call me. No one and I mean no one in this city will be stupid enough to touch you."

John sounds so serious that I have to scamper over and kiss him on the forehead.

"Did you just kiss me like a puppy?" he growls.

"A puppy. Now there's a good idea."

John grunts. "Who do you think will walk this puppy?"

"Um... you, obviously. I'll be in college and since you brought peace to New York, you won't have anything better to do."

"I own a casino, Alexis. That's a lot of work."

I shrug. "Whatever you say, John. Whatever you say."

"A puppy. Hmph. We'll see about that."

"I'm getting ready to stalk my best friend. Aren't you worried that I'll stumble across a stone-cold killer?"

"Nope. That Gabe motherfucker probably bought drugs from the wrong guy."

"You are annoying."

"Yes."

John kisses me and then gives me a pat on the ass. Condescending butthead. I know I'll learn something tonight and I'll bring my phone and some pepper spray. It's not a gun, but if I come across a bad situation, I can use the pepper spray to handle myself. He gives me the address to Cameron and Chloe's alleged meeting place and he advises me on a route I can get to where they won't see me.

"Do you know every back alley in New York?"

"And Jersey," John replies with a grin.

"I can't believe you're letting me walk into literal danger on my own."

"If you can survive Sammy, I trust you. And I have guys five blocks away who owe me their fucking lives. I met that Cameron motherfucker. And broke his fucking wrist."

John did that? I want to scowl at him, but he grunts disapprovingly at the entire idea of Cameron.

"Those preppy kids aren't worth a shit," he says.

"You broke his wrist?"

"Did I say that?" John says. "He broke his wrist. While I was holding it."

"That sounds suspiciously like you broke it."

"Did he look bent out of shape?" John grumbles, trying to distract me with a kiss on the forehead. And then on the neck.

I get ready and avoid John's attempts to distract me with kisses and pressing his dick against my butt so I can flee to the streets. I take the train from East Village to Brooklyn and follow John's somewhat poorly drawn map of the sidestreets on my phone. It's nice walking the streets and feeling safe, even if maybe I shouldn't. If John hasn't gone into overprotective mode, maybe I'm just... fine.

Then again, maybe he's just too confident. I clutch my pepper spray, slightly relieved John didn't give me a gun. I'm not like him. I don't think I would be able to do what he does and I don't want to think about it. He promises he won't have to kill anymore and I believe him. He's my living proof that men can change for love. From the moment he met me, from the moment he saw my absolute revulsion with his lifestyle, he wanted to change. I was never this happy with Cameron. Cameron didn't want to make me happy. He wanted to have me, but how I felt about the situation was entirely incidental.

And then the Gabe thing...

I get close to the place where Chloe works and I disguise myself against the door of a closed office building so I can watch them. I see Cameron walking up to the bar first and then he walks out alone and walks around the corner into one of those side-streets that's not quite an alley, but not quite paved. I can get around there without Chloe noticing and before she leaves the bar if I move quickly.

I hastily cross the street (illegally) and enter the alley from the other direction, hiding behind a trash can. Cameron paces and vapes, clouding the alley in a thick pineapple-scented haze. If he walks too far into the alley, he'll notice me, but he seems to be sticking to the part closest to the street.

"Fuck, Chloe," he mutters under his breath, frustratedly kicking a rock. She emerges around the alley and rushes towards Cameron, wrapping him in a hug. It's like a punch to my gut. What the fuck? Since when are they cool?

Cameron pulls away from Chloe's hug quickly. He looks pissed off and definitely not cool.

"Did you fucking tell her?"

"Can you calm the fuck down?" Chloe hisses. "Obviously not."

"Where is she?"

"You don't deserve to know."

"Chloe, I swear to God–

"What, Cameron? You're going to kill me the way you killed your roommate?"

Cameron turns red. "I swear to fucking God, Chloe..."

"Chill. I didn't tell her and she won't find out. You have rich lawyer parents who got you off the hook. What's the big deal?"

"I don't want her to know what I did. Alexis didn't deserve what happened."

"Yeah, no shit, Sherlock."

"It's not just that," Cameron says. "I cheated on her. That night… I cheated on her."

Chloe hits him. Hard. Then she hits him again. And again.

"You asshole!"

"Can you chill? Someone might hear you?"

Chloe rolls her eyes but lets up on hitting him. "You are… annoying."

"I got rid of the guy who hurt her. That should count for something."

"Is that why you came over here? To make sure I kept you out of trouble."

"Yes. And… to tell you to look after Alexis. I'm transferring to Stanford. My parents think it's for the best considering… everything."

"You should just talk to her," Chloe tells him. "Explain. Alexis isn't some innocent little flower who can't handle life."

Cameron chuckles. "You're right. But she deserves better. I don't want to mess with her head."

Chloe sighs. "You have potential, Cameron."

"Thanks…"

"I have to get back to work. Your secret is safe. I can't guarantee she won't find out but… it won't be from me."

CHLOE LEE, that's where you're wrong…

I WAIT for them to separate and stroll off in different directions, but I don't move from my hiding spot for a long time. Tears wet my eyes and I feel more emotional than I expected. I have my answers, but I don't know what to make of them. I guess I spent too long without texting or calling, so John calls as I walk towards the train station.

"WHAT DO you think of the Hamptons this weekend?"
    "Um... nothing, because I've never been there."
    "Have you been crying, cupcake?"

JOHN VICARI... I don't know if I can tell you the truth.

Chapter 24
The Normal Life
John

Life is normal again. Alexis returns home from her little escapade and says everything's fine. She seems cool, so I believe her and then she starts talking a mile a fucking minute about her science classes at NYU and a professor she's desperate to get an internship with. I offer to threaten the guy so she can get the job and Alexis gives me a twenty minute lecture on morals while making me wash the dishes. I might be the boss outside of our East Village apartment, but she's the boss at home.

The weekend hits and Alexis gets more jumpy the more I talk about East Hampton. I rented a place from one of our new friends in Boston who has a house out there. Darragh Murray's spot is the perfect place for our special weekend. Alexis doesn't know it's going to be special but... I have news for her. And a surprise.

"Are you sure we have to go out there?"

"What type of girl turns down the Hamptons? I gotta take you shopping more."

"Unless we're shopping for sweatshirts and yoga pants, I don't need shopping."

"The beach?"

"Okay. I might like the beach. But I don't swim."

"You don't have to swim. Just look hot in a bikini."

"I have rolls everywhere, John. I won't be playing out your Baywatch fantasies."

"Good, because I don't have Baywatch fantasies. I am very fucking attracted to how you look. *Exactly* how you look right now."

I eventually wrangle Alexis' ass in the car and hit the highway. She sings along to that new Taylor Swift song she likes and then reads out loud interesting comments from this forum she's obsessed with called *Lipstick Alley*. I don't understand half the fucking words coming out of her mouth, but I love her. *I love her so fucking much it hurts.*

I used to think a lot of stupid shit about women like Alexis. If I ever had a capacity to love or be a good fucking person, my lifestyle killed it in me. We *have to* stop killing. We must. I don't know if the Murrays understand. They fucked off back to Boston and they're working with us, trying to keep peace in both our streets, but once they find the fuckers who made problems with us before, violence is a fucking guarantee.

You can't change people. You can't change the mob. It is what it is and perhaps one day, I'll have to kill again, but that day won't come soon – I hope. We get to the beach and Alexis cheers up. She nearly darts off towards the water, but I convince her to enter the rented home for my little surprise.

When I open the door, Alexis gasps. "This place is crazy!"

"The Irish have taste. I'll give them that."

"This place must be what, twenty million dollars?"

"Something like that. Turn this way…"

We walk into the foyer and Alexis gasps again. There's a giant red box (with holes in it) and a white ribbon in the middle of the floor.

"Is that for me?"

"It ain't for me, cupcake."

"Can I open it?"

"It's a present. Yes."

And considering how quiet it is, her present must be sleepy. Thank you, Sammy for not screwing this up...

Alexis approaches the box and tugs at the ribbon. The entire thing falls open and reveals her special present – part one of her special present. Alexis makes a squeal that echoes throughout the house.

"John, you didn't!"

She starts jumping up and down, nearly slipping on the tiles. Then she leans into the box and pulls out her new best friend – a German Longhaired Pointer puppy. She has reddish brown fur that's sleek, soft, and well-groomed. As Alexis picks the puppy out of the box, she wakes up slightly and squirms. Alexis giggles and then gives her a hug. The puppy makes little whining noises, but then takes to Alexis' hug, nuzzling in her arms and falling asleep.

"How the *hell* did you know this was my favorite dog breed?"

"I called Chloe."

"She's adorable, John..."

Alexis sets the dog down and then rushes me. When she hugs me, I feel this profound sense of fucking victory. Making her happy is the best feeling in the world. I get a better rush from this than I ever got from drinking. I love her and I never want to go another day without seeing her smile.

"I fucking love you," I whisper. "Don't forget it."

"She's perfect."

"What are you gonna name her?"

"Poppy," Alexis says. "That's always been my dream dog name."

"Whatever you say, cupcake. Whatever you say."

I let go of her and Alexis gives me a funny look.

"Your eyes are smiling," she accuses. "You don't smile a lot but your eyes are definitely smiling."

"Is that suspicious?"

"Yes."

John

"Close your eyes then."

"What? Do you see how that's more suspicious?"

"Alexis..."

"I'm not going to just–

"Alexis, close your eyes," I command. "Please."

She shuts her eyes and I know I don't have long before my stubborn princess opens them right back up, so I get down on my knees and try not to freak the fuck out. Lucky tried to help me with this part, but I'm not as quick with my words. I don't use as many words as Lucky does and with her, I always seemed to say the wrong ones at first. I was too harsh. Too cruel.

"Open up," I tell her, clearing my throat.

"Why are you kneeling?" Alexis asks. "And why is there..."

She trails off. *Okay, asshole. You can do this.*

"I love you, Alexis. I don't want to stop. You made me a better person and I don't want to lose a woman who could change a dick like me. Make me the happiest Italian man in Long Island and become my wife. *Please.*"

I open the box, slowly. My hands never trembled so much when I pulled a trigger. This is so much fucking harder because I don't know what she's going to say and I don't know if she wants me the way I want her. Does she really want a life at a mobster's side, or will she run off to a dick like Cameron?

Alexis covers her mouth and she reacts by crying. She just bursts into tears and yells, "I can't!"

THIS IS *not* the answer I expected. I close the box and rise, putting it back in my pocket, my ears reddening. This is absolutely not how Lucky said this would go. He promised that Alexis would say yes, that I'd given her the world and showed her my true heart. *She can't.*

"Okay. I understand."

"No, you don't understand!" Alexis half-wails. "I thought I could keep this a secret, but I can't... I've been lying..."

"About what?"

"About what happened when I followed Chloe."

My chest tightens. Did something happen? Did someone hurt her? I'm ready to burn down the fucking world for her.

"What happened?" And who the fuck do I have to kill?

"Cameron did it," she gasps. Alexis' hands rush to her stomach and she breathes in slowly and nervously. I put my hand on her back. "Listen, Alexis. Calm down. You need to calm down."

"I'm sorry," she says, tears streaming down her face. "I should have told you but I didn't know if I should tell you or the police or…"

"Okay, breathe. Take a deep breath and you can tell me the truth."

Alexis follows through with several difficult deep breaths.

"I don't deserve you."

"What the hell are you talking about? I still want to marry you. I just want you to… you know… calm the fuck down a bit."

Alexis gives me a watery, surprised glance. "You're not mad?"

"Uh… no. You found out your ex killed your attempted rapist and your best friend kept it a secret. You needed time to process. I want to be your husband, Alexis. I don't want to let stupid shit get in between us."

"It's not stupid. It's criminal."

"Yeah, and I'm one to talk. I assume that preppy kid isn't worried."

She shakes her head. Yeah, just what I thought. Shit has a way of working out and if it's not my circus, I don't want to fuck with the monkeys.

"I love you, Alexis. Wipe your tears and let me marry you."

"You can get back down on that knee," Alexis says through her whimpers, wiping her face with the edge of her shirt. "Let's try this from scratch."

She fans her face to dry the remaining tears and I get back

down on one knee. I'd kneel a thousand times for her. She's mine – and she always will be.

"Alexis Carter, will you do me the honor of–

RINNGGGGGGG! RINGGGGGGGG!

I HATE my fucking cell phone.

RINGGGGGG!

"I HAVE TO GET THIS," I mutter. Alexis shrugs. She knows what's coming. I answer the phone, ready to *gut* Sammy Zagarella for daring to interrupt my proposal.

"What the fuck is going on?"

"Are you busy?" Sammy asks casually. Am I busy? I want to punch him in the fucking face.

"Just in the middle of proposing to my fucking girlfriend. No biggie."

"Oh. Did I interrupt?"

"Yes, Sammy. You did."

"Well, it's already in the past. I've got a big problem."

"You might have a bigger one by the time we're done."

"THE GIRL IS PREGNANT," Sammy says. "She's 100% pregnant, and she has nowhere to live and I don't know what the fuck to do with her. You're the boss, maybe you can give her an apartment somewhere or–

"Are you out of your fucking mind, Sammy?"

Sammy has been hit in the head far too many fucking time in the past year. Lucky and I have tried our best to ignore the changes in his mental state, but it's getting downright impossible to communicate with the motherfucker. He's lost his fucking marbles and I don't know if he'll get them back.

Killing his son probably didn't help but... we have peace now. We don't have to do that shit anymore.

"Yeah," Sammy mutters. "I am. Lost my fucking marbles."

Sometimes I wonder if he can change my mind.

"Fix it," I tell him. "Get a fucking shrink if that's what you need... and look after that girl. We don't know if our problems are over."

"Yeah. You expect a guy who hears voices to look after an eighteen-year-old high school dropout. That should be easy."

"Life ain't fucking easy, Sammy. Especially not ours. Open your heart. You're about to have a grandchild."

"Fuck, I'm old."

"Yes, and you're fucking interrupting me. So can you deal with your shit?"

"Yes," Sammy says. "After I tell you one last thing."

"What?"

"I still love you like a brother."

Forgiveness. I never expected Sammy's forgiveness. I didn't think any of us expected it and I didn't think any of us were capable of forgiving each other. We've done a lot of bad shit to each other but now we're even, right? I lose my father, he loses his son, we burn our city down and start this shit over.

It's all we've got.

"I love you too, man."

"Get your girl," Sammy says. "Enjoy your life. You might be a cruel motherfucker, but you've done right by her."

I LEAVE my phone conversation to meet Alexis pacing. I hate that she looks worried.

"Was I gone too long?"

"Absolutely," She says. I'm worried, but her face cracks into a smile. "I'm joking."

John

"Oh. Good."

Alexis bounds up to me with her hands on her hips. "Well…"

"Right…"

I get back down on one knee and propose to Alexis without any interruptions, muddling through a speech where I tell her every fucking thing I love about her.

"What do you say, cupcake? Will you marry me?"

"YES! YES! YES!"

I get off my knees and wrap my arms around her, spinning her around. I don't want this moment to disappear, even if all moments must in the end. She's my second chance at life.

I don't even realize how true that is until I set her down.

"I have some news too. I think."

"What kind of news?"

"I might be… pregnant. I know you said you couldn't, but something must have changed because I'm three weeks late."

"Did you take a test?"

Alexis shakes her head but she sighs. "I know I am, John. I can feel it. I'm scared as hell, but… you just proved that I have nothing to be afraid of."

She slides her hands into mine and I want to kiss her and never stop.

"You're right, cupcake. There's nothing to fear at all. I think I'm finally ready to be a dad."

I mean it. After all the shit I've been through, I want this with Alexis. I want to give her everything she wants in life — medical school, a family, a safe home. I want to meet her parents and travel the world with her.

She makes me feel normal and she makes me want to be normal.

"Really?" She asks, giving me one last chance to back out. *I don't want to leave you, cupcake. Never.*

"Yeah," I whisper. "I think I just needed to know my kid

could be safe. I needed to know I could make this a safe world for the people I love."

"We'll be just fine," she says, holding onto me tightly. "I'll be right here with all the medical knowledge required to treat any future cuts and scrapes."

"And I'll be there to take care of anyone who gives them problems."

"Without murder," Alexis whispers, kissing my neck. *I love how her lips feel. I've always loved her softness, from the moment I first held her.*

"No more killing," I whisper. "Not unless I have to."

"John…"

"I'll burn the world for you, Alexis. I can't lie about that."

"Fine," I whisper. "Then I'll try my best to stay out of trouble."

"That would make me *very* happy, cupcake. Incredibly fucking happy."

* * *

THE BEGINNING…

Click here to order Sammy's story
Book #3 Long Island Mafia Romance
https://bit.ly/longislandmafia3

* * *

Sign up to get a text message notification when my next book drops: https://slkt.io/gxzM

About Jamila Jasper

The hotter and darker the romance, the better.

That's the Jamila Jasper promise.

If you enjoy sizzling multicultural romance stories that dare to *go there* you'll enjoy any Jamila Jasper title you pick up.

Open-minded readers who appreciate **shamelessly sexy romance novels** featuring black women of all shapes and sizes paired with smokin' hot white men are welcome.

Sign up for her e-mail list here to receive one of these **FREE hot stories**, exclusive offers and an update of Jamila's publication schedule: bit.ly/jamilajasperromance

* * *

Get text message updates on new books: https://slkt.io/gxzM

Mafia Playmate

https://bit.ly/bostonirishmafia1

Boston Irish Mafia Romance Series

Mafia Playmate

Mafia Property

Mafia Surrogate

Mafia Possession

Mafia Stalker

* * *

Click here for the complete collection:

www.jamilajasperromance.com/catalog

Content Awareness

Read this passage if you require content warnings for sensitive material. I do not give detailed content warnings that will spoil the plot, but be aware of this note.

* * *

This is a mafia romance story with dark themes including potentially triggering content of **all** varieties, violence, frank discussions and language surrounding bedroom scenes and race.
All characters in this story are 18+
Sensitive readers, be cautioned about some of the detailed romantic material in this dark but *extremely hot romance novel.*

Description

A large pink box arrives on Aiden's doorstep with a woman inside.
His mail-order bride arrives in her birthday suit and tied up in knots with a pretty pink silk ribbon.

Aiden never requested a dark-skinned beauty...
His family would never approve of such an impure connection.

Who is this woman? What does she want?
A note in the box reveals the truth...
The woman in the box - *Valentina* - is a gift from an anonymous sender who wants something dark and twisted in return.

Chapter One
Aiden

You have one job in the Murray family. You grow up, you get your marks, you listen to Pa, you marry a nice Irish girl, preferably a blond or a redhead with lighter features.
You do what Padraig Murray asks.
You pray everyday and you keep your rosary wrapped in your pocket. You stay loyal. You keep our bloodline strong.

Pa demands a meeting with me now that I'm back in the city. He claims it's important, but it can't be that important if he wants to meet me during the Red Sox game. It feels good to be home. There's something special about Boston, but maybe that's just it – paradise is wherever our family is.

After Pa, I'll go home and see Roscoe, my Rottweiler. Then get my shit together and call my younger brother Darragh to check in on his training and find out if Rian's around. Over the weekend, I'll head to Leominster to visit Callum and then Sunday after church, stop by to see Ma and Odhran. I brought a gift home with me for Tegan, Rian's daughter, and I can't wait to see my niece's face light up when I give it to her.

Aiden

If there's one thing I don't miss about being home, it's a never ending list of shit to do.

I meet my father at our usual casual meeting spot, Mulligan's, a place where we aren't afraid to celebrate Irish pride. A place where you can catch the Red Sox game and no one can catch your conversation. *It's as much home as anywhere else.*

I spot my father hunched over the bar from the street, his face illuminated by a warm orange bulb as he watches the pre-game announcer talk. I prefer football to baseball, but Pa bets on all their games, so he likes to keep his eye on the Red Sox each season.

When Pa calls, you answer, and he's desperate to know about the affair with the Italians – what the fuck happened, have I found the renegade cousins who pissed off the Italians, and whether I've killed them yet. *I haven't.*

It's all bad news and my ass is on the line if I don't find a way to sort out all the shit that happened in Long Island. At least we're guaranteed peace with the vicious Italians. *Those greaseballs aren't any better than the blacks. 'Trust 'em as far as you can throw them', Pa told me. But for now, we have peace and that's what matters. At least to me.*

I enter Mulligan's and the conversations fall to a hush. *Aiden Murray's back.* I clear my throat and the conversations continue. But there are more phones pulled out than before and two guys sitting in the back leave. I don't hate the reputation I have. Most of the bar fights I earned this cutthroat reputation in were Darragh's fault, but that doesn't change what people say about me.

Darragh, my younger brother, can still throw his weight around in the ring, but he got his practice here, in this fucking place. Our last fight here was over a girl. Darragh kicked some Puerto Rican's ass and a few of our boys jumped him outside… I don't know what happened to the guy after.

My father slides a twenty-dollar bill across the bar to the bartender, Finnegan O'Malley, a one-eared ex-hitman, who in turn fills up two glass pints of amber Sam Adams. Pa's already several drinks ahead of me. *Great. The news can't be that bad then.*

I pull out a bar stool next to my father, who barely acknowledges me, although he must've caught me entering the bar through the reflection on the glass behind the bartender. He shoves one of the pints across the bar towards me. He knows I prefer Guinness, but I don't mind starting with this. I can see my dad's reflection in the glass. He looks older than I remember. He's pushing 70, so I shouldn't be surprised by the large streaks of gray through his slick hair which was once blond, but changed color throughout his life, settling on a dark chocolate brown, like Rian's.

I glance at the television to check the score, but the game hasn't even started yet. I can smell the alcohol coming off of him already.

"You can have a Guinness after you drink this," he says. "I heard you did good work with the Italians."

He sounds raspy, but calm. My tension dissipates. This is just a normal, father-son meeting. Nothing to worry about.

"I didn't find Eoin or Robert. Haven't heard fuck since they all screwed with Vicari," I say as I take a sip of my beer.

"Maybe the Italians killed them," he says. "They're a violent, vicious group of people."

"Yeah."

Like we're ones to talk. Pa's done with his Sam Adams already and waits patiently for me to catch up, as if I could catch up to a man who's been drinking for an hour. At forty, it's not so easy for me to keep up with long nights of drinking. I don't know how he does it.

He waits for me to have a few more sips, his eyes glued to the television. Chris Sale throws the first pitch. It doesn't go so well. My father glances down at his glass and sighs. "It's going to be a long night."

"That bad this season?" I grunt, glancing up at the Detroit batter sliding into second.

I've been too busy to keep up with baseball. My father grunts. Yeah, it has been that bad.

"Any other news?" I ask him, finishing off the Sam Adams. Dad grunts and snaps his fingers for the bartender, Finnegan. The buff, tattooed bartender hustles over as dad orders two Guinnesses without opening his mouth. Bad news if he's drinking Guinness.

"Cops got Rian last week. They're charging him with manslaughter."

Manslaughter?

"What did he do?"

"What the fuck do you think he did?" Dad responds calmly. "He killed somebody, they caught him. That boy's not careful enough and I have to pay to get his ass out of trouble. Maybe some prison time would do him good."

"That's what you said the first three times," I grunt. Sale throws a good pitch and my father's face visibly brightens.

"If it weren't for Tegan, I'd let him spend a few extra years behind bars," Dad confesses. "Your mother won't let me do that to his daughter."

"What's going to happen to her?"

"I don't know," my father says. "No one has seen the kid in a week."

"What?" I growl, sipping at my beer and hoping this is my father's idea of a joke since he sounds dangerously unconcerned.

"What do you mean no one's seen her? Is she with her ma?"

My father shrugs.

Rian's notoriously bad taste in women landed him with a child he should have never brought into the world. She's a sweet girl, but doomed by a mobster father and a whore mother.

Her ma doesn't live in Boston anymore. She wants nothing to do with Rian.

"Where does he say she is?"

"Last time he saw her was the night he got arrested," Pa says before taking a sip of his beer.

"What about the cops? Did they give her to his lawyer or something?"

I don't have a single paternal instinct in my body, but my mind courses with worry over Tegan, despite my father's calmness.

"She'll turn up," he says, pouring more alcohol down his throat.

Fuck, Rian. My brother must be an even worse parent than our father. His daughter's missing and he's behind bars and there's no one else to look for her except…

"I can find out where she is. Once I get Roscoe and take care of–

"It would serve him right if something happened to her," my father says coldly. "Her mother isn't Irish. He keeps fucking up. I'm tired of cleaning up his messes. Now *drink*. This is not why I asked you here."

I bristle at his comment, but it's just Padraig Murray. This is who he's always been and my brother should have had the good sense to keep his dick in his pants. I made it to forty without fathering bastards all over Boston. Rian should have been more careful. I drink a few more sips, but I can't let this go. *Who else will worry about the fucking kid if not me?*

"How the hell did Rian let this happen? Can I talk to him?"

"Best that none of us talk to him. The cops listen to everything. I can get messages into the prison and messages out, but I don't want you talking to him."

"Fine," I grunt, finishing off my first round of Guinness and ordering us another. I try to pay, but my father stops me and then finally answers my other question.

"Your idiot brother trusted a woman," he says. "He wants a mother for that little girl so badly, that he's willing to do anything. He's willing to kill for a woman who doesn't deserve him."

"I didn't know he had a woman," I grumble.

"*Had* is correct," Pa says. "She's dead."

Aiden

I wish I could tell you a chill ran through me, or I had some other human response to my father's announcement. I don't need a university degree to understand what he's implying. Rian had a woman, she got him locked up, so my father had her killed.

"Will that affect his case?"

"No," Pa says. "It was very clean."

"Who?"

"None of your business, Aiden. You worry about your shit, I'll worry about your brother."

I want to feel sorry for Rian, but he deserves it for crossing our father. This is what happens when he pisses off Padraig Murray. More problems for all of us.

"How much time is he facing?"

"Three years since he's been in jail before. I tried to get that stupid motherfucker to get his life together, but your brother just wants to be a fuck up."

"Who's the lawyer?"

"Someone from Nigel & Bancroft."

At least he isn't cheaping out like he did for Rian's first case. I don't want to push my father's buttons, and despite his outward calm, he must be furious at Rian for drawing more attention to us, but Rian has his uses.

"It's Rian," I remind him. "Crazy fucking Rian. We need him out soon. There are some jobs only Rian has the balls to handle."

Padraig snorts. "He takes after my father. Too proud and too violent for his own good."

We created the monster Rian Murray is. He's our responsibility.

"He needs another woman."

"He needs a woman who isn't a fucking spic," my father spits. "At least the child looks white."

"What about this previous woman? What'd she look like?"

"It doesn't matter," he grunts. "She's dead. Now drink. We

have more important things to talk about than your idiot brother and his shitty taste in women."

I drink because Pa commands it. I do everything he commands and have since I was a child. I have the burns and scars to remind me of what happens when you disobey my father. At first, I hated him for what he did to me, but to keep an organization like ours together, you need to inspire fear.

You have to be cruel to survive – that's just how the world works. I can't let Tegan go. The second I see Darragh, I'll ask about her and track her down.

I drink so I don't lose my temper. He doesn't give a fuck about Tegan. No one does. Maybe he's wrong and one of my sisters took her in. But who would do that? Evie's saddled with her drunkard husband and two unruly kids of her own – Katie and Patrick. Kiara's off at university and Maeve's sixteen, too young to have any involvement.

"I need to tell you something important," my father says somberly, as if there could be something more important than my missing niece right now. I'm burning with desire to leave, but if I get up without my father's dismissal, he'll hurt me. Or someone I care about. Not like there are many of those people yet. It's foolish to get close to people in this life.

"Then tell me."

If he notices my tightening tone, my father doesn't acknowledge it.

"There's a plot against my life. I don't know who. I don't know why but... there's someone out there trying to kill me," my father says, the faded tattoos on his knuckles even more wrinkled than I last remember. He's getting older, but aside from his physical appearance, he shows no signs of slowing down. If anything, he's desperate to prove himself more. If he wasn't ordering more killings than necessary, maybe Rian wouldn't be locked up.

I don't want to dismiss his concerns as paranoid, but he's the leader of our family. There's always a plot against his life. It comes with the territory. My father doesn't have to worry because he has us. *Family*.

"Fuck that," I grunt. "No one would be stupid enough to try to kill you. April 2013, four days after the bombing. An entire decade ago. That's the last time anyone tried."

I was thirty back then, old enough to be the one who ended that war before it started. Back then, we only killed when necessary. I got five tattoos that year, one for each kill. Each a painful release, each representing a necessary act to keep my family safe.

My father smirks and keeps drinking. He shrugs. "That's what I thought. But I'm serious. This time is different. This time the bastards might just get me. I'm getting old, Aiden. Most guys in our line of work don't make it this far."

"What happened?" I grunt, urging my increasingly drunken father to get to the point. His cheeks blaze tomato red with alcohol and his blue eyes swim with tears, again brought on by drinking rather than any emotion. He grunts and knocks his biggest gold ring against the bar's surface contemplatively.

If anyone tried to kill him, surely Darragh would have mentioned it. He's responsible for keeping our father alive.

"I feel it in my bones," Pa replies. "Someone wants to destroy our family."

"Yes," I grumble. "Our cousins. But they're gone and if they were anywhere near this city, we would have heard about it."

"I don't know. Something big is coming for us. I feel it."

"We can make decisions based on feelings now?"

"Cut the shit, kid. You know my instincts are good because you're like me. You can smell shit before it hits the toilet bowl."

"I'm home. If anyone tries to kill you, they'll have to get through me, Darragh, and Callum."

My father smirks. "My boys. I'm proud of all of you. Except Rian. He's a piece of shit."

Ah, Padraig. Honest as fuck, especially when he's drunk.

He might not be proud of Rian, but he still loves my brother enough to spring for decent lawyers and to make sure Tegan goes to the best day school in Boston. Once she's old enough, she'll go to Milton or Dana Hall, or another nice private school where she can meet someone to untarnish her sullied blood, that is as long as I can find her. If Rian's behind bars, she could be anywhere. Hopefully not with her mom's people.

She belongs with us, even if Rian made mistakes. She looks like us and that's good enough to cover up his shameful behavior. I don't know what Rian was thinking with that Puerto Rican chick. Tegan's mother was low class.

Let's hope my brother's behavior doesn't come back to haunt all of us. Let's hope his daughter is safe, sound asleep somewhere and protected.

"Thanks, Pa," I mutter, uncomfortable with even this much emotional closeness between us. I love my father, but trusting him too much is dangerous. Rian found out the hard way that it isn't worth it to defy our family beliefs, and it definitely isn't fucking worth it to screw around with the wrong women.

"And Aiden? I need you to hurry the fuck up and find a wife. I'm getting old and I want to retire, but I need a family man to lead this family. You're the oldest. Why the fuck can't you keep a woman? Do I have to send you back to Galway?"

He wants a real answer.

"Not interested in chasing after girls, dad. All they want to do is take your money and ask where the fuck you're going. I've had enough."

"That old dog won't take care of you when you get old."

"Neither will some Boston snob who could take my ass to the cleaners in a divorce."

He laughs, which is the best reaction I can hope for. He quickly moves along to talking about the game and his plans for the business, and then asks me questions about Long Island. They're a mess out there, but doing better under John Vicari's leadership. We're developing a few buildings together and are prepared to make a lot of money in the real estate game. John does cleaner business than his father. Too bad the old man died of a heart attack… that's the word anyway.

"I need you to find a nice girl," my father reminds me once he's almost blackout drunk. He can barely keep his head up. *Great.* I'm not dragging his ass outta here tonight. If he wants to get so wasted he can't sit up straight, I'll leave him for Finnegan.

"We have this conversation every time we talk."

"This time, I'm serious. I want to retire. I don't want you bringing home no spics either like the Duffy boys."

"Fuck's sake, Pa. You can't talk like that around here anymore."

"I can say whatever the fuck I want. I want Irish children. Irish fucking children and I need you to have a wife so I can retire."

"Retire any old fucking day you want," I growl. "It'll be good for you to stop worrying about who I fuck or marry or the fate of the fucking family."

"The fate of the family matters," he says, taking another sip of his newest glass of beer before rubbing condensation off the sides with his napkin.

"I'm too old to have kids," I growl. "I'm too old to get tied down. You and mom were lucky you even found each other."

That's bullshit and we both know it. They stay together because they're Catholic, because back in the eighties, my dad killed someone for her father and won my mother like a prize. He also put a baby in her quickly and then kept her pregnant. There's nothing romantic about their love story or marriage in the Murray family.

"If you can't find a girl, I'll find one."

"The last girl you found me was a crazy fucking redhead who wanted to bring Roscoe Jr. into the bedroom. No thanks."

My father shrugs. "She was white. Do you know how hard it is to find a white girl around here who hasn't been fucking ruined by some fucking Puerto Rican or black guy?"

"What do you want from me, Pa?"

I know what I want. I want an end to this conversation, and I want my father to give me a fucking break about women and dating. All the Irish and Catholic women in Boston know to stay away from us, and the ones who don't learn their lesson pretty fucking quickly.

"Find a nice white girl with big tits and blond hair and get her pregnant so I know you're fucking serious about family. That's what I want."

"Give me time."

He continues, getting to what I suspect was the original point he wanted to make before the liquor got to him. "And get your ass to the site in Back Bay tomorrow bright and early."

"Why?"

This is the first I'm hearing about something wrong at the Back Bay construction site. I know something's wrong because my father doesn't do anything bright and early unless there's a problem to solve.

"You'll find out tomorrow. You just got back. Go home. Pet the dog. Your mom's tired of walking that big fuck. He nearly knocked her over near Harvard Square."

"How is mom?"

"Pissed off."

"Why?"

"Eh. Upset about another woman. It's nothing."

It's nothing. Dad just got his second mistress pregnant and even if we all know about it, we're all supposed to pretend it's no big deal that our elderly father knocked up a Irish teenager who he supposedly hired to clean the construction company office.

I hate how he treats our mother. What's the point of having a family or a woman if you hurt her? There's no getting through to him, but I have to try for my mother's sake.

"You treat her better, pa. Seriously. She needs you."

He grunts. "Get your ass home kid and get a white girl pregnant."

"Thanks, dad."

"If you can't find one, I'll find a good Irish girl who needs a green card and bring her over to you!"

My father is the last person I want picking my romantic partners. I mutter something to him about cutting back on liquor, then I pat my father on the back and leave the bar. This is the closest we've felt in years, but there's still a wall between us and there always will be. I felt closer to him when I was younger, when it was easier for me to justify the life I led. I know I'm a screw up, I know I don't belong anywhere near a woman or a family or any of the fucking things my father wants from me.

He knows it's wrong to bring a kid into this life, but he did it anyway. He knows that we're villains, but he doesn't care. Fuck, I don't care either, I suppose. I'd just rather not ruin a perfectly good woman.

I drive out of the city listening to rock classics on the radio. Just as I turn down my street – I live at the end of a cul-de-sac – I notice the large box on my front step. There are only five large houses at the end of this cul-de-sac, all of us with wide open well-maintained lawns around traditional New England colonial houses.

The box on my front step is fucking enormous – and I don't remember ordering anything for delivery. My hand moves swiftly to the pistol under my seat. I feel no fear as I reach for the gun and slip a mag out of my pocket. I feel ready.

Leaving the city for any amount of time always carries a risk, especially since I didn't exactly leave the place with a house sitter. The last time my teen brother Odhran house-sat, he trashed the place and had a threesome in my bed. I hop out of my black GMC Sierra with the gun under my coat and approach the box slowly, glancing furtively over my shoulder for anyone who might have eyes on me.

The box has holes in it. It's large. Pink. Wrapped in a bow. I reach for the bottom of the box and try to lift it. *Fuck*. It's heavy. I drop the box and I swear I hear a sound coming from inside it. *Is that possible?* I try to peek through the holes but it's too fucking dark and something's telling me opening this box will be a shit-show. It has to weigh about a hundred pounds. Maybe more. I'm no weakling, but it still takes a measure of back strength to lift a box that fucking heavy.

I open my front door and greet Roscoe Jr., my rottweiler, as he bounds towards the door to greet me. His coat looks shiny, the nub of his docked tail wags back and forth. Pa's choice, not mine. He runs up to the box and sniffs at it a bit.

There's definitely something in there and it gets his attention because Roscoe utters a low bark.

"Roscoe, go lie down."

Once he heads off to his bed, I throw my doors open wider and eye the giant box to decide how to carry the fuckin' thing. I would call Rian if his stupid ass wasn't in jail. I could call Callum, but he's still hung up on some fucking girl and won't answer my calls because I won't sugarcoat my opinion of him. Then there's Darragh… He's probably twice as drunk as Padraig. Not a good option either.

I'll have to carry the box myself. I stretch a little and then grab the edges of the box and grunt as I carry it a few feet inside my doorway. I set the box down more gently. *Is there something alive in there?* If it were an animal, I suspect Roscoe would be barking from his spot in the house, but he's laying down as I commanded, gazing at me curiously and wagging his tail.

He's probably wondering why I'm not taking him for a walk since I'm back. *At least he didn't bite the sitter this time.* I close my front doors and then search for an opening on the giant pink box. Finding none, I start with the ribbon and peel it away. The box comes up to my waist. It's *enormous*.

Aiden

If it didn't weigh a hundred fucking pounds, I would assume it's a novelty gift or something extra special from one of my brothers. Which of my piece of shit brothers would get me a welcome home gift? It's not like either of them are here with a six pack of Guinness right now...

I peel the top of the box open and there's another box inside it, also pink. I open the second box and stumble backwards as I expose the contents. I don't mean to act like a fucking idiot, but I nearly fall over, because this is the last thing I expected to find on my doorstep. I just got back to Boston... How long has that box been out there?

Holy fuck, why isn't she screaming?

I GAIN control of myself and approach the box again, heart pounding because my second assumption is that the human female in the box might be dead and that's the reason she hasn't made a sound. The sick thought twists my stomach into an unyielding knot.

I slowly approach the box again, ignoring my heavy breathing, focusing instead on taking in as much information as possible about the situation. I move the flaps of the box open and stare at the woman's face.. Suddenly, her eyes snap open before swiveling around and looking me directly in the eye..

Holy fuck, this woman is alive.

"What the fuck is this?" I grunt to myself. Not to myself. I'm not alone. I dry swallow and run my fingers through my hair. She's black. Someone tied up a black woman in a pink ribbon, wrapped her up like a gift and put her in a box on my doorstep. This has to be a sick joke.

I'm almost too scared to reach into the box and touch her, but I have to touch her to get her out of the fucking box.

Whoever this woman is, she ran into the wrong fucking people and ended up in the wrong living room.

I have tattoos and vows of loyalty to prove how I feel about people like her. "Don't worry. I'll get you out of there."

I don't know why I'm bothering with comfort. I reach into the box and grab her at the base of her spine before hoisting her out of the box and gently setting her on the ground. My stomach lurches. This is some sick, twisted shit. Whoever did this to her stripped this woman naked, bared every inch of her dark skin, the color of Arabica coffee, and wrapped her in a pink ribbon, contorting her limbs and running the ribbon over her bare breasts, between her thighs and in loops around her body so she's wrapped up like a chocolate present.

My body has an unconscious, primal reaction. I could unwrap her like the present she's been wrapped up to be, but I need answers quickly.

She has a gag in her mouth, a round white ball that keeps her lips spread open and hooks at the back. Her eyes roam around the room in terror as I reach into my pocket for my knife. I've killed people with this knife and now I'm using it to save someone.

Her skin prickles with goosebumps as I touch her. I apologize, but I need to brace myself against her to get her free. I press the serrated edge to the ribbon and make the first cut.

I cut her legs free. She groans as her legs fall in a curled heap. She cries out and tries to jerk them again, but however long she's been in that position was far too long for her to have full control of her legs and hips.

"Don't move," I remind her. I touch her skin again and my stomach lurches. Fuck, her skin is so dark. I look pale as fuck touching her and even putting my hands on her drives guilt through me. She's black. She's the wrong kind of person. I run my tongue piercing over my lower lip as I focus on all the parts of the ribbon I have to cut free.

When I have her limbs mostly free, she rolls onto her side,

groaning in pain as her arms and legs curl in an awkward and splayed mess next to her. Even her wrists bend at an unnatural angle. I know she's alive, but the woman still looks dead.

I swallow slowly. What the absolute fuck is this?

"I'll take the gag out, but you can't spit or bite or do anything of that nature. Do you understand?"

She stares at me, but she can't say anything. I approach her mouth slowly and reach around her to find the clasp of her ball gag. I unhook it and take it out of her mouth. She groans again and winces in visible pain as she attempts to close her jaw. She slowly moves her hand to her face and rubs her cheek, groaning.

I crouch next to her, staring at her in awe, knowing that I shouldn't but am completely incapable of taking my eyes off the naked woman in front of me. If her nudity makes her uncomfortable, that hasn't sunk in yet. My cock stiffens inappropriately in my pants and I clasp my hands in front of my dick, refusing to take my eyes off her.

Her breasts are small, but they protrude forward in tiny, dark orbs with nipples that are even darker than her extremely dark skin. Holy fuck, I didn't know nipples came that dark. My eyes widen inappropriately and I pray she doesn't notice my leering. Who sent this woman to me and what exactly did they send her for?

Christ, Aiden. Get a grip. You're staring at her crotch now and it's obvious.

She's waxed completely and my gaze snaps to the bare, dark brown lips. I wonder what this strange woman conceals between those lower lips and what color her flesh is between those thin, toned legs. I clear my throat.

"Who are you?"

"Read the card with the gift," she manages to say, with a raspy voice and an accent I can't place.

"I asked you a question."

"Read the card with the gift," she repeats.

I raise an eyebrow and walk towards the box. There's a large card at the bottom, about 8 x 10 inches, printed on thick paper. I pull it out of the box and read the note, muttering it out loud to myself. *What the fuck is this?*

Dear Mr. Murray,

We hope you enjoy your object. Your task is simple.

Use the object wisely. Have unprotected sex with the object and film a 4K quality video.

Compress the video file and send it to the email address below.

The object may be initially unwilling but both of you will face strong motivation to comply. The object understands that documentation of her existence belongs to us and if she fails to comply enthusiastically, we will destroy her identity.

If we do not receive the video within one week of today's date, you will both lose what's most important to you.

Tegan Murray counts on you to succeed. We have possession of the girl and you would be wise to listen to our orders if you or your family want to see her safe.

Do not call Padraig Murray. Do not call anyone else, or you will both suffer.

It takes less than a second to fire a bullet.

You must comply. When you're finished with said object, it is yours to keep.
Sincerely,
Your Benefactors
OA

"WHAT IS THIS SICK SHIT?" I growl, throwing the card back into the box, causing the woman still kneeling on the ground to flinch. My heart thuds.

These people have Tegan and this woman might know where she is and who they are. I won't be a part of this sick fucking game.

* * *

Chapter Two
Valentina

"You have to do what they say," I say to him. *"Please."*

It's not what I want to say, but these were my instructions if I wanted to survive. I never saw the people who put me in the box, but I heard their instructions and their threats clearly.

My throat burns raw as I attempt to plead with the man in front of me, hoping that he'll spare me. *He's involved with the people who took you. He's dangerous.*

The more I talk, the quicker he'll piece the truth about me together. I don't want this man to know *anything* about me. My voice. It's bad enough that he's seeing me naked. It's bad enough that he's about to take a part of me that I never wanted to give to strangers, that I always wanted to *mean* something.

I want to keep a piece of myself to myself. I've never had that privilege before. I won't have it tonight. He's an utter stranger to me and a terrifying one at that.

The gigantic blond man glowers at me, his blue eyes enough to melt me in place. He's 6'4", his hair looks slightly unkempt. Black ink swirls around his pale skin in a variety of Celtic knots, cursive Bible verses and symbols that I don't understand. *Lots of tattoos. He must be a gangster. Something like that.*

Valentina

I hate that I'm naked, but I'm glad that I'm free. There was nothing but pain in that box. The drugs helped at first, but they didn't last thirty-six hours. That's how long it took to get here from Idaho. Technically, the drive takes twenty-five hours, but I tried to measure time – I have a good sense of it because of the piano – and I know they took thirty six.

There's no getting out of this. Maybe this one won't be as wicked as the first.

"Who are you?" the man growls at me. "Who did this and what the fuck do you have to do with this?"

His anger sends a surge of terror through me as his face reddens with frustration. He has absolute control over this situa-tion and he knows it. I can't afford to freeze and make it worse by proving to him what he already knows – I'm vulnerable, weak and utterly at his mercy.

I position myself to cover my breasts as much as possible as well as my *other* parts, but he's already seen every bit of me. Modesty is entirely pointless.

"My name is Valentina," I rasp out, my voice getting stronger as I tell him my name.

"Is that your real name?" he growls, stepping forward and towering over me.

I'll never know if I had another name. I've been called Valentina since I was a little girl. Sometimes Val, but never anything else. I must've had a life before, but I don't remember any of it. All I remember is Pulsifer. He was my father, my abuser, my everything. I wouldn't call this freedom, but there's still a weight lifted because this is the closest I've ever come to leaving the governor's mansion.

The blond man is even taller than I thought he was. I'm more vulnerable naked and despite wanting to stand up for myself, I shrink back from him.

"Yes," I say as firmly as I can manage.

"Who sent you? Because I'll be damned if I screw around with a n–"

He stops himself, but my skin feels a flush of outrage and humiliation as his lips hover over the n-word. I want to hit him, but I don't know what type of man my new master is yet. A racist. That part I understand. He's not the first racist I've had to deal with. He might be the richest though. *He lives in a mansion.*

"Who sent you?" He roars. His face reddens as he screams and his creepy blue eyes look bloodshot. I shouldn't cross him, but I stopped giving a fuck about what happens to me a long time ago. I've already experienced the worst.

"I don't know. All I know is they want you to do what's on that note."

I don't want that. I have to go through with it, but I definitely don't start off wanting that monster anywhere near me.

"No," he growls, his jaw tightening. "I... This is fucking ridiculous. Tell me who sent you, woman."

His anger mounts and my fear intensifies. I'm no stranger to racism, but for the word to nearly fly off the tip of his tongue like that. *How can someone who looks like that be so ugly inside?*

He reaches into his jacket and I know he's reaching for a gun before he pulls it out. The men who sent me here weren't any better than the man who received me as a gift. My throat tightens and I try not to lose control of my bladder as he pulls the pistol out of his jacket and points it straight at me.

Men are all the same and they're all violent disgusting pigs who will put a bullet in an innocent woman's head if she gets in their way. They'll use us up and spit us out and there isn't a man alive capable of real love...

"If you shoot me, you'll die," I state plainly, trying to sound like I have control of the situation. I'm not lying, but I'm also not stupid enough to mean that as a threat either. "And whoever you love enough for them to threaten will die too."

"I don't give a fuck," he snarls. "Who sent you?"

I don't believe that he doesn't care. I sense a crack in this man beneath his outrage. His anger cloaks his genuine concern. If he wanted to kill me, he would have done it already.

"Do I look like I was in control of the situation? You have

their instructions. Are you going to do it or not?" I say to him sharply. Talking to him like this could be dangerous, but he doesn't react to my strengthening voice or sharp tone.

"Am I going to rape you?" He growls, lowering the gun. "Is that what you're fucking asking me?"

He has a thick accent which I can finally place. *Boston*. I'm in Boston, or close enough to Boston that men sound like Matt Damon in *Good Will Hunting*. I don't know anyone in Boston, but maybe that's for the best since I don't know any good people. Never have.

I don't respond to him. He reads the card to himself again and mutters a long string of curse words. I'm already naked and despite his apparent hesitation, the man hasn't offered me clothes. He doesn't know if he's going to do it yet, but I do.

He's going to have sex with me.

"You have to follow the instructions," I say to the terrifying blond man pleadingly. He still hasn't told me his name and I don't know if he will. He might worry I'll go to the police. "At least according to them." Hopefully he thinks of another solution since he's clearly some type of gangster.

I've been through enough shit to know that the police don't care about women like me. The police have *never* cared.

"This is a crock of shit," he hisses, spittle flying from his mouth as his face reddens with pure vitriol. "I have *never…*"

He glares at me like I'm responsible for this. Every inch of my body aches and I have little patience for this bastard acting like I'm the fucking problem.

"Never what?"

He glowers. "I've never been with… I don't… I don't fuck black women."

His voice drips with disgust, but I don't mind because I find this man's racism equally repulsive. He's more bothered by my race than the fact that I arrived on his doorstep naked, wrapped in ribbons, and sent to him in a box.

"You have to follow their instructions. I don't know what happens to you if you don't, but I know what happens to me."

I'll be lost to my past forever.

"Who fucking sent you?"

"I don't know."

I should have expected his next actions. He's a sicko, because the people who sent me only send gifts to sickos. My boss… My *old* boss was probably worse than this man. He was certainly much uglier, but all cruel men are the same.

He quickly racks a bullet in the chamber before re-leveling the gun to my face so I am forced to stare directly down the barrel.

"Kneel," he commands without wavering. I can see in his eyes that he's capable of shooting me. He runs his long pink tongue over his lips. He has a piercing through his tongue, a giant gold knob with a Celtic knot in the center. *What the fuck?*

My knees ache and I can't stop myself from groaning as I obey him. I have no choice but to listen to him despite the pain shooting through me. My stomach turns and if I'd eaten anything in the past 48 hours, it would've come up on this rich white man's hardwood floor.

My head lolls forward and I struggle not to cry out as more pain surges through my legs.

"Who sent you?"

"I don't know," I answer truthfully. If I had those answers, I would disappear in the middle of the night and find some way to get my real identity from the people who own me, or I suppose owned me before him.

"You must've come from somewhere," he says, his finger hovering near the trigger. It never occurred to me that he could do worse than hurt me, that he could kill me. *But he might. The men who did this to me never considered that.*

"My master sold me."

"What the fuck?" he snarls. "What the fuck does that mean?"

"I grew up… I grew up in a house with an older man. He sold me when I turned twenty-five."

"Sold you to who?"

"I never saw. I just know… I know what kind of company he keeps."

"Who was your master?"

"Governor of Idaho. Ezekiel Pulsipher," I respond as calmly as possible, even if just saying his name brings back flashes of horrific memories that still torment me every night. Who needs sleep, right?

"I don't know who the fuck that is," he spits. My chest swells with odd satisfaction that there's a corner of the universe not entirely ruled by Ezekiel.

In any other situation, his confusion would have been confusing. Old Zeke was a king in his universe and I wasn't the only girl in his harem. *He owned me since I was six years old. I don't want to tell this criminal about that, but I wouldn't feel sorry if this psychopath turned on my old master. I wouldn't feel sorry if these modern slave owners met this monster.*

I glare at him. I'm not here to give him an explanation. He's not the victim here, I am, and judging by his accent and other cues slowly coming into view, I'm on the other side of the country with no identification, no proof of who I am…Nobody knows I'm here.

It doesn't matter that I'm alone, I have to survive. I don't know what life will be like on this side of the country, but this is the best chance I've had to escape my entire life. *I can fool this white man. I know I can.*

"Why would someone do this?" He snarls.

"Maybe you're a criminal. Maybe they want revenge," I offer, perhaps pushing him too much with my attitude. His body tenses when I say the word *criminal*. Men. They think they're so careful with their emotions, but they get careless when they're underestimating you. Men get careless when they think they have the upper hand.

"I can't do what they want," he says, keeping the gun fixed at my head. This does little to warm me to him. "I can't screw... If my father found out... he would paint the sidewalk with your brains."

Charming. Now I have a definitive answer about the extent of this man's criminality.

He sets the gun on the table behind him and re-reads the card for the third time. His face turns several shades of red.

"This is sick," he spits, glowering at me with familiar, racially motivated revulsion. In most situations, I can't actually know if a man is racist. I have proof about this man.

"You have to. Whoever sent me paid a lot of money. You messed with powerful people," I tell him. "And they have someone you love and if you don't do this–

"I haven't messed with anyone," the man growls, interrupting me. "Get up."

I thought the pain shooting through me would knock me unconscious, but I had too much pride to ask him for relief. I slowly rise, my limbs barely cooperating. I look and feel ashy. I hate that I missed my routine. Spend a any amount of time in a box and you will miss the most damning prison you had before. My body still aches.

He looks me in the eye and I'm too scared not to meet this man's gaze. He's a predator and showing a predator fear gives them permission to pounce.

"My name is Aiden."

Aiden. I shouldn't care what his name is, but hearing it makes me consider him differently. The name sounds forceful and as rooted in his heritage as his Celtic tattoos.

"Great," I reply softly, unclear about what to do with the information.

He clears his throat and speaks again, "I thought you should know before we..."

"So you changed your mind?"

I shake before my body knows I'm shaking. This has happened before. Men have *taken* my body several times. Ezekiel *owned* me and believe me, he made good use of his property. Aiden. The name sounds Irish, but the man standing in front of me is All-American. He's 6'4" tall with *very* pale blond hair, but a thick crop of it. It's nice to see a man who isn't bald and who clearly works out. He's very muscular and the gun is out of the way, which sets me at ease.

"I don't know who sent you, woman. But I intend to find out. Seems like the best fuckin' way to do that is follow their instructions."

I knew it.

Aiden reaches for me and I fight my gut reaction to flinch. I don't want him to know how much I fear him. I want him to worry that I'll stab him in his sleep. I want him to feel like he's risking his life every time he rapes me.

Aiden puts his hand on my shoulder. I expected his touch to be rough, but it's very soft.

"Do they have anyone you love?"

I don't want to tell him, but his blue eyes harden and I sense that I'd better tell the truth if I want him to get this over with. His hand cups my shoulder too gently for me to describe. After the sharp angles and the pain of having my body squeezed into a box, his softness is surreal.

"I… I don't know."

"I don't want to hurt you. I won't rape you."

"If you don't have—

"I know," he growls. "But I won't hurt you. You have to consent. I…"

"I belong to you," I tell him, refusing to look away from him. I want him to gaze into my eyes and see a human being. A part of me desperately wants to shame him. It's hard to stare into those eyes and not feel something. He has intense and expressive eyes.

"No," he whispers. "You belong to yourself and once this is over, I'll have to let you go."

I fight back laughter. He won't let me go. I know men like Aiden better than he can even understand. I've lived my entire life in a world of pain and depravity.

"They'll hurt you if you don't do it. Surely my life isn't as important as yours."

"You're right," he growls. "But I've never fucked one of your kind and I don't intend to rape you either. That's not *my* thing."

He says it with the implication that he knows someone who prefers rape. And there he goes with the race talk again. *One of my kind…*

"You have to do it."

"Then agree to my terms."

"Terms."

I don't phrase it as a question and I don't want to sound too eager either.

"I'll give you money."

"So I won't be a slave, I'll be a prostitute."

His face reddens. "I'll send you away. You said they have someone you love. So you have a family?"

"No. I don't."

His hand drops from my shoulder and I glance down at his crotch. Despite Aiden's assurances that going through with this is the furthest thing from his mind, his dick bulges from his jeans. The bulge sends a deep surge of discomfort through me and my head swims.

There's no escape. All my smart-mouthed comments and my internal pleas that I might be able to survive this… I have to go through with it.

"What do you want, then?"

"A place to rest my head for a few nights. Time to get on my feet."

"Done."

He clears his throat. "I'll film it on my phone. I just... I've never..."

Aiden suddenly leans forward and kisses me. His lips surprise me with how soft they are when they first make contact. I want to scream, but it's a good kiss that draws me into Aiden's world instantly. His smell consumes me. His fingers claw at my cheeks as he holds me suddenly and keeps me still so he can kiss me.

Before Aiden, kisses felt like... cottage cheese. I want to push him away but the kiss is too fucking good for me to break away from it. I don't want to upset him, anyway. When he breaks away, his cheeks are red.

"I'm fucking dirty," he says and the revulsion in his voice tells me that he means it.

He doesn't look like he hated the kiss despite the words coming out of his mouth. He leans forward again and kisses me. This time, he spreads my lips apart and slides his tongue into my mouth. The piercing teases my tongue, sending a shiver straight through me. It's better than the first kiss and I kiss him back. He's the first man I've ever kissed back, the first man who has kissed me well enough for me to even try.

Men have done so many horrible things to me in my life and not one of them has kissed me properly. Aiden pulls away again and he pushes hair out of my face.

"We'll do this in my bedroom. Go upstairs. Third door on the left. Shower first."

Shower first. I don't like his tone, but I can't exactly blame him for it. I've been trapped in a box for several hours in a row and I probably smell exactly like it. At least he isn't pointing a gun at me anymore, and doesn't kiss me like a gross, perverted old man. He kisses me like... he would be a good lover.

That's another experience I've never had, another sad truth about my life that I never want to dwell on.

It hurts to walk up the stairs, but my body revels in the most freedom I've had in days. I almost want to race up the stairs to get to the bathroom quicker, but I walk patiently to the top and follow Aiden's instructions to find his bedroom. I can hear Aiden talking to his dog, telling him to stay on his bed for the next little while while he's busy. His house smells new, even if it's an old colonial that has probably been around since Boston's founding.

The bedroom is *extremely* neat. The floor smells clean and as my bare feet touch it, I feel like Aiden's right to wrinkle his nose at me. I'm the dirty one. *But he's sexually aggressive, and a racist one at that.* I can hear him following me up the stairs. He walks slowly, but he has a heavy gait. That may come in handy later if he tries to sneak into bed with me when I want to sleep. If I need to fight him off. That type of thing.

I had to fight off Pulsifer sometimes. That got easier as I got older. Aiden's a lot bigger than some decrepit governor of Idaho.

I find the bathroom door open and I walk inside. He has a clawfoot tub that could hold seven people. Judging by the perverts Pulsifer normally deals with, Aiden probably has had seven people in this tub at once. It sickens me to think what other secrets he could have. I flinch as he appears behind me. For a man with a heavy gait, he can apparently walk quietly when necessary.

"Get into the shower. Take your time. I'll set up the camera."

He sounds nervous, which makes me nervous. I imagine him being completely cruel. A monster would be crude and quick. Monsters *really* want you to cry. Aiden doesn't have any of those traits. He glances at my breasts, his cheeks redden and he swears under his breath.

"I can handle the shower," I say to him. He stares at me for a few seconds before leaving the doorway. I relish this alone time. I'm too grateful for my survival to think about escape. I wish I could tell you otherwise, but this is the truth. I grew up being passed around America's dirty underworld. Escape stopped being a real consideration when I turned eighteen and realized this was my destiny – permanent sexual slavery.

I clean myself as best as I can and try to ignore the numb feeling spreading over my body as I anticipate Aiden's actions. Most men are very rough. You can close your eyes and do your best to block out the pain, but nothing stops the dirty feeling of being powerless and having another person use you like an object.

Once I'm clean and have spent as much time in the shower as I think I can get away with, I step out and grab one of the insanely fluffy white towels hanging from the rack. As soon as I put it on my skin, the luxurious warmth spreads through me and the towel is so soft that I get a momentary feeling of safety.

I've carved out a life for myself despite my circumstances. I don't want anyone to feel sorry for me. I've learned how to play the piano. All the men who owned me had books that I enjoyed reading. I write poetry too, though none of it is good enough to share. Who would read my poems, anyway? Certainly not this blond hunk of muscle. His brain is probably the size of a pea.

He returns to the doorway and scowls as he watches me dry myself, reminding me that he's oversized and perpetually disgusted by me. I'm not shy about him seeing my body. He's seen it all anyway and he's going to have sex with me on camera, so there isn't a point in pretense.

"I took a vow that I would never touch a woman of another color," Aiden growls, sounding angry with me, like it's my fault that I'm black and he's racist.

I don't respond to him.

"I don't know if I can get hard," he says. "You might have to work to get me off."

I purse my lips. I have to ignore his suggestion that I'm too ugly to arouse him. White men. I try not to generalize them, but it doesn't help that all the men who have hurt me have had brilliant blue eyes, just like Aiden's. He has more of a pretty boy look, but he still has those cruel blue eyes.

"Have you done this before?"

"Yes."

I'll respond to his direct questions, but other than that, I have nothing to say. It's not like he cares.

"I'm sorry."

I give him a curious look, but I don't say anything. It's smarter not to say anything.

"If it helps, I'll make it good for you," he says in a gruff and gravely voice.

Don't bother. I want to say something cutting, but I don't want to anger him. Violence and sex are intertwined in the male brain, especially men like Aiden, a giant clearly used to getting what he wants.

This time, not responding to him provokes cheek redness. White men are always turning red when their feelings are about to take over. I brace myself for another racist comment.

"Whoever sent you must know my family. They must know about our beliefs and I want you to be clear about mine. I know my history and my heritage. I believe firmly in the superiority of my people over all others. This will not change because I stuck my cock in you," Aiden says, his voice trembling with rage as he stares at me.

I drop the towel. I'd rather him finish this than continue listening to his racist tirades.

I don't flinch, even if I want to. His words cut me deep, but Aiden, for all his complaints, still reacts like a man. His gaze drops decisively to my breasts and his teeth instinctively sink into his lower lip. His supposedly difficult to rouse cock bulges forward in his pants. *It doesn't look like he's struggling to get hard at all.*

He's even redder than before and his left hand clenches into an angry fist. I hope he's not the hitting sort. Those are always harder to deal with.

"Get on your knees," he commands, asserting power over me as my naked body renders him powerless to continue his racist little speech. I don't defy him. Despite my complete disgust with

Aiden, pleasing him represents my best chance at survival, so I consent to his commands.

Any position on my knees still hurts. If Aiden cares, he doesn't show it. He walks towards me and crudely thrusts his hips into my face. His trousers smell like cigarettes and beer. His pants pockets bulge with car keys and a few other objects I can't identify. A simple, brown belt cinches over his dark blue denim.

His thighs are thick and muscular, barely held back by his pants. My heart quickens as he shifts his stance to his left side, cocking his hip. I glance down at his shoes. Brown boots. The tips are probably steel, so I don't want to do or say anything that could provoke him to kick me. I'm in enough pain as it is.

"The camera's over there," he says. "We'll have to move. I just wanted to see if you would obey me."

He leans forward and kisses the top of my head. *He's fucked up. It aches down here on my knees and I'll have to get up again.*

Aiden commands me to my feet and I follow him back out into his bedroom. He shows me where he has his cellphone set up on a bookshelf right in front of Sun Tzu's *The Art of War* and an extremely tattered copy of *The Holy Bible.*

"Kneel there," he commands, pointing to a spot in front of the lens. "It's already recording."

I obey him and quietly kneel before Aiden, facing away from the camera. He walks into the frame and commands me again, "Look up at me. I want to see your face."

When I gaze at him, he frowns with that mixture of revulsion and disapproval I already recognize as his gut reaction to me. Despite his cruel facial expression, he's still hard. I can still see the bulge in his jeans and it's terrifyingly huge the closer he gets to me.

"I don't cum from getting head," he says. "But I doubt you can arouse me without it. Take my dick out."

He's so full of shit. This man has the biggest erection I've ever seen. *He doubts I can arouse him? Something is making him unbelievably stiff and there's no one else in the room but me.*

Taking my time to remove his cock from his jeans is the only way I can postpone it. I've seen dicks before, and most of them are completely unpleasant to look at. Many of the ones I've seen are shorter than my pinky finger. The governor called some of the world's most depraved men his friends.

Aiden remains resolutely planted in place, glowering down at me as I unbuckle his belt and then slip the jean button through the loop before unzipping his pants. Because of his muscular butt, I can't rely on his jeans to fall off on their own. I hook my fingers through the back, making contact with Aiden's ass as I pull the jeans down. As I ease his jeans over his ass, I can't help but notice how deliciously round and muscular his ass feels. My hands fight the urge to cup his firm glutes and focus on the required task - getting his dick out of his jeans.

His breath catches as the jeans slide down, revealing an equally toned and muscular pair of thighs. He has tattoos everywhere, but the thigh tattoos are the most alarming. *Choose death.* He has a skull, several Celtic knots, Bible verses, and intricate designs woven together in a tapestry of a criminal's life.

A pair of crisp white boxer briefs cling to Aiden's thighs. More details of his bulging cock become apparent to me. The monster curves slightly in his briefs, the thick head oozing fluid that creates a wet spot where the tip touches the fabric.

The elastic waistband of his boxer briefs sticks to his hips and as I remove his underwear, I expose more tattoos and worse. He has scars and partially healed wounds all over his body, not to mention more muscles. He's the most muscular man I've ever seen this close and it feels wrong to notice.

All the men who fucked me were ugly and cruel with bodies and tongues that failed to arouse me. This man might be a sick motherfucker but at least he's handsome. It's a small comfort, but I've never touched a man with such well-defined muscles, and the least I can do is appreciate it.

His cock springs free and juts forward with all the arousal Aiden claims he doesn't feel. His body doesn't lie. I haven't even touched him yet, but his cock already protrudes with pure enthusiasm. Once I get the briefs over his ass, they remain taut and stretched around his thighs.

I can't help but stare at Aiden's dick. I've never seen one as big as this. His dick is nearly the length of my forearm and it's thick, with a dusky pink color. The tip reddens immensely, like he's sore from how hard he is. *His dick is so red.* Tufts of trimmed dirty blond hair cover the base of his cock and his shaft is so heavy, his erection leans to one side.

Clear fluid oozes from the tip.

"Don't just stare at it. The camera's rolling."

He probably doesn't mean to be insensitive. He's nervous about this too. It's not like he wants me in this position. I grasp the base of Aiden's cock to hold it up and he makes an uncomfortable grunting sound. He pulses with heat and saliva pools in the corners of my mouth against my will.

He's huge. I run my tongue over my lips so I can get them wet enough to stretch around Aiden. I lean forward and he grunts, nearly jerking back.

"I can't…"

I grasp his shaft tighter. It's too late to back out of this. Before Aiden can pull away from me and deny both of us a chance at survival and escape, I run my tongue over the head of his cock and lick up every drop of the clear fluid emerging from the tip. Aiden's next groan sounds more like an uncontrollable moan of pleasure.

Pleasing him is good. Pleasing him will bring this to a quicker end and I'll have a much greater chance at survival if I please him. The thought occurred to me that once my use has run out, he'll kill me, but I can't dwell on that. If pleasuring this man ensures my survival, it's what I'll do.

I tighten my lips around the smooth, bulging head of Aiden's big cock. He makes an ungodly pleasurable groan as I get his dick head wet with my spit and prepare myself to take the length of that enormous thing down my throat. If I gag, he could hurt me. I have to make him like it. We're being filmed, aren't we?

I tighten my lips more and get Aiden's dick even wetter. His next groan is even louder than the first and he touches the top of my head instinctively before remembering himself and jerking his hand away from me.

Men enjoy having lips around their cocks, but this man really likes it judging by the moans coming out of his mouth. I flatten my tongue along the underside of Aiden's shaft and then slide the full length of his dick into my mouth.

Tears prickle in the corners of my eyes as I stuff every inch of Aiden's dick in my mouth. He groans with pleasure again and I tighten my lips around the base of his cock as I feel the tip tickling the back of my throat, threatening my gag reflex to erupt. I squeeze my eyes shut and focus on breathing slowly through my nose.

As the tip of Aiden's cock touches the back of my throat, he moves his hips slowly with one thrust, and then he erupts. His climax happens so quickly that we're both equally surprised. The tears threatening to pierce the corners of my lids fall freely down my cheeks. I make a gagging sound as Aiden pumps thick ropes of cum into my throat.

The first warm gush fills my mouth and as Aiden tries to remove his cock from the sticky deposit of fluid between my lips, even more spills from the tip and he leaves my lips, face and mouth a mess of cum as he stumbles away and gains his composure after a few steps, making the conscious choice to put as much space between us as possible. There's surprise evident on his face, especially his eyes. *They're terrifying.*

I cough once and try to swallow the cum in my mouth, but that does nothing to remove the thick ropes coating my face and lips.

"Fuck," he says. "I've never..."

"I'm fine..." I whisper, leaning forward, trying to wipe the cum off my face and not wanting to look Aiden in the eye out of pure humiliation. I look ridiculous, I'm crying and there's cum all over me. I worry he won't go through with the instructions on the card. Then what? I'd rather stay here, thousands of miles away from the governor than to *ever* return. If Aiden doesn't finish this, I don't know who might come looking for him.

Aiden crosses the room, standing straight in front of me with his cock hanging limp. My body tenses with uncertainty. I can't predict how he'll react. He crouches in front of me, forcing me to gaze at him with concern. *Is he going to hit me?*

We're face to face and Aiden takes his finger, places it beneath my chin and turns my face so I'm staring him right in the eye. We're still on camera, but it doesn't feel like it. This moment is just for the two of us.

"That was the best head of my life," he whispers. "Once we make this fuck tape, I'll pay you back for that with my tongue. I owe you."

The touch of his finger and the intense blue gaze feel romantic, but Aiden's words emerge with a business tone. There's no romance here. I nod slowly and he rises to his feet.

"Get up," Aiden commands. "Get on the bed and face the camera."

He won't look at me as he commands me this time. I don't want him to look too closely. He's seen more than I would show a stranger, if I ever had control of my life enough to make the choice not to. I avoid gazing into the camera lens directly, but I obey Aiden and position myself in all fours on the bed.

I feel lewd on display like this. I tilt my head downward so my hair falls down over my shoulders to cover my breasts from the camera's view. It's not exactly modesty, but it's the closest I can manage given the circumstances.

I glance over at Aiden through my peripheral vision. He's hard again, with barely any time between this and his previous orgasm. The way he spoke about his ability to cum, I expected a man with some type of sexual dysfunction, not a seconds-long refractory period.

Chapter Two

My throat tightens as I imagine my body stretching to accommodate that thing. I nearly choked on Aiden's dick in my mouth. That enormous thing could make me bleed if he isn't careful.

"Arch your back," Aiden whispers. "I want to see your ass."

It might be my imagination, but I swear his voice shakes like he believes the words emerging from his mouth represent the worst taboo. He approaches the bed slowly with that gigantic cock jutting from his hips.

"I've never filmed something like this," he murmurs as he draws closer. Aiden presses his large hand to my lower back tentatively. His hand is so fucking warm. His warmth spreads through me and I squeeze my thighs together to avoid any biological reactions to his touch.

I can't control my response to him. Aiden moves his hand down my lower back over my ass cheeks, his palm curving around my soft cheek. He makes a low growling sound in the back of his throat as he touches the inside of my thigh and discovers my wetness.

"That will make it much easier," he murmurs in response to my wetness. I think that'll be it, but Aiden slides his finger through my juices, swirling his index finger in slow circles through the juices on one thigh before moving to another. "But this is the only time. I don't fuck around with black women. Understood?"

I don't answer him. I just nod. If I'm going to have sex with this racist, I want to get it over with quickly. Judging from what happened before, maybe this won't last long. That's my best hope.

* * *

Click here to order Mafia Playmate:
https://bit.ly/bostonirishmafia1

Forced To Surrogate

Sample these chapters from my Amalfi Coast Brotherhood Italian mafia romance series while you wait for the next mafia romance series.

If you enjoy dark & twisted mafia romance stories, you can binge the entire completed series on your eReader.

Enjoy the free chapters.

FORCED TO
Surrogate

JAMILA JASPER

Description

The last thing Jodi remembered was a shot of tequila.
Next thing she knows,
Italian sociopath Van Doukas has her chained in his basement...
And he's claiming she agreed to become the mother of his child.

There's a detailed contract and everything... with her signature.
Jodi will do whatever it takes to get away from him...
But she doesn't count on the 6'7" Italian Stallion being skilled
with his tongue and excellent in bed.

* * *

Click here to read *Forced To Surrogate*:
https://bit.ly/amalficoast1

Series Titles

Forced To Surrogate
Forced To Marry
Forced To Submit

Content Awareness

dark bwwm mafia romance

This is a mafia romance story with dark themes including potentially triggering content, frank discussions and language surrounding bedroom scenes and race. All characters in this story are 18+. Sensitive readers, be cautioned about some of the material in this dark but extremely hot romance novel. The character in this story is **forced by circumstance** into her situation.
Enjoy the steamy romance story…

* * *

Click here to read *Forced To Surrogate*:
https://bit.ly/amalficoast1

Chapter 1
Produce A Pure Italian Heir
Van Doukas

There aren't enough cigarettes in the world for meetings with my father. The boss. Tonight, I meet with him to discuss something 'very important'. He calls everything 'very important', but tonight, I know exactly what he wants from me.

He wants me to kill again, this time for my foolish sister, who can't seem to keep herself out of trouble. Everyone in the family heard about what happened to Ana by now. That idiot Jew was foolish enough to put his hands on her with witnesses and expect nothing to happen? That's not how the Doukas family works, which he'll soon learn.

You mess with the Doukas family, we retaliate. If the Jew had any wits about him, he would disappear from the Amalfi Coast and head for the mountains or Sicily, or somewhere we don't have ears. He could go to Albania like Matteo. Maybe then we wouldn't find him. But fuck, I don't want to carry out another hit. Why can't that lazy fuck Enzo do it? Or better yet, Eddie. I carried out my first hit when I was two years younger than him. We spoil the new generation and wonder why our family falls apart.

None of this would be my responsibility if Matteo would get over himself and come down off his fucking mountain.

I stop my motorcycle and approach my father's front door. The all white old European style mansion sits on an excessive and opulent lot on the coast, right above the cliffs with a long path to the beach, a 'fuck you' to the tax collectors and the government who want to stop us from doing business.

Most of my siblings still live here, but I prefer keeping myself far away from papa and his… associates.

I can hear the party from the entrance. Seriously? On a fucking Tuesday afternoon? I assumed he called this meeting because he was working for once. He's intertwined in a different business based on the noise filtering outside. Please, Lord, let me not walk in on my father having sex with a model… *again.*

I open the front door to our old family home without knocking and immediately regret it when a completely naked foreign woman runs giggling toward the door, too high and drunk to feel self-conscious, exposing her completely nude body to a stranger. At least I didn't find her twisted in bed with papa, although this isn't much better.

"Oh! Good afternoon, sir!" she teases me in crude Italian, spinning around to show off her assets. *Whore. Foreigner. Her tricks possess little interest to me.* My brothers Lorenzo and Matteo would sway more easily.

"Where's my father?"

She giggles and spins around again. Fucking hell, I wish the ground would swallow me up. My father's prostitutes do not interest me.

"Your papa?" she says, standing to face me with her legs slightly apart, daring me to ogle more of her body. I have no interest in whores and I want her to answer my fucking question.

Before I can answer, another one of my father's toys saunters into the foyer, naked. This one is young—she looks eighteen just about—far too young for my father. I grimace and keep my gaze firmly fixed away from the nude females. Just because the men in my family are bastards doesn't mean I have to follow suit.

If we don't conduct ourselves with respect, how can we expect the respect of the Amalfi Coast?

"Yes. My father. Sal," I grunt, failing to hide the irritation in my voice.

The woman ignores my irritated tone with her response.

"Oh, he's in the back with Boyka. I can take you there after we take you to bed upstairs."

How much is he paying these women? We're still struggling to get Jalousie off the ground and he spends all his money on Slavic hookers.

"Not interested. I have a meeting with him."

"Are you sure?"

I don't dignify them with a response. I walk past the girls, keeping my eyes away from their bodies. Where the hell is my father? I pass the long hallway with the family portraits and follow the loud music and the louder giggling from near the pool. The familiar sound of pool jets betrays papa's location.

He's in the fucking hot tub again, I know it. He spends all fucking day in the hot tub, dishing out orders and expecting work to happen without him lifting a fucking finger. It's a fucking miracle anything gets done around here.

My father chuckles loudly, and I brace myself before approaching him. He's the boss and you don't question the boss, even if he's your father and even if he cares more about partying and women than our family — than our future.

When I enter the back patio, the pungent smell of tobacco and marijuana surrounds me. Judging by the bottles of vodka on the ground, the piles of cigarette butts and the other piles of detritus, they've been at this fucking party since last night.

Fuck. I put the cigarette tucked behind my ear into my mouth and approach my father's outdoor speakers, unplugging them and stopping the little dance party happening around his hot tub. Three women, each wearing next to nothing with their tits out belly dance for him while he chuckles loudly, his fat stomach causing waves in the hot tub. When the music stops, they stop too and look up at me indignantly.

They don't have to ask who I am. The ones who don't know Van Doukas can tell that I'm related to Sal. I have my father's eyes, but thankfully, I don't have his overweight body or his bald head. The girls make booing sounds at me, but I brush them off.

"I'm here for our meeting," I say sternly to papa.

He chuckles and nods. "Yes. The meeting. I almost forgot."

Almost? He doesn't look like he's fucking prepared for a meeting.

Papa dismisses the girls, except for one — Boyka. She slides into the hot tub next to him, twirling his thick plumes of chest hair around her fingers and sliding his freshly cut cigar between his lips. Nauseating. Papa coughs after a puff and taps the cigar over the edge of the hot tub.

"You're early."

"I'm twenty minutes late."

"Oh?"

"Papa, you said it was important. Shouldn't we conduct this business alone?"

None of the girls are dumb enough to rat on Salvatore Doukas, but unlike my father, I don't see the sense in taking risks.

Boyka's hand moves down my father's chest and I don't want to imagine what sorry shriveled part of him she touches next. I just want my orders so I can get the fuck out of this bachelor pad.

"I'm getting old, Van," he says. "I'm getting old."

He didn't call me down here to bitch about his old age. I furiously puff on my cigarette, waiting for him to get to the fucking point. Papa grunts as Boyka touches something... sensitive. Cristo...

Watching my father grunt through a hand job might be the only thing worse than watching him stick it to a woman.

"Do you mind postponing your fucking hand job until later?"

Boyka's hand rises guiltily from the water and I choke down bile. She really was touching the old fuck. I shouldn't swear at him or set him off. Papa might seem old, but he can have me killed. Any of my brothers would do it if he gave the command. Tread carefully, Van.

"Maybe I should leave," Boyka says, giving me a flirty glance as she plays with her tiny pink nipples.

"Yes," I snap. "Please get the fuck out of here."

Papa scowls. "Be respectful, Van. Boyka is a very dear—"

"I said please."

Papa smirks. "Boyka, return in thirty minutes. If we're not done…"

"We'll be done," I interrupt, glowering at my father. I don't have all afternoon for his games when I have the club to attend to.

Boyka reluctantly leaves.

"Are the women in this house allergic to fucking clothes?"

"None of them are allergic to fucking anything."

I'm not doing this with the old man today.

"Why did you call me here?"

I start another cigarette. I keep swearing I won't touch another, then I spend five minutes around papa and change my mind.

He leans back in the hot tub, displacing several pints of water over the edge.

"I'm tired, Van," he groans, leaning back and rubbing his forehead.

"From working?"

My father doesn't pick up on the sarcasm. He hardly leaves his fucking hot tub anymore, and he hasn't done anything even remotely resembling working at either of the nightclubs, restaurants, apartment complexes or construction sites around town.

If it wasn't for me and Enzo, he wouldn't have the fucking

time to boink Boyka or whatever the fuck he does with all these young Slavic women.

I still have to tread carefully around him. He's still my father, my boss, and I must obey him.

"Yes," he says, coughing. "From working. I need someone to take my place and lead the family soon. I want to retire, Van. You and I both know I need a break."

He spends every fucking day on vacation while his sons and nephews run his businesses. Vacation? We're the ones who need a fucking vacation.

"Perhaps you should contact Matteo about that."

My older brother spent his entire life preparing to be the boss. It's not my fault he fucked off, leaving his worthless children with us, I might add. I'm already halfway through my fucking cigarette and he hasn't closed in on the point.

Papa scoffs. "Matteo hasn't left Albania in four years. He left his children, his business, his fucking money, and he's not coming back. Give up on him."

"You're the one who trained him for the role. Send Enzo after him. Better yet, send his fucking son."

I don't want to go into the mountains to bring my jackass older brother back and I don't want to have this conversation with my father.

"Why don't you go to Albania?"

"Every time I'm in the same room as Matteo, he tries to kill me," I remind papa. I love Matteo, but he isn't exactly easy to get along with.

I'm surprised a woman tolerated him long enough to allow him to give her Eddie.

"Fair. But I need a replacement, Van. I don't want to be the boss anymore. I can't take the stress much longer."

Stress? What stress? Does my father seriously think sitting in his fucking hot tub banging whores counts as a job?

"Have you considered the role?" He asks before I can spew something disrespectful in my father's direction.

"Why would I want to be the boss of this fucking family? It's filled with degenerates, fuck-ups, people who need more violence to be kept in line. I kill enough as it is. You don't want me to be the boss and nobody in this fucking family wants me as the boss."

"People respect you, Van."

"People fear me. There's a difference."

Papa nods. "Exactly. Personally, I think you would make a good boss."

"I disagree."

But I don't completely. Yes, the job would be horrific and I'd have even more blood on my hands than I do now by the end. I could bring honor back to our family, clean the streets of our scum, stop the Jews from fucking with our shit… but I can't. Not with Matteo gone. Even in the fucking Albanian countryside, he would find out what I did and Matteo would kill me.

"No," Papa replies calmly. "You don't. But I agree with your assessment that you're not quite ready."

"I never said that. I said I didn't want the job."

Nobody smart wants my father's job. He spent twenty years walking around with a target on his back before he built up enough trust, enough loyalty, enough captains in the streets of Italy to ensure his safety. I don't want to lose my freedom.

"You didn't have to say anything. I know my son."

"Hm."

Arguing with my father is entirely senseless.

"You need an heir, Van."

"What?"

"I will give you the leadership of this family without the ritual, without the sacrifice and without the financial investment required. All I want is an heir."

"Why don't I go up to fucking Albania, then? Because I can't produce a child out of thin air."

Papa chuckles. "Don't you have women? If you want a

woman… I filled this house with them. I have very young ones too. Eighteen. Nineteen. They make good mothers."

"I am not interested in fucking teenagers."

"Then find a whore like that old Greek Pagonis fuck. I don't care how you get the heir. You can prove how serious you are by giving me a child. I'll be generous. I'll give you a year."

"I don't want this role," I snap. "So the likelihood I'll produce an heir is slim."

Papa laughs, which only infuriates me further. There's nothing funny about bringing a child into the world.

"You can't lie to me, Van. You were always the most ambitious child. Maybe it's because you were smack in the middle and we didn't pay any attention to you. Who fucking knows?"

My father spent little time raising any of us, except for Enzo, and look how that fucking turned out.

"Thank you for the psychoanalysis."

Every time I visit my father, my desire for alcohol increases exponentially, along with my cravings for nicotine. He brings the worst out of everyone, especially me.

"No problem," he says, again ignoring my sarcasm.

"What happens if I don't produce an heir? Eh? You still need someone to take your place."

"I make this offer to Lorenzo if you don't produce what I want."

"What?" I would have at least expected him to mention one of our cousins, one of the very obedient captains from the northern coast, or even fucking Eddie, Matteo's 18-year-old son, would be better than my irresponsible fuck of a brother. That old fuck really knows me well because he just said the only thing that could get me to reconsider his stupid fucking offer.

"You heard me."

"Lorenzo would ruin this family. For fun."

"I know. And it would become your responsibility to save it. You would have to act as the boss to save Lorenzo from himself. You might as well earn the position."

Fuck this old man…

"I don't want a family life, papa. I don't want the fucking wife or the fucking family. I want this life. It's what I'm good at. Business. Killing. More killing. That's who you taught me to be."

I'm not a man who can picture himself kicking around a football with my children or taking them to the beach. I'm not built for seducing women for more than a night and dealing with the danger of introducing them to my life or worse, hiding it the way papa did with our mother.

He can pretend it's not his fault what happened to her, but we all know the truth. No woman deserves our life. I can't afford to react. He loves when he can draw a reaction out of me.

Papa continues, as if my reaction is irrelevant. "Part of this life means having a family. I can't expect my other children to carry on my bloodline."

"Matteo has a son. You have a fucking bloodline. Why don't you make him the fucking boss?"

"Eddie? Eddie will not survive long the way he lives."

"That's a way to talk about your grandson, eh?"

"Have another cigarette, Van."

I'm already on my fucking third. But I'm not in a position to turn down his offer, considering the shit he wants me to deal with right now. An heir? I thought he wanted me to kill someone. Producing an heir in a year… It's just fucking impossible. I stick the cigarette in my mouth and light it.

"You can't let the family fall apart. We aren't the only people who would suffer. What would happen to our people, good Italian people, when the only people around they can get money from are the fucking Jews, who hate our guts?" He says.

I can't let his guilt trip work on me.

"I want an heir."

"Hm."

"Consider what you would sacrifice by turning down my offer, Van. It's not just about the family. It's power. You act like you're a fucking saint, but you are my son. You enjoy power.

You're just too much of a stuck up cunt to let yourself enjoy it."

"Thanks papa."

"You're welcome. Now, onto the matter of the Jew."

Fuck. I hoped my father would only piss me off one way today, but if we're discussing the matter of the Jew, I won't leave here tonight without an assignment. Someone else could easily do this job, but he wants me to kill. Because I'm good at it.

"I suppose none of my other brothers have the free time to do this?"

"I don't care. I need you to do it. The cunt offended this family."

"Perhaps we waste too much time retaliating for every offense. Ana told you to drop it."

I'm taking a risk just questioning his order, but he's pissed me off so much that I stopped caring.

"Decision making isn't women's work. It's our work. The man signed his own death warrant. I want it done soon. Call me when you finish the job."

"Hm."

"If you don't like the way I run this family, Van, you know what to do. I want to retire. Make an old man happy."

Drugs and whores are the only things that make my father happy.

"An heir," I scoff. "You want me to have a fucking bastard child to continue your bloodline? A bastard won't have any loyalty to his family. Children have a mother and a father, a mother they spend all their time with. If I fuck some poor woman, you won't have an heir. You'll have a problem on your hands."

"Then get creative. If you need to get the baby and kill the mother, do what you must."

What's happening to this family? When did we lose our way and talking about murdering women for our own ends? Papa...

This life changed him. It was slow, but it changed him completely. Too bad there's no getting out.

"Thank you for the advice."

"You're welcome. Now get Boyka back in here and get the fuck out. I need relief."

"Good evening, papa."

I drop my cigarette on the ground without bothering to step on it. Maybe my father's right — it's time for him to retire. But how the fuck will I get an heir? I need help.

There's one person I can call on for assistance in these matters. I don't like involving the Greeks in Italian business, but… they're our cousins. She answers after a few rings and it sounds like she's at a nightclub. She has an inordinate amount of time for parties…

"Ciao?"

I can barely hear her over the sound of the music.

"Miss Pagonis. It's Van."

She giggles. "Duh. What's happening? You finally have work for me?"

"How soon can you come back to Italy?"

Chapter 2
Single AF On The Amalfi Coast
Jodi Rose

I'm the last single woman in my family.

Three months in Italy, and I haven't had so much as a kiss, but my younger cousin Raven gets married to her college boyfriend and he looks like a dream. I drop a congratulatory comment on her photo, but my heart sinks.

You ugly, Jodi. Get used to it and stop chasing all these men out of your league. Settle with Kyle. He's the best you can do. Maybe mama was right. I'm not the marrying kind, anyway. I spent all my dating years focused on school and look at where that got me...

"Edo!"

The bartender gives me a sympathetic look. Ugh. Edo is so hot. Too bad all the hot guys are gay, especially in Italy, apparently.

"What happened?"

"Look at this."

I show him my phone and Edo cracks a smile. "Beautiful! Is she your sister?"

"No, my cousin. She's getting married and here I am... single... again."

And I'm running away from my problems with a one-way ticket to Italy. When my family finds out I'm not coming back, they're going to lose their minds. Everyone already thinks I'm crazy for leaving Kyle...

"Fuck your ex, Jodi. Seriously, fuck him," Edo says with all the passion of a best friend, even if we barely know each other.

I have major regrets about getting drunk my first night here and spilling all the drama about my ex-boyfriend to a bartender, but at least it made us fast friends. Although I'm not sure if Edo just likes the fact that Americans tip, unlike our Italian friends. He always has a way of scamming some extra euros out of me. At least he's a damn good listener.

I groan and dramatically lean against the bar as I make a proclamation that I wholeheartedly believe.

"I'm never going to get with another guy again. This is it. I'm dying alone."

I've read the statistics. Or at least I've read what women on Lipstick Alley say about the statistics. I'm a thick, well-educated black woman who is tired of the dusties and has real ass standards — according to the internet, I'm dying alone.

Edo grins and shakes his head. Since he learned I was American, he's done everything in my power to take me under his wing since I got here. I just hate getting too far out of my comfort zone, so I've ditched all his invitations to visit the local clubs in favor of spending my nights drinking cocktails alone and checking social media. I'm in Italy. I should have daily adventures and bread. I can't forget the delicious ass bread.

"You will not die alone," Edo says. "At least not without trying... my latest cocktail creation."

Edo does a dramatic dance before revealing some clear beverage that looks like some horrible mix of vodka, vermouth and orange juice.

Good. I want to get completely fucked up.

"That looks... clear."

"You'll love it, I promise."

"Will drinking really make the pain go away?" I muse, twirling the glass around so the little orange peel swirls inside it.

Kyle. Why do you always miss the ones who fuck you up the most?

Hopefully, this drink will get my ain't shit ex off my mind, but let's be real. What I really need is a summer romance. Ha. Like that's going to happen in a country where half the people think I'm a prostitute because of my skin color.

"Yes. It will. Absolutely." Edo replies with a wink.

"Cheers." I swirl the drink around despite Edo's repeated claims I ruin his creations by doing that. I pour it down my throat and taste a pleasant citrus flavor before a powerful vodka burn. It takes everything in my power to get the rest of the drink down my throat. Whew! That was a damn burn.

"What the hell did you put in that?"

Edo winks, but offers no response. Tricky ass Italian.

"My shift ends in ten," he says. "I'll take you out tonight to Jalousie. No getting out of it this time to watch *Empire* in your apartment."

How the fuck does this skinny ass white boy know me so well already? I shake my head, prepared to reject his offer to take me to the club, but Edo won't let it go. He wriggles his brows suggestively.

He loves regaling me with stories about all the shenanigans that go down at the Amalfi Coast nightclubs. I'm not really a nightclub girl. Small bars like this one fit me better, but didn't I come to Italy to have fun? Meet someone? I should put in some effort.

The only men who give me any attention are the creeps on the beach who say so much nasty shit to me in Italian that I'm glad I don't understand.

Maybe I'll meet better men at the club, especially a club with a fancy ass French name like this one. Jalousie. Wait… Edo's mentioned Jalousie to me before in the past.

"Ain't that the club with the mafia shootout you told me about?"

I don't believe half the shit that comes out of Edo's mouth, but he loves regaling me with stories about the real Italian mafia, which he claims is apparently far worse than any mafia in Long Island or Staten Island. How could anyone who lives in one of the most beautiful parts of the world hurt and kill other people? I think he likes telling tall tales to impress tourists.

I get people on Staten Island killing each other, but the Amalfi Coast? Hell fucking no. The sea is perfectly blue, the air smells fresh constantly, and it's plain peaceful out here. Italians have a rich culture, amazing food, better wine and the guys here are hot.

Not every guy, but when you walk down the streets here, you definitely encounter more than a few hotties. They all dress like supermodels, too. I've never seen so many regular ass people sporting Gucci and Fendi.

"Yes," Edo says. "But you're here for 9 more months, right? Have a fling. Don't tell him your real name… and disappear. You can find a hot and incredibly rich man to spoil you during your trip."

"Wait… is this a gay club or my type of club?"

Edo chuckles. "The guys are hot. I didn't say they were gay. You haven't earned your way into going to a gay club with me yet."

"Wow, Edo. I thought we had something going here."

Edo shrugs. "My private life is my private life. That's how it is in Italy. Your private life, on the other hand, is my playground. I'll introduce you to people. I know people who frequent Jalousie."

"Hot guys?"

"Eh…"

"Hot straight guys?" I correct myself before he answers. I don't want Edo tricking me into going out for nothing.

"Not exactly… I have a girl friend in town who goes all the time — Cassia Pagonis."

He says the name like I'm supposed to know who the fuck that is.

"Who the fuck is that?"

Edo chuckles. "A very fun girl with very hot brothers."

I perk up a little until Edo tells me they're all married. Great.

"Great. They're married…"

Before Edo can reassure me (again) more customers wander into the bar and Edo scurries to the other end of the bar to take orders.

I gaze into my phone again, looking at pictures from Raven's wedding. My cousin looks gorgeous, but I can't help a twisted pang of envy. I know it's wrong but… will that ever happen for me?

My homegirls from college keep sending me articles about the sorry state of marriage for black women. Alyssa says that we need to divest completely from marriage and just have fun.

My idea of fun isn't keeping a collection of all "my dicks" in a private folder on my phone. I want the real fucking thing! Even if the world loves reminding me that 'the real thing' only happens for white women or black women with the lightest dusting of melanin… I want to believe in love.

I scroll past Raven's pictures and my feed is all babies, new puppies, new jobs, new houses, new apartments, new husbands… new everything. Before Italy, I was just doing the same old shit. I wanted to shake things up. I don't know why my life hasn't transformed entirely. I'm in the prettiest place on earth — the Amalfi Coast.

Edo's shift ends, and he calls my name from the other end of the bar, beckoning me over to the cash register.

"Any tip for me today?"

"I saw you slip that five euro note out of my wallet. I think we're good."

Edo shrugs. "Sorry, this job doesn't pay well."

"I get it. I'll pay for our drinks tonight. Happy?"

"Incredibly."

I shouldn't be offering to pay for anyone's drinks, honestly, but I tell myself that I'll worry about all the damn money I'm spending once I get back to America. I have nine months of freedom and then I can worry about these damn bills and loans and everything else.

Edo drags me off my stool, and we step outside into the cobblestone street. I'll never get over how beautifully blue everything is here. The streets smell like the ocean, pastries, wine and cigarettes, of course. People sell jewelry and fruits on the streets and the Italian accents are… gorgeous. My Italian's still crap, despite Edo's best efforts to teach me a few phrases.

At least I don't have to hear all the street harassment thrown my way, which is plentiful. Edo replies defensively to a grey-haired man who calls something lewd in my direction and grabs me tighter. "Fuck these guys," he says. "You aren't that fat."

I swear, I'll never get used to how fucking blunt they are. But I appreciate Edo doing his best to defend me. We can hear the music from Jalousie echoing down the street before we get close.

"Isn't it early for the club?"

"Why are you so fucking American?" Edo asks, linking arms with me. "Relax."

"EDOARDO!" A shrill voice with a strange accent calls from across the street. I know Italian accents by now, at least how people from the Coast sound when speaking English, and this girl sounds different.

"That's Cass," Edo says to me, a smile breaking out across his handsome face. "Chin up. She'll love you."

Edo waves to the girl across the street and she struts over to us, sticking her hand out to stop the cars making their way down the cobblestone streets. They don't even honk as she passes.

The first thing I notice about her is how striking she is. She's tall, with curly dark brown hair pinned up out of her face and flowing down her back. She's wearing crazy high heels, like all the European girls do, a short leather skirt and a tight black leather crop top.

With her dark red lipstick, she looks like a film noir femme fatale… and she stares like one.

"Edo… is this your American friend?"

She turns to me and smiles. Shit, her accent might be strong, but her English is perfect. Cass's hair falls over her shoulders, her curls carrying a soft eucalyptus scent.

"Jodi Rose," I say, happy to have some female company around here, not like there's anything wrong with Edo. "Nice to meet you."

She takes my hand, three silver Cartier bracelets sliding down her wrist. Wow. Her bracelets aren't the only expensive item of clothing she has.

"Cass Pagonis. I'm sure Edo has told you all sorts of horrible stories about me."

"I did not!"

Edo definitely did. But Cass doesn't seem like a crazy party girl. She rolls her eyes and brushes him off.

"I'm here on the Coast working for my cousin's family," Cass says. "I'm from Thessaloniki. My idiot brothers want me back next week, unfortunately. But I could use a night out before I go."

Edo claps his hands. "Yay! Party time. Too bad Jalousie only caters to the most chauvinistic mafia pigs you can imagine."

"I thought you said they were hotties?!"

"They are," Edo says. "But they might be assholes."

Now he tells me. Edo would have said anything to get me out of my damn apartment. I hope I don't regret it.

"Watch it," Cass cautions, an impish smile on her face. "Those chauvinistic mafia pigs are my cousins and brothers."

Edo shrugs. "Fine. Fine. But I need dick too. Gay rights."

Cass swats his shoulder.

"Edo, why don't you let me take her for the night? There's no one at Jalousie for you, and you can go meet up with Klaus or… that other one."

Edo suddenly straightens his back and reminds both of us that just because he's gay doesn't mean he's given up on old world chivalry.

"I can't send Jodi off with a stranger," he says.

I appreciate the sentiment, but I don't know if Edo would do much damage against… any man who weighed more than his slight 108 lb frame.

"I'm fine," I tell him. "Seriously."

"I'm armed anyway," Cass says. I think she's joking, but neither of them laughs. Is she serious? She doesn't look armed, and she looks more like a model than someone who knows how to use a weapon.

I could use a female friend in my life over here. I've got plenty of female friends back home, but they all want to talk about Kyle and my "healing journey". They don't want to hear that I'm still lost after all these months.

Edo shrugs. "If you insist."

"I insist," I tell him. "You've done enough taking care of me. Plus, I'll get to know my new friend… Cass."

"Exactly," Cass says. "Jodi… I think we can become wonderful friends. We can swap stories about Edo."

"There are no stories about Edo," he chimes in. "Because Edo is an incredible friend and a better bartender."

"Shoo," Cass says. "I can handle things from here."

Edo doesn't quite walk off, but he checks his phone and begins texting furiously to plan his next move.

"It's the last time they have DJ Fat Camel playing here. We'll dance, drink and later, I'll take you home, yes?"

"That sounds good to me."

"Well, you have my number if Cass abandons you on the top of a Ferris wheel," Edo says as he swipes four times quickly across his screen and then shoves his phone into his pocket.

Cass rolls her eyes. "I have done nothing of the sort. Get out of here, you big drama queen."

"Ciao!"

Cass and I say "Ciao!"

Edo walks down the cobblestone streets and lights a cigarette before disappearing around the corner. Cass breathes a sigh of relief and turns to me.

"I just think you're perfect," she says.

Weird comment to make, but I mumble a gracious thank you, assuming something got lost in translation.

"Do you have friends with you?" Cass asks, taking out a hand mirror and fixing her bright red lipstick.

"No. I'm here solo tripping. Had a quarter life crisis and… here I am."

"Do you like Italy?" she asks genuinely. Her eyes are so intense.

"It's beautiful."

"Not as pretty as Greece," Cass says. "But I agree. Shall we go in?"

"We should head to the back of the line," I say, my stomach knotting as I see the line stretched around the block. I hope we can even get into the club.

Cass grins, unperturbed by the growing line outside Jalousie.

"My cousin owns the place. Come on, we go in through the back."

Before I can protest, she takes my hand and we walk around a back alley that smells like trash, vomit and again — cigarettes. Cass drags me over to a door and surveys me once before touching the handle.

"Very proper outfit. Excellent. Let's go. Ready to dance?"

I nod, even if I'm nervous. Sure, I'm trying to have an adventure tonight, but I just met this chick. How do I know she isn't crazy? Well, she has Edo's backing, so at least she'll be a good time. Edo definitely knows how to have fun if his clubbing stories are even 55% true.

Cass punches in a six-digit code and the back door to the club opens. I can smell the club before I hear the music and Cass drags me in through the back before I can second guess myself. What am I really doing? I don't know this chick at all and I agreed to go clubbing with her? Is Edo's word really enough?

Once we're in the back door, a man appears. He's tall, with dark brown slicked back hair, tattoos all over his arms and grey eyes. He has broad shoulders, but is otherwise lean and very muscular. He's handsome, but it's too bad he smokes. I can smell the cigarettes from a distance.

"Cass? What the fuck are you doing here?" he asks, seeming genuinely upset.

"Shut the fuck up, Enzo," Cass snaps, her expression changing suddenly into a disapproving scowl. "I have business here."

The man smirks. He's around Cass' height, but he looks... greasy.

"Is that her?"

"Mind your fucking business."

Cass pushes him hard so we can get past him. The grey-eyed man's eyes land on me and he runs his hand over his jawline before snickering.

"He's going to kill you."

"Shut up," Cass snarls. Enzo laughs and raises his hands in defeat.

"Enjoy your night," he says to me in a sing-song voice. For the first time, I feel real hesitation. But Cass grabs my hand and drags me inside of the club.

Cass drags me all the way to the tables and chairs surrounding the dance floor, chatting excitedly and peppering me with questions about America. I struggle to understand her accent at first, but then I get into the rhythm of her voice and it's easier for us to communicate.

I have to listen in so hard that I barely scan the room we enter. At least the nightclub has a nice interior, and it doesn't seem like any ghetto shit might pop off. Another Edo exaggeration, it seems. I relax as Cass sets me up at a small, two-person table.

"I'll get you a drink. Wait here. If anyone comes to talk to you, tell them you are with Cass Pagonis. That will shut them up."

Before I can protest, or offer to come with her, Cass disappears. Shit. I guess I have to wait here. I already have five texts from Edo about the hotties he met at the club a few doors over. Damn, he moves quick. I've been here for weeks already and I still haven't met a heterosexual male who hasn't been an incredibly old and excessively horny man offering for me to be his 'African prostitute' — offers I have obviously declined.

Cass returns quickly, before I have any time to worry with two shots, each one with some blue flavoring at the bottom.

"Okay, Jodi. This is to a long and beautiful friendship between us, starting with one crazy night, yeah?"

I nod. "Hell yeah. I've never done anything like this before."

I blurt out the last part nervously, but Cass has a way of soothing me. She just smiles and nods. "Don't be scared! I'm a good Greek girl. Now come on… we'll take the shots together."

She counts us down.

"1… 2… 3…"

I take the shot — and it's the last thing I remember about that night.

* * *

Chapter 3
Not An Italian Woman
Van

"**W**hat the fuck? Cass!"

"I did what you asked. I have a girl in the back of the Escalade. I did an excellent job. She took the pills very well."

I slam the door shut. Cass must have given this girl elephant tranquilizers because she doesn't even fucking flinch.

"I gave you a list of characteristics, you Greek bitch."

"Careful, Van. Gal's in a boat a few miles off the coast. Don't make me call him on you."

"I said blonde. I said twenty-one. I said 5'4" tall, and I said thin. Does the woman in the back of this fucking Escalade look anything like I told you?"

My voice trembles with rage and that irritating Greek cousin of mine just smiles and fishes a hand-rolled, loose cigarette from her skirt pocket.

"Do you have a lighter?"

"You sound bored. Don't you understand I could shoot you dead and drop your fucking body in the sea for this?" I growl.

Cass snickers. "You could try. Now, do you have a fucking lighter or not?"

I slam the lighter into my bratty cousin's outstretched palm.

She lights her cigarette, that impish smile across her fucking face. Never trust a Greek bearing gifts. Why the fuck didn't I remember that before calling her? I only called the little brat because she likes money enough to keep my secret.

"What were you thinking?"

"Men don't know what they want," she says. "That's what I was thinking.'

"No! I know exactly what I want. I wanted a small, blond woman who belongs in the life, not a foreigner... not an African."

"Ignorant cunt," Cass snaps, slamming the heel of her boots into my calf. "She's African American. They're very cultured."

I want to break her in half. If she didn't have three of the most annoying brothers, perhaps I would.

"I don't want her."

"Too bad. She's what you get."

That little shit... Cass nonchalantly smokes. Doesn't she have a child now? That poor baker's son must be at home caring for her brat while she fucks with my life across the sea. If she didn't have a child, I would have at least attempted to smother her by now.

Instead, I'll give my bratty Greek cousin another chance to do the fucking job right.

"Go out again and find exactly what I asked for."

"You idiot. I drugged her and set her up for this. If she wakes up, she could go to the police, and this happens in your new nightclub? I'll be in Greece and your stupid club will be bankrupt. Does that sound wise?"

"Fuck, Cass. How could you fucking do this to me?"

"I didn't know you were so racist, Van."

"It's not racist. Fuck. I don't expect you to understand."

"Do you know any other words besides fuck? I'm leaving. I did what I came here to do. Sandros is waiting for me on the boat."

"I'm never hiring you again."

"You always say that. Why don't you trust me, cousin?"

"Because you're an evil Greek bitch. That's why."

Cass laughs like I paid her a compliment.

"That's going to be my next tattoo. Her name is Jodi, by the way. She seems very nice. I think she has a good curvy shape too. But what do I know? Ciao, Van."

She leans forward and kisses me on the cheek, leaving the red print of her lipstick behind. I rub my forehead as she walks off. Fuck. I've made a huge mistake and now I have a drugged woman in the back of my fucking car.

I call Enzo. Because he's the brother you call when you have a drugged woman in the back of your car and you need to go kill a Jew.

"What do you want?"

"Meet me at the beach."

"What part?" Enzo huffs. He wants to know if this is for a murder or a party. He'll know by my answer.

"Southern shore. I have a problem."

"Killing David tonight?"

My jawline clenches. "Yes. But I have another problem. I can't do this alone."

"Can't you get Eddie to do it?"

"No. I need you…"

Enzo can be a lazy fuck sometimes.

"See you in ten."

"Be there in seven."

Fuck. I get into the car and glance behind me at the woman laid across the leather seats of my Escalade. Jodi. I've never seen a woman like her in my life. She's confusing, and she's definitely not what I wanted. I need a woman I can produce an heir with—a surrogate to give me a child and then disappear. What the hell was Cass thinking disobeying me?

She's more proof we need to tighten the hold on our family. Nobody respects the Doukas name anymore.

She's still asleep when I get to the beach. I peer into the back seat at her chest rising and falling. At least she isn't dead. I don't have the stomach to dispose of two bodies tonight. Enzo rolls his car next to mine, rolling down the window and expelling an enormous cloud of marijuana smoke.

"You showed up high?"

"Relax. I also brought Eddie."

"Ciao, Uncle Van."

"Why the fuck did you bring Eddie?"

"Didn't you bring someone?" Enzo smirks, which means he probably noticed Cass at the club earlier and pieced everything together. She's still in the back of the Escalade and I don't need my fucking brother or my idiot nephew involved with this.

The last thing I need is Enzo dragging out my personal business for his habitual mockery.

"Shut up. Where's David tonight?"

"Gambling. As usual. Does Ana know we're doing this?"

My brother irks me sometimes. "Do you think Ana fucking knows?"

"Why so upset, brother? Working with the Greek cunt didn't work out? Who could have predicted that…"

"Shut up, Enzo."

Eddie glances up from his phone for the first time.

"Either of you have a cigarette?"

"You're too young to smoke," Enzo says.

"Fuck off. You're only three years older than me," Eddie protests, throwing a powerful punch on Enzo's shoulder. My brother doesn't flinch.

"Doesn't matter. He's your superior. You listen to him," I growl. If papa had taught them discipline from the beginning, neither of them would be like this. Now it's my responsibility whenever we go out to remind these fucks what *cosa nostra* is really all about. Our way of life is falling apart.

Eddie shrugs, and Enzo hands our nephew a cigarette, giving me a knowing look. After what we do tonight, he'll need more than a cigarette. We both remember our first kill and it wasn't pretty.

After two puffs, Eddie grins. "Are we working or what? I have more cunts to catch tonight."

"Quiet, Eddie," Enzo grumbles, tapping away on his phone. "Okay. I've got him. He's five blocks away."

I wonder what weapons my brother and nephew brought tonight. We'll need more than my pistol.

"Who is he drinking with tonight?" I grunt. How many motherfuckers will we have to take out?

Enzo shakes his head. "You won't like this."

"Five other men from his family. We can't be sure he'll leave the place alone."

"We need someone to lure him out," Eddie suggests. "A prostitute. Or a woman who can act like one. I'll get my girlfriend."

"You're still seeing Zara?"

I told Eddie to leave Zara alone after the last incident. I don't want to deal with another domestic problem.

"Why should I stop? She always takes me back."

"At least she makes a believable prostitute," Enzo says, shrugging. Eddie laughs, not even bothering to defend the woman he claims to love. Yes, she's a foreigner, but that shouldn't matter if he's chosen her. Love. This is what papa wants me to fight so hard for? Whatever he has for this family isn't love, and I have no intention of repeating his mistakes. I'll leave love for the younger generation, although Eddie doesn't leave me with much hope.

"Show some respect," I growl. "We're not using Zara."

Eddie puffs out his chest, but he's careful not to push me too hard. I'm just as likely to put out a hit on him as anyone else.

"Why not? She's mine to use," he says defiantly until I raise my eyebrow and silence my nephew.

Unfortunately, my idiot brother speaks up in Eddie's favor.

"We don't have a choice," Enzo says. "Unless you have someone else for us to use?"

The smirk on his irritating fucking face tells me he knows exactly who and what he's asking for. Bastard.

He knows what Cass did for me. Either that, or he suspects. My face betrays nothing. Unlike my father and Matteo, I don't let Lorenzo get under my skin.

"I have nothing for you."

"Except the unconscious immigrant in the back of your car," Enzo replies calmly, stealing another cigarette from Eddie's shirt pocket. All they fucking do is smoke and run women. Maybe my father's right and I need to take control of this family. My stomach lurches at that thought, combined with the knowledge of the woman in the backseat of my car.

"Why bother drugging and kidnapping a prostitute if we can't even use her?"

"If he doesn't want her, I'll have her," Eddie snickers, taking the lit cigarette from Enzo and taking a huge puff.

"Put out the fucking cigarette. We don't need a lure, we need patience, something you stupid fucks know nothing about. We drive to the Jew and we wait for him to exit alone. We trust he will exit alone. If we can't get him tonight, we get him tomorrow night. Understood?"

My tone sets them straight this time. Enzo puts out the cigarette. They can't disobey direct orders. Even if they might not fear me, they both fear papa. Then again, judging by Eddie's averted eyes and sheepish glances, perhaps I'm more terrifying than I thought. Matteo would have whipped them into shape. I hope Albania is worth it, you stupid fuck.

The boys get into Enzo's car and he drives away first. I want to take my time out here on this beach, with this woman, and assess this mess of a fucking situation. Never trust a Greek bearing gifts. How many fucking times has papa warned me about the Pagonis family? They're tricksters. I wipe my sweaty hands on black jeans and open the back of the car.

Fuck you, Cass.

She couldn't have made a bigger effort to deviate from my

exact specifications for what I wanted in a woman — and, more importantly, what I wanted in a womb. How am I supposed to produce an heir with... her? I specifically said blonde. This woman couldn't possibly come anywhere close to blonde. And her skin color...

My stomach twists in an incomprehensible knot as I stare at her unconscious body, a tight party dress barely covering her thick thighs. Her thighs are... large. Everything about her is larger than the typical Amalfi Coast club girl. She doesn't look like she's afraid to eat anything denser than lettuce, to start. She has curves. Very full curves. She's not my type, but my cock doesn't appear to get the message. I feel like a fucking teenager.

She isn't suitable for this job, but perhaps she'll have her uses. I'll examine my prize later. I have to kill the Jew before the woman wakes up. Considering how little Cass obeyed my instructions, I may not have much time. I follow Enzo's route to the bar where the Jews hang around, shooting dice and drinking like the rest of us. I have nothing against the religion — it's the people. It's tradition.

Our families have been at war for generations. They blame the past on our people, even if two generations ago, they were the ones bankrupting humble Italian families and taking ears and noses as collateral for unpayable loans. Without the family, without the protection and organization under papa and his trusted advisors, they would have owned all of us, kept us no better than slaves.

So no, I don't hate the Jews — but I have pride in myself and my family. I am an Italian man. Nobody owns me.

Enzo texts me when he's in position. This is the boring part. I stop the car and allow everything to settle into pure silence — except for a soft sound in the back seat. Snoring. I find the sound unsettling. I spend nearly every waking moment that I can alone, so her soft noises remind me that there's a stranger, another fucking problem, lying in my back seat.

The crowd around the Jewish bar thins shortly after our

arrival. It's late enough that couples and foreigners and groups of students on vacation spill out of the bar and onto the cobblestone streets. Foreigners don't care who owns which bar or which club. They just want to spend their money, blissfully unaware of the work that goes into keeping Italy their playground.

I know the man I'm going to kill. We're friendly. In public, us Italians hold nothing against the Jews and they hold nothing against us. Our war happens in secret. I attended school with David. We played football together in high school. Tonight, I'll chop him up into several pieces and… well, you'll see how it goes.

After an hour, Enzo finally messages me. Eddie saw him and he's leaving through the back, drunk and stumbling home alone. Eddie has eyes on him, but we'll need to move the cars to get him. Easy. I command Enzo to pick him up since he has Eddie on the street. We'll take him to the beach. It's the best place for a born and raised Italian to die.

We drive thirty miles up the coast to the beach where we work. You don't shit where you eat, right? The woman sleeps peacefully in the back seat the entire time. It's for the best. Enzo and Eddie wait for me to get there, only pulling the Jew out when I leave my car. They might be fuckups, but when it's important, they make an effort at obedience.

He doesn't struggle and not just because of the gun Eddie presses into his stomach. He knows his time has come. Everyone in the life knows this is most likely how we're going to die, a bullet to the fucking head that's had our name on it for years.

"Take his hood off. He knows who we are."

Enzo obeys, but Eddie keeps a tight grip on the Jew before removing the cloth hood from the man's head. He raises his gaze instantly.

"I don't want to do this," I tell him.

"Don't give me the speech, Van," David chokes out. "Just finish it. Don't draw it out."

"You know what you've done and why this is happening. We have to send a message."

"I have money, Van. Enough money to set the three of you fucks free. You could leave Italy. Forever. Money. Information. I have anything you want."

Every man behaves differently when he faces death. Death isn't pretty. You piss and shit yourself in front of other men. You cry for your mother. You deny what's happening — and with the Jew, you attempt to strike a bargain. You attempt to give your killer what he wants, hoping he sets you free and allows you to disappear. Believe me, you get this far and free yourself, you want to disappear.

The Jew has made a grave miscalculation. I will never and would never choose money over family. Even if it's just my sister Ana, who I strongly dislike.

"We don't need money from you people anymore."

"I know. I know... But Van... we have history."

"Fuck, I'm tired of this. Uncle, can I shoot him?"

"Eddie, no. That's not how we do things."

Enzo puts his hand on the man's shoulders and nods. "Yes," he says. "We give them time to pray to their God and whisper any last words before we gut them and stuff their dicks in their mouth."

Now the man takes a piss. I swear I could fucking kill Enzo for scaring him. That's the last thing we need.

"I promise we won't desecrate your corpse. Now pray if you must."

"I have a request," David pleads.

"Hm?"

I don't like the idea of a dying man making requests, but considering Enzo just pushed him to the edge of fear, I feel a touch generous. Just a touch.

"My chain. Give it to my daughter. Please. That's all I ask. I want her to know that I was thinking about her."

"Your daughter is three. She won't remember you," Enzo says. Fucking hell, I want to kill my brother.

"Don't listen to him. Eddie, take the chain. We'll do what the man says."

"Take my gun off him?"

"He won't run," I say to him, but of course, I can't exactly make these assurances. It's just a guess. He's alone with three armed mafiosos on the beach. He would have to be an idiot to run. I make a very incorrect judgment about our captive's intelligence. As Eddie lowers his gun and begins removing the man's star hanging around his neck, he shoves his elbow into Eddie's side and throws a hard kick toward Enzo before taking off down the beach.

Stupid fuck… I take off after him, pulling out my gun as I run. The poor bastard isn't quick — something I would have considered in his position. He played football with me. He should know who he's dealing with. I throw my leg out and catapult the Jew to the sand. He cries out as his body goes flying. Enzo and Eddie catch up with me as I trip and roll over, holding my gun aloft. I can't stop what they're about to do now. The Jew made a mistake by running.

Enzo throws a hard kick into the man's side. Eddie laughs as blood spurts from the man's face. They beat him for a while until he can't make any other sound except a whimper and a prayer. When he prays, I stop them with my hand.

"Before you die, we'll be needing that information you promised?"

He looks up at us as if he won't say anything. Then I watch the defeat flow from his face. Information. He'll give it up to us. The Jews have strong bonds, but not as strong as ours. They don't kill the way we do, so their people don't fear giving up information. At least I can justify this to myself.

I killed a man for information sits better with my conscience than killing a man for Ana. If I don't follow orders, I'll be the one kneeling on the beach next. I can't have that happen.

This isn't exactly going in the order I planned it, but I still need that information. The man gazes up at us, blood in his mouth, his eyes glued shut and swollen. He's already half dead.

"What do you need to know?"

Enzo whispers the question in quiet Italian. The man shakes his head.

"You're messing with the wrong people."

"Thanks for the advice," Enzo says. Before I give the order, he empties his gun. Two in the man's head and one in his chest. My stomach tightens. Even Eddie's eyes spark open, stunned. The worst part of all happens after the gunshots — a loud, blood-curdling scream. The three of us turn around to see her standing there, wide-awake and screaming her head off like a banshee.

My woman…

Fuck.

✳ ✳ ✳

Click here to read Forced To Surrogate:
https://bit.ly/amalficoast1

Extremely Important Links

ALL BOOKS BY JAMILA JASPER
https://linktr.ee/JamilaJasper
SIGN UP FOR EMAIL UPDATES
Bit.ly/jamilajasperromance
SOCIAL MEDIA LINKS
https://www.jamilajasperromance.com/
GET MERCH
https://www.redbubble.com/people/jamilajasper/shop
GET FREEBIE (VIA TEXT)
https://slkt.io/qMk8
READ SERIAL (NEW CHAPTERS WEEKLY)
www.patreon.com/jamilajasper

JAMILA JASPER

Diverse Romance For Black Women

More Jamila Jasper Romance

<u>Pick your poison...</u>

Delicious interracial romance novels for all tastes. Long novels, short stories, audiobooks and more.

Hit the link to experience my full catalog.

* * *

FULL CATALOG BY JAMILA JASPER:

https://linktr.ee/JamilaJasper

Patreon

13 SEASONS OF SERIAL CHAPTERS

NEW preview chapters published WEEKLY on my Patreon.

Read all 6 seasons of *Unfuckable* (Ben & Libby's story)…

Unfuckable

For a small monthly fee, you get exclusive access to over 375

chapters of my first completed bwwm dark and spicy serial romance, as well as the spin-off serial...

Despicable

The second serial, despicable has 300 chapters available for all Patreon subscribers to access instantly and... we officially have a **third completed spin-off bwwm romance series.**

And yes you get access to all of this at the $5/month tier with more benefits at more pricey tiers.

The third serial is about Clover + Thomas. Thomas has a shocking connection to a character in the second serial and Clover is an all-new African American female lead.

Powerless

This series has three *very long* "seasons" of chapters, the length of five full-length novels all-together.

You will probably have over three months of binge-reading before catching up to current content, making this one of the most 'bang for your buck' author Patreon subscriptions out there.

Don't take my word for it.
Check the post history:
www.patreon.com/jamilajasper

Patreon has more than the ongoing serial...

⚡ INSTANT ACCESS ⚡

- NEW merchandise tiers with **t-shirts, totes, mugs,** stickers and MORE!
- **FREE paperback** with all new tiers
- **FREE short story audiobooks** and audiobook samples when they're ready
- #FirstDraftLeaks of Prologues and first chapters **weeks** before I hit publish

Patreon

- Behind the scenes notes
- Polls and story contribution
- Comments & LIVELY community discussion with likeminded interracial romance readers.

LEARN MORE ABOUT SUPPORTING A DIVERSE ROMANCE AUTHOR

www.patreon.com/jamilajasper

* * *

Thank You Kindly

Thank you to all my readers, new and old for your support with this new year.

I look forward to making 2023 an INCREDIBLE year for interracial romance novels. I want to thank you all for joining along on the journey.

www.patreon.com/jamilajasper

* * *

Thank you to my most supportive readers — my Patreon subscribers!:

Carla
Jonathan
Kelly
Jessica
Jasmine
DARSHELL
Dawn
Tiabuena3
Leigh
Yvonne
Ashlee
Crystal
Marshybabyyy

Shout

Quaniquequia

TK

Kayla

Shronda C.

Ma-Eyongerie

Kayla

Chantell

Kheiara

ophelia

Vickie

Cass

Kamil

Kaela

Love

Miryam

Charlene

Summer

Lola

Eryn

DD Davis

Symone

Deborah

Beatrice

Valescha

Khadija

makhalaab

Kaya

Glitter Garden

SavageSam

sybil arroyo

Ncsportsfan79

Jessica G.

Danielle

Yola

Joslin

Alexciz

Stacia

Ayanna

Asia

Hailey

Kaya

Nikki

Naomi O.

Jessica J

Chakiya

Noelle

kourtnee

Martha

Nikki Valentina

xjkpop

Valeria

BlkBae

SweetS

Msteeq

Rhonda

Darrah

Killa

Shavon

Misty

India

Kassandra

Imani

Nala

Chantell

Benvinda

Roger

Lexi B

Zapphire

Vbrooks

Tasha G

Kiera

Valencia

Stacy

YANITZA

Texansgurl76

Emma

Tinette

Jenny

Mariah

Nale

Tanisha

Trenita

Shelle

dulcemaria413

Shanice

Letarsha

Tania

Neeka

Julia

Linda

Lisa

Jiannie

Jillian

Tameka

Asia

Scarlette

Olwyn

R W

Fayefaefee

Brianna

Tiffany

Katie

Diamond

Kera

Tia

Love Reading

Dominique

Sheria

Jennifer

Georgette

Monique

Wendolyn

King Turtle22

Jessica

Nic M.

JustChill

DJC

Atira

TheeLastHokage

Yvonne

Chrissy

Janelle

Rian

LaRonda

LaRonda

Deanna

dlawson382

Jasmine

Haley

Belinda

Sercee

Yvonne

Jadelock

Farah

Tamiya

Quin

J.Payton

Geek Girl

Ashley

Rubi

Pilar

Sandra

Jurnee

Anni

Shannet

Joneesa

GlitzyHydra

Amanda

Barbara

Brianna

Jamica

Lyons

MARY ANN

Marketia

SarahD

LoverofHawaiiHearts

ceblue

Yolanda

MonaGirl Lewis

Dianna

Mary

amna

Nysha

fayola

Ty

Abria

Shyra

Andi-Mariee

Jamila

Naee's World

KEISHA

Jennett

Fredericka

Candece

Chante

Pholuv

Lydia A

Sabrina

JM

Jackie

Mo

Natrilly83

Ashaunte

Tolu

Margaret

Wendolyn

Lori

Dionne

ZLB

Kristina

Nicol

ELBERT

A. Harris

Jesi

Brenda

Desiree

Angela

Frances

LaShan

Only1ToniD

Debbie T.

Tiffanie

April L

shawnte

Kay

Lisema

Yvonne F

Natasha
Colleen
Julia
Amy
Jacklyn
Shyan R
Kiana B
Pearl
Javonda
Sheron
Maxine
Dash
Alicia
margaret
Love2Read
Juliette
Monica
Sandhya
MaryC
Trinity
Brittany
June
Ashleigh
Nene
Nene
Deborah
Nikki M
Dee
TyKira
Kimmey
Laytoya
Shel W
Arlene
Judith
Mary

Shanida

Rachel

Damzel

Ahnjala

Kenya

momo

BJ

Akeshia

Melissa

Tiffany

sherbear

Nini J

Curtresa

REGGIE A.

Ashley

Mia

Tink138110

Phia

Sharon

Charlotte

Assiatu C

Regina

Romanda

Catherine

Gaynor

BF

Perpetua

Tasha G

Henri Ann

sara

skkent

Rosalyn

Danielle

Deborah J

Kirsten

ANA
Taylor R.
Charlene
Louanna
Michelle
Tamika
Lauren
RoHyde
Natasha
Shekynah
Cassie
AnnaBooms
Keitheena
Nick R
Gennifer M
Rayna
Anton
Jaleda
Kimvodkna
JaTonn
Jazmine
Anoushka
Raynischa
Audrey
Valeria
Courtney
Donna
Patrisha
Jenetha
LaKisha J.
Ayana
Taylor
Christy
Monica
FreyaJo

GRACE
Kisha
Christine
Alexandra
Amber
Natasha
Stephanie
LaKisha
kristylove7
Cynthea
DENICE
Latoya
monifacd .
Doneishia
Mariah
Gerry
Yolanda T
Yolanda P
Susan D
Phyllis H
Alisa K
Daveena K
Desiree S
Kimberly B
Robin B
Gary S
Stephanie MG
Georgette A
Kathy
Marty
JanetDaniels
Megan
Shelle
Delores
Janet

Lydia
Phyllis
Freda
Charlott R

<u>Join the Patreon Community.</u>